PRAISE FOR ONE SHARK, NO SWIM

"Lehua Parker's writing style is so fine that you can't help but marvel at what she has created. It is not easy to write a novel that would suit children and adults alike. ...A perfect dose of humor make this book an ideal read for any age group. ...The books are fantastic. Period." — **Tales from Pasifika**

"...a great follow up to the first book, *One Boy, No Water*. ...I will warn you the ending will leave you with a *wow* and scrambling for a next book." **–Eastern Sunset Reader**

"Lehua Parker's books are simply delightful. So intriguing and well-written, you can't help but turn pages to see how these legends-come-to-life will affect Zader and his family." **–L.K. Hill,** *The Botanist*

"A trip to Hawai'i for the price of a novel." **–Eric Bishop,** *The Samaritan's Pistol*

ONE SHARK, NO SWIM

THE NIUHI SHARK SAGA BOOK 2

LEHUA PARKER

MAKENA PRESS

ONE SHARK, NO SWIM
By
Lehua Parker

One Shark, No Swim is a work of fiction. Names, characters, places and incidents either are the product of the author's imagination or are used fictitiously. Any resemblance to actual persons, living or dead, events, or locales is entirely coincidental.

Hardback ISBN: 978-1-949429-03-9
Trade Paperback ISBN: 978-1-949429-04-6
eBook ISBN: 978-1-949429-05-3
Audiobook ISBN: 978-1-949429-10-7

Published in the United States by Makena Press.

For information on subsidiary rights, please contact the author at:

AuntyLehua@LehuaParker.com

For Dylan and Shelby

Remember, no matter how much fun
your father says night diving is,
he's from Montana.

CONTENTS

The Lauele Universe   viii
A Note About Language   ix

1. Kalei Comes Ashore   1
2. Research   6
3. Analysis   11
4. Dreaming of the Girl   17
5. The Box   22
6. Scotch Tape and Heels   25
7. The Promise   29
8. Hill Slide Blues   33
9. Uncle Florence Nightingale   37
10. Nu'uanu Road Trip   41
11. Uncle Kahana's Heart   46
12. Land Surfing   50
13. The Science Guy   55
14. Waiting   61
15. Coming Home   64
16. One Lump or Two   67
17. Aloha, Mary Poppins   72
18. Eyes on the Back of Your Neck   78
19. Salting the Wound   82
20. Confession is Good For the Soul   86
21. Coming Clean   91
22. Piqued   95
23. The Game   96
24. A Knife that Knows Your Hand   104
25. Stalk   113
26. K-Pop Divas   114
27. Art Park Guy   119
28. All in the 'Ohana   123
29. Blank Paper   129
30. Secrets   132
31. The Competition   138

32. Reef Walk   144
33. Second Dinner   149
34. A Blade that Knows Your Heart   152
35. Survivor   158
36. Broke 'Okole Old Man   162
37. Brothers   168
38. Fight Like a Shark   174
39. Hoping It's Haupia   181
40. Dessert   186
41. Tools, Not Toys   191
42. A Taste of Raw Fish   195
43. Raw Fish Dreams   200
44. Lipstick Warrior   202
45. Jackie Chan Wannabe   209
46. Lauele Girlz   215
47. Bump   220
48. Origins   224
49. Revelation   227
50. The Writing on the Wall   232

   Glossary   240
   Discussion Guide   250
   Acknowledgments   252
   About Lehua Parker   254
   Also by Lehua Parker   255

THE LAUELE UNIVERSE

The Lauele Universe is full of stories that explore the intersections of Hawai'i's past, present, and future. Not all of the stories are about Zader or the Niuhi, but many Lauele Universe stories feature characters and events described in the Niuhi Shark Saga.

Zader Stories
Niuhi Shark Saga Trilogy
Book 1: *One Boy, No Water*
Book 2: *One Shark, No Swim*
Book 3: *One Truth, No Lie*
Prequel
Birth/Hanau (Zader's Birth)

Lauele Universe Stories
Nani's Kiss
Pua's Kiss
Rell's Kiss (Rell Goes Hawaiian)
Tourists
Under the Bed

A NOTE ABOUT LANGUAGE

Aloha!

The Niuhi Shark Saga takes place in an imaginary location on Oahu, Hawai'i, called Lauele. Like most islanders, the characters use common Hawaiian and Pidgin English words and phrases when speaking from the heart. Most of the time, it's easy to understand *plenny small kine fish* means *plenty of small kinds of fish*.

However, some words like *hanai* (adopted) or *'ohana* (family) are harder to figure out. Whenever you're unsure, head to the glossary. There's also an online Hawaiian Pidgin English dictionary, free reader's guide, and more activities on http://www.niuhisharksaga.com/.

I hope Zader's adventures in *One Boy, No Water*; *One Shark, No Swim*; and *One Truth, No Lie* give you a little taste of island living. Drop me a line and tell me what you thought. I love to hear from readers.

A hui hou,

Lehua Parker

AuntyLehua@LehuaParker.com

ONE SHARK, NO SWIM

KALEI COMES ASHORE

Sashimi
A Japanese delicacy of very fresh and thinly sliced raw fish.

The night Kalei's Niuhi shark head broke the surface of the large saltwater pool at Piko Point, his thoughts were consumed with sashimi.

Raw 'ahi tuna glistening like rubies on a bed of green cabbage would definitely hit the spot. He smacked his lips, remembering the taste of shoyu and wasabi hot on his tongue and how the flavor of cheap wooden chopsticks lingered in the back of his throat long after he'd swallowed each morsel.

Can't forget to chew, he thought. *Humans chew.*

For Kalei, eating fresh 'ahi was no big deal, but having someone else catch, clean, and serve it on a platter was once in a blue moon special. When a sashimi craving hit, there was only one place to go: Hari's in Lauele Town, Hawai'i.

With the moon as his only witness, Kalei gracefully shifted from Niuhi shark to human form. Blinking salt from his newly human eyes, he pulled oxygen deep into his lungs.

The first human breath burns like smoke from a fire. Gills are so much better.

In the middle of spiting seawater's tang, he paused.

Blood.

His nose twitched.

He opened his mouth and inhaled again, feeling microscopic flecks trickle past his teeth to coat the insides of his cheeks. There were three different kinds of blood in the air, all centered near Pohaku, and none of them very fresh.

The strongest is fish blood—a deep water fish, not something from the reef. Smells like the best belly part of the fish, not the rubbish head or tail. Not crab bait, then. There's a hint of banana leaves, too. Someone's lunch?

He sniffed again.

No whiff of spice or rice. Not even a trace of plastic wrapper. Now why would somebody place a prime slice of raw fish on a banana leaf in front of Pohaku? It's like—

An offering?

Interesting.

Pohaku was a sacred round 'aumakua stone that sat guarding the water's edge at Piko Point. Roughly the size and shape of a basketball, Pohaku was often mistaken for an ancient Hawaiian fishing god leftover from the days when stone and wooden gods dotted beaches and hills, but the truth was much more intriguing. Most days, Pohaku was content to watch surfers on the Nalupuki-side of Piko Point or families splashing at Keikikai beach on the other.

Most days, but not all.

Kalei craned his neck—one of the few advantages to his human form—and searched for the blood's source. His eyes confirmed what his nose told him: whatever smelled like a chunk of deep water fish on a banana leaf was long gone.

"Who remembered you, Pohaku, but forgot you don't like fish?"

Pohaku didn't answer—at least not in words. Pohaku spoke in mental images and emotions—when he condescended to communicate at all.

"Too embarrassed to tell the story? Don't worry. I know it's not your fault. Humans are short-lived and stupid."

Kalei opened his mouth, letting the breeze tickle his tongue. Like a wine connoisseur, he concentrated on each bloods' distinct note and ignored the flavors of jasmine, seaweed, and hot asphalt.

"I know blood when I smell it, Pohaku. There's fish and two other kinds of blood here. Why?"

Silence.

"Still not telling? Fine. I'll figure it out for myself."

Kalei pulled himself completely out of the water and onto the lava flow. Holding his arms high above his head, he gently pulled on each wrist until the joints in his shoulders, elbows, and wrists popped. Giving his back a twist and bending his knees, he frowned at his missing right toe.

After all these years, I'm still not whole.

In the water, the missing tip of his tail never affected him, but in human form the lack of a big toe threw off his gait. Awkward and clumsy on land, he appeared the very opposite of Niuhi: sleek and lethal. Kalei wiggled his remaining toes and smiled.

Humans are fatally foolish. Even an octopus understands the benefits of camouflage.

Standing firm with both feet on the ground, he felt the lava rock buzz, buzz, buzzing like a beehive. Curious, he drew another lungful of air, hunting for a trace of the second kind of blood.

"Human, older than the fish blood, and it splattered onto you, you naughty 'aumakua. There are speckles along your side where the tide cannot wash it clean. Is some-wanna-be-chief making old-time human sacrifices? Has someone mistaken you for a war god? Don't get a swelled head. People these days can't tell their 'okoles from their elbows."

Kalei sighed.

In his mind Kalei felt Pohaku's slow indignation bubble to the surface as he sent the image of a husky boy falling, then cupping his bloody nose as he hurried to shore.

"Just a clumsy boy with a bloody nose? How sad. Makes me yearn for a wanna-be-chief brave enough to beat his war drums and raise the old gods."

With the second blood scent fixed in his mind, Kalei inhaled to discover the source of the third.

"There's a trail of blood drops from where the boy with a bloody nose landed next to you that goes all the way to the beach. Near the pavilion, there's a faint whiff of his pee that dribbles along the road. Odd. He's too old for wetting his pants. Feeble-minded, perhaps?"

He clucked his tongue.

"Can you imagine, Pohaku? Humans are so disgusting now; in the old days we never had this problem. The soft-headed were given back to the gods. Everybody's so sensitive nowadays, it gives me a rash."

Kalei spun, crushing pipihi and too-slow hermit crabs beneath his heel. From Piko Point, he looked across the dark lava flats towards the lights at Hari's Grill and Convenience store.

Sashimi and TV soon. With luck, there's a sumo match on.

But I can't leave until I know what the blood and excitement bubbling along this lava flow is all about.

He scratched his arm, considering.

"Nice try, Pohaku, but you know as well as I that a kid's bloody nose from a trip and fall doesn't leave behind this delicious caffeinated champagne buzz in the reef. This energy is too intense for something that simple. Something big happened here. There's more to it than you're telling."

Kalei opened his mouth and throat wider than a human could and gulped down great gasps of air.

"I taste conflict—a fight? No—there's real fear here. The boy feared for his life. Who hunts boys, Pohaku?"

Silence.

"I know you know, you old forgotten thing. There's a third kind of blood here that's as fresh as the fat boy's. They're connected. It's the memory of the fat boy's fear that's pulsing through these rocks, the kind of fear that comes from a predator's chase. You know I can't allow that. Not here. Who dares hunt boys in Lauele, Pohaku? Who are you protecting?"

Kalei crawled along the rocks, trying to identify the third blood.

"It would be easier if you just told me, Pohaku. You know I'm going to find out."

He set his nose against the lava, inhaling bits of seaweed and crab shell, but it was useless; in his human form his senses were too blunted for this kind of delicate detective work.

"I can't believe you're making me do this," he said. "You know how much I hate to change!"

In two strides he dove back into the big saltwater pool. The water boiled, then parted to reveal the tip of a massive Niuhi shark snout. The shark floated over to Pohaku and daintily sniffed.

Kalei erupted out of the water, changing into human form mid-air. Landing, he swung his foot to kick at Pohaku.

"Niuhi!" he yelled. "A young male was hunting here—and he's definitely male. It's not Maka or Pua's blood."

He wrinkled his nose and closed his eyes, all thoughts of sashimi banished. He clenched his fists, nails digging into his flesh.

"Who dares to come around here, Pohaku? I know you know!"

But Pohaku sat still as stone.

2

RESEARCH

I ka nana no a 'ike
By observing, one learns.

On TV, the shark jaws unhinged in slow motion, the rows of teeth gulp, gulp, gulping the half-frozen fish carcasses, slicing through the heavy rope strung through empty eye sockets, and untethering the rotting mass from the side of the dive boat.

"Crikey!" said the narrator from the safety of the shark cage. "That was close."

From my perch on the living room couch, I snorted into my guava juice, the straw almost going up my nose.

You call that close, I thought. *Brah, try swimming outside the bars.*

The great white shark cruised past the cage, its flat black eye watching the divers wave chunks of melting fish through bars wide enough for lenses and arms, but not heads or snouts. I paid close attention to the way the shark moved, watching to see if it would reveal its nature in ways Australian researchers never considered.

The shark's after the bait. It couldn't care less about the divers.

I rattled the ice in my glass, careful not to touch the condensation with bare skin.

Not Niuhi.

I took another sip as the dive team scrambled back into the boat.

"Confunit! Now you, Alexander Kaonakai Westin?"

Three names!

I jumped up from the couch, narrowly avoiding dumping ice and guava juice down my front.

"Uncle Kahana!"

"That's right, Zader. Drinking and eating in the living room. Busted. Spill your drink, and it's a trip to the emergency room for sure. If the ice doesn't blister you, your mother's lickin's will."

Uncle Kahana and his dog 'Ilima stood in the doorway between the kitchen and the living room. More than just my great-great-uncle, he was the person who found me abandoned on the reef at Piko Point when I was a newborn and brought me to my Westin 'ohana, the family who adopted me and raised me as their own. He was the one who taught us about my water allergy, about how a single drop of water on my skin burns like acid, and how I can't eat raw seafood or rare meat because they give me nightmares.

Uncle Kahana claims we're all 'ohana by blood as well as by adoption because his Aunty Lei had the same allergies, but he won't tell me who my birth people are or where they live except to say Hohonukai-side, which isn't on any map. It drives me crazy, but he keeps saying, "Patience, Grasshopper," like some gray-bearded kung fu sifu in a bad Chinese movie.

Uncle Kahana had his hands on his hips and his head cocked to the side.

Not a good sign.

"I hui'd the house from the back, Zader, but you never answered," he said.

"Sorry, Uncle. I didn't hear."

'Ilima stood next to Uncle Kahana, panting a little and wagging howzit with her tail. I love 'Ilima. She's been Uncle Kahana's shadow and part of the family from before I was born.

Wait, I frowned, thinking about it.

That would make her over 120 in people years.

I blinked.

No way, that can't be right.

As I continued to look at her, she dropped her eyes and tail. She licked her lips and put her nose to the ground as if all she was thinking about was the next snack she could hoover from the carpet.

Uncle Kahana followed my eyes to 'Ilima and her new obsession with the floor. Suddenly, her head lifted, and her eyes gleamed. Perking her ears, she made a beeline for my bag of jalapeno jerky on the coffee table.

Uncle Kahana dropped his hands from his hips and muttered, "Yeah, I wanna see you take just one bite, titah."

'Ilima sniffed the bag.

"Go for it. I dare you. You're gonna be scraping that carpet with your tongue, bumbai. Remember the Mexican buffet? Remember jalapenos? Remember fire-futs fo'days?"

She got a little closer and inhaled. The spicy jalapenos went right up her nose. 'Ilima snorted and backed away, blinking at me like I was some kind of monster who'd popped her favorite balloon.

"Yeah, that's what I thought, 'Ilima," Uncle Kahana said. "Discretion is the better part of valor, no matter how delicious you think the jerky."

'Ilima shook her whole body and flopped on the carpet, eyes watering.

Uncle Kahana turned his attention to the TV.

"Why are you watching this crap, Zader? I thought Jay was the one fascinated by Shark Week shows."

Jay's my hanai brother, my almost twin from different parents. Last fall Jay had a shark scare while surfing at Piko Point. For a long time all Jay would watch was Shark Week shows, but before eighth grade ended, Jay had gotten over his fear and was back surfing.

When I turned on the TV this morning, he sat with me for a minute or two, then wandered outside to wax his surfboard for the millionth time. This summer Jay was helping Nili-boy coach a junior surf camp, and I thought he was taking it all way too seriously.

I shrugged. "Jay's surfing again. He doesn't care about shark shows now."

I looked down at my glass wrapped in a dish towel and inched my big toe deep into the carpet. I didn't like talking about sharks or surfing. I pretended I didn't care about things like going to the beach or playing soccer without worrying about sprinklers coming on or having to carry a stupid umbrella and wear shoes everywhere I go. But the truth was I hated being different in ways that made me *special*.

Special is way overrated.

Last summer, Uncle Kahana helped me figure out a way I can be out on the lava flow near the action and not stuck at the pavilion. I look like a space alien freak in all my gear—long rubber hip waders, a jacket with a hood, a deep-sea diver's helmet, and vinyl gloves—but at least I can sit at Piko Point and feel like I'm part of the surfers lined up for the next wave.

Since I can't surf, I spend a lot of my time drawing what I see in the tide pools at Piko Point. Some people think I'm a good artist; it's how I got into Ridgemont Academy for ninth grade. My painting of a ti leaf lei on the bottom of Jay's surfboard even helped him get back in the water after his shark scare. But I'd trade all my sketchbooks and pens for surfing in a heartbeat.

Back when Jay was afraid of sharks, he watched Discovery Channel Shark Week reruns twenty-four seven. Mom hated it then and doesn't like it now that I'm watching them. I'm not afraid of sharks, exactly. I watch for a different reason, one I haven't told anyone.

If Mom knew, she'd approve even less. She'd probably throw the TV in the trash and send me to counseling.

Uncle Kahana said, "If Jay's surfing again, why are you still filling your head with all this shark shibai?"

Is that why Uncle Kahana and 'Ilima are here? Did Mom send him to talk to me?

Before I could answer, 'Ilima sneezed more jalapeno dust, rocking her whole head back and forth.

"You sure you don't want a bite? Just a little taste, 'Ilima," Uncle Kahana teased.

'Ilima gave Uncle Kahana stink-eye and sneezed a third time, but turned her head so no doggy germs got on my snack. She's polite that way.

"Seriously, Zader, what's with all the shark shows?" Uncle Kahana wasn't giving up.

"Research," I hedged.

3

ANALYSIS

Kahuna Niuhi
An expert in the ways of the Niuhi; a human who speaks with Niuhi.

Uncle Kahana said, "Research? For what? School's over. It was pau last week."

On TV, the dive crew was back in the boat, heading toward shore. The narrator was talking about the long strings of buoys that held nets stretched along the mouth of the bay, pointing out how they keep swimmers and tourist dollars safe.

Good, a diversion.

"You think they work?" I asked, lifting my chin to the TV.

Uncle Kahana glanced at the screen. "No," he said, "they don't. If anything, they attract more sharks to the area."

He sank into a chair next to the couch. 'Ilima curled near his feet.

"Why?" I asked.

"What do you mean, why? It's obvious."

I pointed at the TV. "Earlier in the show, that guy in the green shirt said stringing fishing nets between the deep ocean and the beach is necessary to keep sharks away from people. He said if all the sharks that got caught in the nets made it to the beach, tons of people would get bit."

Uncle Kahana rolled his eyes, but before he could speak, I held up a hand so I could keep talking.

He gave 'Ilima side-eye and turned to the TV.

"Mmmrph," he said.

"Now according to the other expert, the one in the blue shirt, the nets don't work because they attract sharks."

Uncle Kahana started nodding.

"The sharks come because they're curious about the nets."

Uncle Kahana stopped nodding and started to frown.

"He says the nets disrupt the electromagnetic forces in the ocean, confusing the sharks."

Uncle Kahana shook his head from side to side, reminding me of a great white sawing through frozen fish heads.

"You listening, 'Ilima? That's their expert opinion. Codeesh!" he said.

He rubbed his forehead and pinched the bridge of his nose.

"That's it, 'Ilima. We're making our own documentary, except ours is going to be about first aid for shark bites. We'll put 'em on the internet right next to the videos of the all baboozes who like to hand-feed sharks. Think of all the lives we'll save."

'Ilima chuffed and flopped on her side.

Uncle Kahana pointed at the screen. "Use your eyes, Zader. What do you see?"

The images were horrifying. All kinds of fish, sharks, turtles, and even dolphins were tangled in the nets. Lurking in the distance on the deep-sea side, I saw bullet shapes of sharks, cruising. They were waiting for the camera crew to move on so they could move in, I was sure.

"The sharks aren't confused. They come to the nets because of all the dead and dying. It's snack time," I said.

"'Ae, Zader. That's right. Something has to clean that mess up."

"Niuhi?"

He narrowed his eyes at me, but didn't change his matter of fact tone. "Would you eat a pilau hamburger you found on the sidewalk or would you go buy a fresh one?"

"They're common sharks," I said. "They aren't aware. They aren't Niuhi."

Uncle Kahana nodded as he watched the images on screen.

"When you were a kid and the hukilau fishermen lowered their long nets off Keikikai beach, you said a Niuhi shark came."

He sighed and wiggled a little in the chair, fussing with a cushion.

"Yes," he said.

"The Niuhi shredded the nets and bit people." I swallowed. "He ate them."

"A few," Uncle Kahana said, squishing a cushion.

"On the program it showed tons of long nets out in the ocean. They've been there for years. Uncle Kahana, where are the Niuhi?"

Uncle Kahana prodded the cushion some more then lifted the bottom of his t-shirt. He picked at an imaginary speck along the hem.

"Uncle?"

"Hah?"

"Where are the Niuhi?"

"Niuhi? Ocean. Where else?"

"I mean over there." I waved my hand at the TV.

He peered nearsightedly at the screen. "Where?"

"On the TV!"

"What?"

"Niuhi!"

"Niuhi?" He squinted his eyes and canted his head. "No, that's just a regular hammerhead. Now they're showing common white tip. Get plenny on the reef."

I heard a suspicious noise like a dog chuckle, but when I looked down 'Ilima quickly made a sneezing sound too tiny to be real. While I kept starting at her, she smacked her lips and licked her nose.

"Allergies," Uncle Kahana said.

I wanted to give him stink-eye, but I didn't dare. Uncle Kahana was also my Lua instructor, a Hawaiian form of hand to hand combat similar to karate or kung fu. He didn't look like much, but I knew he could tie me into a pretzel without breaking a sweat.

I tried again. "Uncle Kahana?"

"Yes, Zader?"

"Last Christmas you told me a story about your father. He didn't want the fishermen to use hukilau nets off Keikikai beach because that would make a Niuhi shark come. You said Niuhi sharks don't like long nets because they trap everything—good fish, bad fish, things nobody is going to eat. It's wasteful. Those nets on TV are bigger than any hukilau net I've ever seen. Where are the Niuhi?"

Uncle Kahana and 'Ilima exchanged another look. 'Ilima immediately put her head down and closed her eyes. She squiggled, making herself comfortable on the carpet. Her breathing slowed as she started to snore.

"Chicken," said Uncle Kahana.

She snored louder.

He turned to look at me. "I don't know," he said.

"What?"

"I don't know." He pointed at the TV. "That's Australia, not Hawai'i."

"But you're the expert! What do you mean you don't know?"

He rubbed his chin. "You missed the point, Z-boy. People have been fishing a long time with all kinds of nets. The nets aren't the problem. It's where they're used. Fishing with hukilau nets off Keikikai beach is kapu—it's forbidden. Breaking kapu has consequences—that's what my father was trying to tell the fishermen. The Niuhi shark coming was the consequence of breaking the kapu."

"So Niuhi sharks are like cops? They show up when laws are broken?"

My words made Uncle Kahana's eyes bug out just like a big fat bufo. He opened his mouth, but no sound came out. I jumped up, alarmed at the rising purple in his cheeks and forehead and the pale tight circles around his mouth and nose.

"Uncle?"

'Ilima rushed to her feet, leaped onto Uncle Kahana's lap, and jammed her cold nose in his ear.

"Aiiiieee," he gasped, sucking in a bellyful of air. "Water," he croaked.

I ran to the kitchen, jammed the yellow dishwashing gloves on my hands, flipped on the water faucet, and filled a glass. By the time I made it back to the living room, his purple face had faded to red, and he was breathing normally.

"Uncle?" I held out the glass.

He took it from my gloved hand, waving his thanks before swallowing half of it. 'Ilima was back at his feet, her head tilted up with worry.

"Alexander Kaonakai Westin, you will be the death of me yet." He took another swallow. "And you, 'Ilima! What are you trying to do? Sticking your wet, clammy nose in my ear! I'm lucky my spirit never jumped out of my body just to get away from your ugi nose!"

'Ilima chuffed and licked Uncle Kahana's hand. She lay back down at his feet, but didn't take her eyes off him.

He motioned me to sit while he drained the glass. I slipped off the gloves and threw them onto the coffee table, checking my hands for blisters or pain, but the gloves were dry inside and had protected my hands from the water.

"Sore?" he asked.

I shook my head. On the TV the credits were rolling.

He cleared his throat. "Zader, hear me. Niuhi sharks are not cops. Cops aren't bosses. They just uphold and enforce laws created by governments; they don't make them. Niuhi sharks are like old-time Hawaiian chiefs. They are the law." He coughed and cleared his throat again. "You aren't going to learn about Niuhi by watching TV."

"I know."

"So why? You like watching big teeth chomp in slow motion?"

Uh, yeah.

I loved watching razor-edged teeth sink into anything—live seal, frozen tuna, fake surfboard—it didn't matter. I liked the way the chum looked oil-slick on the water too, like ocean rainbows when the light hit it just right. But somehow, I didn't think Uncle Kahana would see it the same way. Jay thought I was crazy when I tried to explain. He said it was morbid—one of our last vocabulary words of the school year.

Uncle Kahana was still looking at me, waiting for an answer.

I shrugged.

He rolled his eyes. "Fo'real? You like watching big bites in action? That's it?"

I picked at a scab on my arm, unsure if he would laugh or not. Finally, I decided.

"Uncle Kahana, you ever have dreams?"

4

DREAMING OF THE GIRL

Ho'omaika'i
To give thanks; a blessing; a favor.

"Dreams?"

'Ilima sat up and leaned against Uncle Kahana's leg. His hand dropped to her head.

"What kine dreams, Zader?"

"Never mind," I said.

"No, not never mind. What kine dreams are you having, Z-boy?"

"A while ago I had a dream about this girl—"

"—ah, maybe you better talk with your Dad about that."

I stopped and gave him a *look,* the one that most people couldn't meet. Uncle Kahana blinked a few times then swallowed.

"An'den," he said, causally waving his hand for me to continue.

"I'll show you."

I went to my room and came back with my sketchbook open to a drawing of Dream Girl.

Uncle Kahana took the book from my hand and tipped it toward the light coming in through the front windows.

"Hmmm," he said.

'Ilima nosed Uncle Kahana's leg. Uncle Kahana adjusted his grip, allowing her to see the picture. Her eyes went wide as she turned from my sketchbook to Uncle Kahana to me then back to the book. She gave herself a shake, faked a snort, and then settled down again at Uncle Kahana's feet, front paws over her nose.

"No kidding," Uncle Kahana muttered.

"What?" I asked.

"I said she's pretty."

That wasn't what he'd said.

I shrugged. "I guess."

"So what're these dreams about?"

I took a deep breath. I couldn't do it alone anymore; it was time somebody knew what was happening to me, someone who could give me some advice and help.

"Uncle Kahana, for years I've dreamed about this girl."

I told him about Dream Girl and how I had these vivid dreams about strange places and people and how she and I would sometimes fly high in the sky and spy on a man who scared us both, a handsome Man With Too Many Teeth. I flipped through the sketches, explaining what I felt and saw in the dreams. Uncle Kahana nodded in all the right places and studied the pages as I talked.

"But these are just dreams, right? Nightmares, some of them, but still all in your head, Zader," he said.

I bit my lip.

Uncle Kahana will either believe me or call Mom and tell her there's some-thing seriously wrong with me. Either way, there's no going back.

I said it as fast as I could, like a tsunami wave striking the shore.

"I saw him. The Man with Too Many Teeth. I saw him on the reef at Piko Point."

Uncle Kahana locked his eyes on my face like laser beams.

"When?"

"A while ago. I was wearing all my waterproof gear."

"Dive helmet, too?"

"Everything."

"Zader, this is important. Did the Man with Too Many Teeth say anything to you?"

"No. He just ignored me."

"Ignored you? Standing on the reef in a deep-sea helmet, hip waders, long sleeve rain jacket, and bright yellow gloves?"

I rubbed my forehead, thinking back.

"It was like I didn't matter."

"Beneath his notice."

"Yeah."

He let out his breath in one great rush.

"Hubris," he muttered. "Ho'omaika'i."

"What?"

"Nothing," he said. "It doesn't matter."

He waved a hand, pushing it all aside.

Uncle Kahana said, "So he passed you without speaking, an'den?"

"I hele'd on out of there as fast as I could. He was heading out to Piko Point. I didn't look back until I was all the way to the beach pavilion, but he was gone by then."

I paused, remembering.

"He had a slight limp."

Uncle Kahana reached up and rubbed his temple. "Of course he did," he mumbled.

He sat there for a minute, looking at the TV, but not seeing whales breeching or blow holes spouting.

"But Zader, what does all this have to do with Shark Week shows?"

Back to the start of our conversation, I squared my shoulders.

"I had another dream. In this one it was night. I was standing at Piko Point with Dream Girl. She was angry, huhu to the max. Said I ruined everything."

I closed my eyes.

"She said her name wasn't Dream Girl. It's Ka-Maka-O-Ka-Moana, Maka for short. She said he's coming after me. She called him Kalei. I think that's the Man with Too Many Teeth's name—Kalei. Then she—"

'Ilima nudged my hand with her nose. I opened my eyes and placed my hand on her warm head.

"She what?" Uncle Kahana pressed.

Get it over with.

"She called me brother, ripped a ti leaf lei off her wrist, and threw it at me. She dove into the deep saltwater pool at Piko Point and . . . and turned into a shark," I said.

'Ilima whined and pushed harder against my leg. Uncle Kahana sat frozen in his chair, his mind far away.

"She swam out the tunnel to the open ocean," I added.

He blinked and turned to me. "But it's all a dream, right?"

I shrugged. "I wasn't dreaming when I saw Kalei on the reef. Maybe it's all more real than I thought."

Uncle Kahana looked past me, not meeting my eyes when he spoke.

"Zader, think about it. What you saw was a man walking along the reef who reminded you of some scary boogieman you saw in a nightmare. That's it. He didn't threaten you; didn't speak to you; he *ignored* you. Why? Because he was just some guy out for a walk, that's all."

Whining, 'Ilima turned from me and put her paws up on Uncle Kahana's knees. When he didn't look at her, she barked a single sharp staccato bark right in his face.

"Quiet, 'Ilima," he snapped. "I know what I'm doing."

"What?" I asked. "What are you saying? You believe me, right?"

Nothing was making sense.

'Ilima jumped away from Uncle Kahana and came back to me. I could feel her chest rumbling. She pinned her ears flat against her head and glared at Uncle Kahana.

He didn't seem to care.

I patted 'Ilima's back, confused.

Why is Uncle Kahana acting like it's all in my head? If anyone would understand, I thought it would be him.

He rolled his shoulders and leaned back in his chair.

"Nah, no worries Z-boy. It's classic teenage fantasy: a beautiful, elusive girl; a bad man out to get you; hints about your birth family, not just a regular 'ohana like the Westins, but a special magic shark family. Of course a kid who's allergic to water is going to dream about swimming! It's your allergies. I bet you had Dream Girl dreams after eating meat that was still a little too pink in the middle. You did, didn't you?"

I nodded slowly. "Yeah. I guess you could say that."

"See? Listen to your Uncle: eat extra veggies, cook the steak super-well, and no more Shark Week shows! Then you'll have no more night-mares. Guaranz."

'Ilima chuffed and gave Uncle Kahana stink-eye, but he kept fiddling with the bottom of his t-shirt and didn't look up.

He was right about my allergies triggering dreams. I'd figured out a long time ago that if I accidentally ate meat that wasn't completely cooked or crab that wasn't really crab at dinner, I'd have Dream Girl adventures when I went to sleep.

But the last dream wasn't brought on by food. I'd dreamed about Maka that night because I'd held my shark tooth necklace in my hand when I closed my eyes and wished to see her again. That was the first time I'd dreamed about Maka because I willed it. It was the only time she ever told me her name, said the name of the Man with Too Many Teeth, and turned into a shark.

I didn't know what these dreams were, but I no longer believed they were random flights of my imagination. I had good reason. I opened my mouth to tell him, almost went back to my room to show him the dried ti leaf lei I kept hidden under my bed—the one Maka threw at me when she said that I needed it more than she did.

I formed the words in my mind to tell him how I found it laying on my chest when I woke up and how it proved Maka existed, but what came out instead was this: "Uncle, why you here?"

5

THE BOX

Lanai
A covered porch or veranda; where you pile your slippers before entering the house.

"Oh," Uncle Kahana said, waving a hand toward the front of the house, "from Hari's. I brought you guys the box."

"The box?"

"It's in the driveway. Go. Shoo. Out of here, now. 'Ilima and I have something important we gotta do."

He flapped both hands at me and picked up the remote from the coffee table.

When I didn't move, he added, "What are you waiting for? Go!"

There was too much to think about. Escape was a relief.

I got up from the couch and headed toward the front door.

"Umbrella!" he called.

I clicked my tongue in exasperation, but picked up the hated thing from its place next to my shoes.

Just like a convict with an ankle monitor.

"It's not going to rain," I grumbled.

"Better safe than sorry, Zader. Shoes, too," he called. "You and I are going to talk story about dreams some more. Just not right now. 'Ilima and I are busy."

As I reached to shut the screen door, I heard 'Ilima yip.

"I heard what he said, 'Ilima! I handled it."

She nosed at the remote in Uncle Kahana's hand.

"Because we came to watch TV, not talk story," he said.

She jumped on the couch and pouted.

"We'll talk about this later! You wanna watch the show or not?"

She spun in a circle three times before lying down with her head as far away from the TV and Uncle Kahana as possible.

He flipped the channel, and I could hear a studio audience applaud.

Whatever. Obviously more important than me.

Squinting a little in the bright sun, I walked down the front steps to find Jay squatting next to the biggest cardboard box I'd ever seen.

"Wow!"

He looked up. "I know, yeah? Uncle Kahana said Hari got a new big screen TV. He mounted it on the wall under the new covered lanai. We get the box!"

At Hari's Grill and Convenience Store things were changing. In addition to carrying everything from tooth brushes to poi and dive watches, he'd recently converted the side of the store into a covered patio enclosed on three sides, but open to the wind, rain, and sky on the other. Called Hari's Lanai, it had a simple cement floor, a couple of ceiling fans, and a scattering of tables and chairs. It was the kind of place where old futs nursed coffee and played cards, surfers grabbed snacks, and kids stopped to slurp blue raspberry slushes on their way home. The quick grill menu was mostly burgers and island-style mixed-plates heavy on the salt, ginger, garlic, and chili pepper water, just the way Hari liked them. It was the only convenience store or fast food place in Lauele.

Mom said Uncle Kahana had lived in the apartment on the second floor above Hari's store since she was little. Uncle Kahana joked that Hari's new lanai made a great living room, but if Hari started a karaoke night, he was finally moving. Hari said not to worry, there would never be a karaoke night—nobody wanted to take a chance that Uncle Kahana sing.

"Hari's Lanai now has a big screen TV?" I asked.

"Uh, yeah, lolo brain. See the box?" Jay tapped it with his foot.

As he shifted his weight, I could see his back muscles ripple through his t-shirt, his shoulders broader than ever after spring surf competitions. Jay was built strong and lean, with long-fingered hands that hinted at his future height. Mom said he ate so much now, she swore he had hollow legs.

I knew the feeling. Sometimes I stopped eating not because I was full, but because I was tired of chewing.

"Did Hari hook it up to satellite?" I asked.

Jay looked at me like I was crazy. "Kinda hard to watch anything around here without it, yeah? With rabbit ears, you only get PBS. That's all Uncle Kahana watches at his apartment."

"So if there are 'uku-billion channels on Hari's new monster TV just downstairs from his apartment, why did Uncle Kahana come all the way over here to kick me out of our house so he could watch TV?"

"You don't know?"

"What?"

"*Oprah.*"

I felt my jaw hit the driveway. "Not," I said. "No way."

"Fo'real. Every weekday morning at our house. Usually, we're still in school."

I flashed to an image of the morning gang at Hari's—the pau hana fishermen, cane haulers, and pineapple pickers who drank coffee and played trumps and backgammon—listening to Oprah's life lessons. It was only the fear of tears scalding trails of fire down my cheeks that kept me from crying as Jay and I collapsed on the grass laughing.

6

SCOTCH TAPE AND HEELS

Ridgemont Academy
A privately endowed high school for exceptional students.

Half an hour later, Jay and I were putting the final touches on our awesomest project ever: a cardboard sled shaped from Hari's TV box. It was huge. We were sure we'd break land speed records racing down grass hills. We might even catch air.

Jay nudged me. "Try look."

"What the—"

Charlene Suzette Apo tottered across her driveway, wobbling in her mother's old high heel shoes.

Char Siu was our calabash cousin and Uncle Kahana's only other Lua student. Like me and Jay, she was headed for ninth grade at Ridgemont Academy in the fall.

Unlike me, Char Siu and Jay got into Ridgemont on early acceptance. For a while it had looked like I'd be walking alone to public school at Lauele High in the fall, starring in the role of 'Alika Kanahele and Chad Watanabe's daily punching bag. All through Lauele Elementary and Intermediate, the Blalahs had hassled me, especially when Jay wasn't around. I'd been scared of being on my own, but things changed before the end of eighth grade, and I know I would've been okay. 'Alika and I worked our differences out in a fist fight at Piko Point.

Sorta.

When you're thirteen, sometimes the pecking order in the food chain gets a little confused.

Char Siu was teetering in the high heels when her ankle rolled near her mailbox. I winced. Quivering like a circus performer on a high wire, she kept her balance.

Jay bumped me again.

"Don't look!" he hissed. "No eye contact!"

"What's up with her eyes? They look funny," I said.

"Don't look her in the eyes!"

"What? Why?" I asked.

"Howzit, guys!" she called.

She bobbled again when she waved her hand, but stayed upright.

"Too late," Jay moaned. "You made eye contact. She's coming over."

Char Siu pranced over the curb and struck a pose, hands on her hips and one shoe delicately balanced on its point.

"What do you think?"

Jay didn't glance up. "We're busy, Char Siu."

She thrust her lip out. "You never even looked."

"You're wearing your mom's old church shoes. Why? Did 'Ilima eat one of your slippahs?" Jay yawned.

"I gotta practice, Jay. Lisa Ling told me all the girls wear heels at Ridgemont."

Jay turned to me. "You ever see Lili wear heels to school?"

I shook my head. "No."

Our sister Lili was going to be a senior at Ridgemont next year.

"Her friends?"

"No."

"Sounds like Lisa-kine shibai to me," Jay said.

"You just don't know, Jay," Char Siu said. "We're not in intermediate anymore. All the girls our age wear 'em. You'll see."

"Good thing we're not girls," I said. "I wouldn't last a minute walking around in those shoes. Poho, that."

"Hard for run li'dat," Jay said. He looked up at her. "Hard for see li'dat, too."

"It's called makeup," she said.

"I've seen makeup. My mom wears makeup. Lili, too. Her stuff is all over the bathroom. But makeup doesn't make mempachi eyes li'dat. That's something else."

I looked a little closer. Char Siu's eyes did look bigger, rounder, like she'd opened a door and giant spiders jumped out. One eye twitched and then stuck half open-half closed.

"What's wrong with your eye?" I asked.

"Nothing!"

"Then why is it sticking to your face like that?"

"Ho!" Char Siu reached up and peeled something off her eyelid. "The stupid Scotch tape won't stay. I told Lisa it wasn't right."

One eyelid looked normal now and the other still looked like it was keeping track of a man-eating bug. She reached up and peeled something off the other eyelid and suddenly she looked normal.

Well, normal for Char Siu.

"You put *tape* on your eyelids?" Jay's eyes bugged out like a bufo's.

She sighed. "Lisa said it would make my eyes look bigger."

"Why do you want big eyes?" Jay was fascinated.

"I don't know. Lisa said it was important."

"Why?" I asked.

She shrugged. "Because Lisa and I are going to be riding the Ridgemont school bus together."

"So's Tunazilla. She's wearing tape, too?" Jay asked.

Tunazilla was really named Petunia Kanahele. She was what Aunties called big-boned and boys called Godzilla-lite. Nobody liked Tunazilla, not even her mother who dumped her with her grandmother to raise along with Tunazilla's cousin, 'Alika, one half of the Blalah bully brigade. Somehow Tuna got accepted into Ridgemont's ninth grade class on full scholarship ahead of me on the wait list.

She sings; I draw.

Kinda puts my life in perspective. I try not to think about it too much.

"No. Tunazilla does not wear scotch tape on her eyelids," Char Siu said, exasperated.

"Why not?" Jay asked.

"'Cause she's Tunazilla, stupid-head."

"And Lisa—"

"—Isn't. Get it?" Char Siu said.

"No," Jay said.

"Does Becky Walters wear tape?" I asked.

Becky and Lisa hung out together, but Becky wasn't going to Ridgemont next year.

"No. She's haole," said Char Siu. "She doesn't need to."

Jay and I exchanged a look, mystified.

"Guys, Lisa and I are going to Ridgemont next year," she said.

"Yeah?"

"Ninth grade."

"So?"

Char Siu looked at us for a moment then shook her head. "Clueless."

THE PROMISE

Blowing bubbles
Selling an unlikely story.

Char Siu kicked off the heels and threw them across the street where they bounced on her front lawn. She rubbed her eyes, wound her ponytail into a loose bun, then knelt down next to us.

"So what're we making?"

"Sled," Jay said, relaxing now that Char Siu was herself again.

"I don't think that's right," she said, eyeing the cardboard box. "It looks too square."

"Chillax, Char, we're not pau," I said.

"Yeah," said Jay, "we never even added the fins, yet."

"I dunno; I've never seen a sled like that. When my family went to Tahoe last winter all the mainland ones were made of plastic, not cardboard."

I threw my arms out wide. "You see any snow around here? You only use plastic sleds if there's snow. We're making a *grass* sled. When we're done it's going to fly so fast the grass going catch fire!"

I kicked my stupid umbrella out of the way as I checked out the box's edges.

She's right. Too square.

"Jay, hand me the knife."

"Here."

From underneath a scrap of cardboard he pulled out the biggest, sharpest knife from the kitchen.

"Hey! That's your mom's best chopping knife!" Char Siu said.

"So?" Jay said.

My other hand secretly tapped the pocket where I kept *my* knife, the small folding one I used for carving drift wood. It was still there. I'd gotten into the habit of carrying it around with me; I like the way it feels in my hand, like an extension of my thoughts. I keep it razor sharp, honing the blade nightly against an old-fashioned whetting stone I hide in a drawer on my nightstand.

When Jay said we needed something to slice through cardboard, instead of reaching into my pocket for my knife, I told Jay to get Mom's chopping knife from the kitchen. I don't know why—cardboard, wood, they're both former trees—but I felt cutting common cardboard with my blade wasn't right. It's be like using a gold chalice for sprunch or wearing a tuxedo to surf.

"Does Aunty Liz know you guys are using her favorite knife?" Char Siu asked.

I gripped Mom's knife tight and stretched out the box with my other hand.

"No," I said, "and she's not going to, right?"

I gave her small-kine stink-eye as I sawed through the cardboard, curving the sides down in the front.

"What do you think, Jay?" I asked.

Jay circled our box, brushing the hair out of his eyes.

"I think cut here, Z. More aerodynamic."

"Yeah!" I started hacking away at the sides again. "We can duct tape this part and that part together like this."

"Aunty Liz is gonna notice," Char Siu said, "when she goes to make dinner and the knife is so dull it only dents the vegetables. Cardboard *ruins* a knife edge. That's why box cutters have razor blades."

"Chee, Char Siu, no worry; Uncle Kahana gave us permission," Jay said.

"No way," she said.

"Fo'real," I said. "He's in the house. Where do you think we got the box? Anyways, you're wrong. Mom'll never know we used the knife."

"Yeah," Jay said, "Plus she's working late. Guaranz we'll have pizza for dinner. No veggies to chop."

Char Siu dug her heels in. "I know Uncle Kahana never said you can use the good knife to cut *cardboard*."

"Uncle Kahana told us to go play outside, and that's what we're doing," I said.

"He said to use our imagination. Our imagination says we gotta use the good knife to make a sled. Plus how many kids around here have a grass sled, hah? You're just jealous," Jay smirked, his air of superiority thicker than volcano smoke.

"No act, Jay. I know you guys copied this from *Calvin and Hobbes*," she sneered. "I saw you reading the comic book in the library instead of doing research for Ms. Robinson!"

She waited.

Smoothing the edges of the duct tape, Jay and I ignored her.

Annoyed, she played her trump card.

"I'm telling!"

She flounced toward the porch, arms folded and nose high.

Oh-oh.

Jay jumped up with the knife and dashed around the side of the house, heading for the back door.

"Okay, Char Siu," I said to her back, "it's your funeral."

She stopped, one foot on the first stair. "You blowing bubbles, Zader."

"You wanna bug Uncle Kahana when Oprah's on . . . " I shrugged. "It's your funeral."

"He won't care."

"Today Oprah is interviewing people who can eat their weight in chocolate."

"Shibai."

"Fo'real. Then Oprah is talking about how she adopted an entire

31

African village. First time they ever had chocolate was 'cause of her. First time they ever had *toilet paper* was 'cause of her."

"Bulai. Everybody get TP."

"Not. And they only drink coconut water and stuffs li'dat, 'cause there's no good water where they live. Super tough drinking only coconut water with no TP. Ho, sad, yeah?"

Char Siu was weighing her options. If Jay was right about Uncle Kahana's secret *Oprah* habit, chances were good that Uncle Kahana was more likely to take it out on the tattletale who interrupted than the kids breaking the rules. But backing down now meant losing face. I didn't think Char Siu could stand that.

She stuck her chin out. "Okay. I won't tell if you let me have the first ride down the hill."

"Shoots!" I said.

"No!" puffed Jay, running back to the front yard. "Too late, Char Siu. Go tell. See if we care. Nyah!" He stuck his tongue out.

"Nyah, back!"

Char Siu stuck out her tongue and wagged it, shaking her 'okole, too.

"It's too late for you, Jay! Zader already said I get the first ride."

She put a hand on her hip and thrust out her chin.

Jay and I flashed side-eye.

We agreed.

"Okay," said Jay, "you get the first ride. But you gotta swear never to tell."

"Cross-my-heart-and-hope-to-die, stick-one-needle-in-my-eye, I'm never telling Zader and Jay ruined Aunty Liz's best chopping knife! Okay?"

I nodded. "Okay."

When Char Siu made a promise you could count on it.

8

HILL SLIDE BLUES

Kuku
A low creeping weed that grows in large grassy areas and vacant lots with thorny burrs that stick to
everything.

We futzed around with the sled a little more, adding a rope handle and gluing fins until Jay finally declared it perfect.

I grabbed my umbrella, and we loaded the sled on top of Char Siu's skateboard, half dragging, half pushing it to the pavilion between Keikikai and Nalupuki beaches.

On the hill behind the pavilion, the summer grass was dry and clipped so short that red dirt showed through in patches.

Itchy.

"Ready to take 'em up?" Jay asked.

I eyed the angle of the hillside.

"You sure about this?" I said, "That looks—"

"Fine. It's fine. Let's go," Char Siu said, lifting one end of the box.

It took us forever to grunt the sled to the top, but the payoff was worth it. While the slope to the pavilion and parking lot was long and smooth, the far side of the hill was much steeper and ended in a deep ravine. During heavy rainstorms it filled with run-off that drained into the ocean, but most of the time the gully was dry and full of broken and discarded things like shopping carts and rusty hubcaps.

Holding onto the sled, I peeked at Char Siu's face. Staring down the ravine, I saw her lips tighten and her forehead wrinkle. I caught Jay's eye and he grinned wickedly. He nonchalantly looked down over the edge then rolled his head and shoulders.

"Eh, Char Siu," he said, "you going baby-side or man-side?"

"Girl-side," she said.

"And which side is that?" he asked, winking at me.

She's not that crazy.

"This side, stupid head," she said, pointing down to the ravine.

"Wow, Char, that side's like dropping in on a sixty foot wave!" Jay crowed. "Think you're man enough?"

I shook my head. "Never mind what Jay says—girl-side, man-side, whatevers-side—that's one monster drop."

"You think? Too steep maybe?"

But before I could say yes and give her an out, Jay jumped in.

"What? You chicken?" Jay asked, giving her side-eye.

"Not!"

"Chicken."

"Jay—" I said.

"Bocka-bocka-bock!" Jay stuck his elbows out, flapping them like wings.

"This? Pshhtt! This is nothing. Last year I skateboarded down Rags-dale Avenue, eyes closed. This," she sniffed, waving her hand, "give me a break."

Ragsdale? That street is so steep that from the bottom you have to lean back to see the top!

Ho, Char Siu, you better check your pants! I smell smoke!

Jay cocked an eyebrow at me.

"Ragsdale's, huh? All the way in Nu'uanu?" I asked.

"So?" Char Siu said.

"So how did you get there, Char Siu? Mynah bird?" Jay said.

"No, no, no!" I said. "She waved her magic wand and—"

"—and a flying unicorn swooped down—"

"—farting cupcakes and fairy dust—"

"—and said, 'Hey, little girl! I know a great place to ride a skateboard—'"

"—and . . . and . . . "

Jay and I held our sides gasping for air.

We couldn't top each other fast enough.

Char Siu sighed. She knew there was only one way to make us stop.

She gripped both sides of the sled, took a deep breath, and flung her stomach on the cardboard, hurling herself headlong down the ravine side of the hill.

The slick cardboard rocketed over the parched grass.

"Cheehooooo!" shrieked Char Siu.

"Awesome!" breathed Jay. "Look at her go!"

Oh, no!

"Char Siu! Lean left!" I called.

She doesn't see it!

"Left!" I shouted.

"Aieeeeeeeeee!" screamed Char Siu as the lip of the box clipped the top of a half-buried rock, flipping the sled and Char Siu high into the air.

The sled landed upside down, bounced twice, and thundered to the bottom where it came to rest near a couple of plastic grocery bags and an old tire. No real damage.

Char Siu was not so lucky; she landed on her face and skidded to a stop in the middle of a kuku patch.

"CHAR SIU!" we shouted, tumbling down the hill.

She lay there in the dirt, not moving, not speaking.

"We killed her!" Jay cried.

Heedless of the kuku's thorns, I dropped to my knees and touched her shoulder.

"Char Siu! You okay? Say something!"

"Aaaaah."

"She's alive!" Jay said as we high-fived. "That was rad, Char! Like pearling on land!"

"Land pearling!" I said.

"Wiping out without the wave, titah!"

Charlene Suzette slowly raised her head.

We blanched when we saw the kukus poking out from her cheeks and chin. She looked like a dog that lost a battle with a porcupine. As she eased her way up, I saw thorny burrs sticking everywhere, in her clothes, arms, and thighs. Her palms were scraped raw, and she had a big strawberry on her right knee. I could smell the salty blood tang as it oozed to the surface from all the pin pricks and scrapes. Her clothes were streaked with dirt, and she had bits of dry grass and twigs caught in her hair.

"Char?" Jay asked. "You okay? Really?"

She glared at him then checked her knee. She dabbed at it, wiping the blood from her fingers on her shorts. She started picking at the kukus in her left hand, not looking at us, not saying a word.

"Eh, you not going tell, right, Char Siu?" Jay asked.

9

UNCLE FLORENCE NIGHTINGALE

Lolo-palooza
What happens when a bunch of feeble-minded, crazy people get together.

When we walked in the front door of our house, Uncle Kahana didn't say a word, just motioned us to the kitchen and got the first-aid kit from under the sink. It took him twenty minutes to dig out Char Siu's kukus with the tweezers and a needle, twice as long as the ten minutes it took to stop Jay's bloody nose.

Ointment on her raw palms, a bandage on her knee, hair brushed out, and an ice cold Diamond Head lemon-lime soda held to her cheek, Char Siu flexed her right hand and shook it. She sucked her knuckles, wincing.

"Sore?" Uncle Kahana asked.

"A little," Char Siu said.

"Good," muttered Jay from under a bag of frozen peas.

"Next time punch somewhere more soft, like his stomach," wheezed Uncle Kahana.

"Or his head," I giggled.

"Ha ha. So funny I forgot to laugh," Jay said. He lifted away the bag of peas and gingerly probed the sides of his nose. "How bad?" he asked.

"Not bad," I said.

"For a bull dog," Uncle Kahana said.

"More like a pug," Char Siu said, "that ran into a wall."

"At least I don't look like a porcupine!" Jay snapped.

I snorted.

"What you said, Mary Poppins?" Char Siu rounded on me. "Where's your umbrella, hah?"

I hated that thing; hated that I had to carry it everywhere; hated that it made me different—and Char Siu knew it.

"Shut up, Char Siu!" I said, balling my hands into fists.

"Guys—" Jay said.

"Oh, wait. My mistake. You can't be Mary Poppins because Mary Poppins *cared* when someone got hurt!"

Char Siu's eyes started to well.

"I said lean left! You never listened," I said.

"I leaned left!"

"Then how come you went straight?" I snapped.

"You think you can do better?" Char Siu growled.

"Guys—" Jay said.

"Better than a girl!" I snarled.

"You take that back, Zader!"

"No! What you're going to do? Punch me like you punched Jay? Go, try!"

"Guys—" Jay said.

Char Siu filled her lungs and opened her mouth.

"Enough!" roared Uncle Kahana. "Bunch of stupid heads, all of you!"

"What did I do?" Jay whined.

"You carried the sled up the hill with these two lolos. I bet it was your idea to make a sled out of the box in the first place," said Uncle Kahana.

"Zader helped," Jay mumbled.

"And together it was just one big lolo-palooza fest! You guys are lucky she didn't break her neck."

"We just wanted to slide down a hill like mainland kids," I said.

"I thought—" Jay started.

"You thought what, genius?" Uncle Kahana put the tweezers away and gathered up the paper towels.

"Nothing," said Jay.

"Spill it. I wanna hear how come Char Siu looks like a pin cushion."

"I thought it would be like surfing," Jay said in a rush.

Uncle Kahana froze.

'Ilima leaned forward.

"Surfing?" Char Siu asked.

"I thought if we made a sled, Zader could—"

"Surf," I finished. "You thought I could feel what it's like to surf."

He shrugged. "Yeah," he said.

Uncle Kahana reached out and patted Jay's shoulder. "You had the right idea, Jay," he said, "but the wrong place and the wrong kind of sled."

"Yeah, no snow," Char Siu said. "If Zader wants to know what it feels like to surf without going to the beach, we're going to need a lot of shave ice."

"Shave ice! Snow!" snorted Uncle Kahana. "Who needs it? Small kid time, my cousins and I went mud sliding up Nu'uanu Valley. You want to surf on land, that's the best place!"

"How?" Jay asked.

"How? *How?* Get in the car," said Uncle Kahana. "Eh, 'Ilima, we go!"

'Ilima scrambled out from under the kitchen table, bolted past the front door, and raced to Uncle Kahana's junkalunka car parked on the street. She jumped through the open window, then turned back toward the house, tongue out and tail wagging.

She yipped.

"We're going to Nu'uanu?" Jay asked. "Now? Today?"

"That's what I said! Clean your ears! I'm going to show you kids how real Hawaiians slide!"

He paused, remembering me.

"Eh, don't forget your umbrella, Zader," he said. "Nu'uanu's a rainforest, yeah? C'mon!"

"Rainforest? Really?" I asked.

It seemed dangerous; I doubted Mom would approve.

I was all in.

Uncle Kahana checked the sky.

"No worries, Zader. I've been watching the weather. It hasn't rained in a week, even Nu'uanu side. Nothing's going to be dripping."

"Okay."

"But bring the umbrella just in case. And maybe your waders and jacket, too. Just in case."

"Okay, but I'm leaving the helmet," I said.

The clothes are bad enough.

"Eh, Charlene Suzette," nudged Jay, "want to bring your skateboard? You can ride down Ragsdale's with your eyes closed."

"Skate down Ragsdale's with your eyes closed? You got a death wish?" Uncle Kahana shook his head. "If the hill doesn't get you, the traffic will. Forget the skateboard. Kids, get in the car!"

1 0

NU'UANU ROAD TRIP

Morgan's Corner
A place where people often have strange, inexplicable experiences.

The ride to Nu'uanu took forever, us kids in the back with
'Ilima and Uncle Kahana up front.

At the start of the old Pali road, Char Siu rolled down her
window, sucking in the cool, green smell of the rainforest. I rolled my
window down, too, and tipped my head out, watching tree branches
stretch over the road and blot out the sky, their tentacles black against
the blue.

I filled my lungs with the smells of ginger, maile, mud, and rotting
mangoes, pushing away the car sickness that crept in the back of my
throat whenever I rode along twisty and narrow roads.

Jay was stuck in the middle, feet perched on the hump that covered
the drive line.

Riding shotgun, 'Ilima's head was hanging out the window, the
wind blowing her ears sleek. She caught me watching her and ducked
back into the car, grinning her doggy grin at us over the seat.

"Okay, gang," said Uncle Kahana, "we're almost to Morgan's
Corner. No worries; I'm going to park a little bit past it. And we're

going to make sure we hele home before dark." He peered up at the sky. "Looks like we can't stay too long."

"What's Morgan's Corner?" Char Siu asked.

Uncle Kahana looked at her through the rear view mirror. "You never heard the story?"

"No," Jay said.

"None of you?"

We all shook our heads.

"Codeesh! You guys don't know anything!"

"How're we supposed to know if nobody tells us?" I asked.

Uncle Kahana blinked. "You're right, Zader, how're you supposed to know if nobody teaches you guys, hah? My kupuna told me all the old time stories; stories that are not really stories, you know?" He rubbed his chin. "Now, who's *your* kupuna?"

We looked at each other and shrugged.

He puffed out his cheeks and blew. "Me, you lolo heads! And Aunty Liz and Uncle Paul and Aunty Amy and Uncle Glen! All your elders! We're your kupuna. And your kupuna have the kuleana, the *responsibility*, for your education."

Uncle Kahana paused for a moment to scratch his chest through his t-shirt.

"Now your parents are good at school things like English and math and modern kine stuffs like computers. But I know *real* kine stuffs; things you need to know to really *live*."

He reached out and ruffled 'Ilima's ears.

"Past time to pass it on, eh, 'Ilima? Time to teach."

He cleared his throat.

"Okay. Morgan's Corner. One night this guy and his wahine—"

'Ilima yawned the biggest yawn ever and blinked sleepy eyes.

Uncle Kahana glanced at her then looked at our faces in the rear view mirror.

"What, 'Ilima?" he said.

'Ilima threw her eye wide, looking like she'd never get to sleep.

He pursed his lips. "Too scary?"

She chuffed and looked out the window, so disapproving I could feel it coming off her in waves.

He's not going to tell us. He thinks we're too young.

"Eh, I think you're right, titah. Nightmares. Better we save that story for later," he said.

"Noooo!" I moaned.

"Uncle Kahana!" Jay wheedled, "We can handle it!"

"Yeah!" Char Siu said.

But before the begging really got started, 'Ilima put her front paws up on the door frame, shoved her head and shoulders out the window, and bark, bark, barked, her tail thumping like a pahu drum against the seat-back.

Uncle Kahana slowed, pulled off the road, and parked beneath a huge mango tree.

"Nah, pau story already."

We groaned.

"Fo'real. We're here. Everybody hele out."

'Ilima leaped gracefully through the window and immediately started sniffing, nose to the ground and whining a little in the back of her throat.

Jay followed her. "What did you find, 'Ilima? Mongoose?"

She glanced back at Jay, then tipped her head back and let loose a long baying wolf howl.

"Ugh! Chicken skin when you do that, 'Ilima!" Jay said, rubbing his arms. "Like fingernails on a chalkboard!"

With great drama, 'Ilima slowly put her nose back to the moldy, leaf-covered ground and continued casting about in ever widening circles.

Char Siu slammed the car door. "What's 'Ilima doing?"

"Ah, nothing," said Uncle Kahana, giving 'Ilima stink-eye. "She thinks she's a blood hound tracking a scent. Hah, 'Ilima? You think you're the Hound of the Baskervilles? No more late night PBS for you!"

'Ilima ignored him in favor of whatever smell she was following.

Uncle Kahana sighed and flapped his hand toward a jacaranda tree.

"The trail to the top is over there. Let's go," he said.

"Wait! Do I need the waders or not?" I asked.

I really didn't want to haul the smelly boots all over the rainforest.

Jay reached out to the nearest bush and shook it.

"Dry," he said.

Uncle Kahana kicked the dirt, and a little puff jumped out.

He shrugged his shoulders. "What do you think?"

I shook the rubber waders, considering.

"Hot," I said. "Heavy."

"Leave 'em then."

I chucked the waders into the backseat.

"Umbrella?" I asked, hopeful that for once I'd be as free as Jay and Char Siu to run and climb.

"Bring 'em. I'll hold it for you while you slide," said Uncle Kahana with his back to me. He was busy looking at the trail.

"Why?" My lower lip crept out.

I tried to suck it back, but it wouldn't stay. Uncle Kahana would listen to reasonable questions. Pouting ended conversations in ways I never won.

"We're only little bit crazy, Zader, not stupid," Uncle Kahana said gently. "Bring 'em just in case. Do you really want to get caught out here in the rain?"

"No," I mumbled.

The thought of getting caught without protection terrified me. I imagined that like the Wicked Witch in Oz, I'd slowly melt into a puddle of goo.

Fine! I'll take the umbrella. And the little dog, too!

'Ilima grinned like she'd heard my thoughts, but when she caught me looking at her, she turned away and batted a rotten mango with her paw.

Not a doggy care in the world.

Yeah, right.

"Uncle Kahana, you want me to roll up the windows and lock the doors?" Char Siu asked.

"Why?" Uncle Kahana asked.

"Uh," Char Siu paused, considering Uncle Kahana's junkalunka car.

"Leave 'em," Uncle Kahana said. "Nobody around here is going to bother my car or anything in it."

"Why not?" Jay asked.

We'd seen plenty of junkalunka cars made worse by vandals before. Lauele ravine was littered with them.

Uncle Kahana turned to him, eyebrows raised.

"Everybody around here knows better."

11

UNCLE KAHANA'S HEART

Makule
Old; aged.

Hiking to the bottom of the hill, we wound our way through low lying ferns and under kukui, hala, and hau trees, the sound of Jay and Char Siu's slippahs snick, snick, snicking through thick sticky mud. In my shoes, I paid attention to where I stepped, choosing matted dead leaves and fallen branches over suspicious bare dirt. We walked for a while, always moving toward the sound of rushing water, until Nu'uanu stream appeared down a gully on our right.

I was glad to stop for a moment while Uncle Kahana pretended to check that we were going the right way—after all, there were only three ways to go: up the hill in front of us, around it to the left, or back the way we came. Even Jay looked a little tired. Surfing was definitely easier than hiking in this heat.

'Ilima continued to cruise along, wandering away from us when something caught her eye and coming back when she lost interest. She casually glanced toward Uncle Kahana then did a quick double-take, cocking her ears.

I followed her eyes and really looked at Uncle Kahana.

His face was a little puffy. I could tell he was dragging a bit, wilting in the heat and humidity.

"Zader, come," Uncle Kahana called, waving me over and putting an arm around my shoulders. He pointed up a steep hill. "You see over there, that trail that switches back and forth?"

I squinted.

"Yeah, I think so," I said.

"Good, good," said Uncle Kahana. "Now I'll go up first—"

'Ilima interrupted with two sharp barks.

"What?!" Uncle Kahana said, putting his hands on his hips. "It's just the top of a hill! I swim farther every day holding my breath underwater!"

'Ilima growled low in her throat as she walked to where the trail started to climb.

"Kulikuli, 'Ilima! Hush! I can do it. It's no big deal," Uncle Kahana snapped.

'Ilima stopped rumbling. Looking Uncle Kahana right in the eye, she sat down in the middle of the trail.

Uncle Kahana wagged a finger at her.

"Enough games, 'Ilima. Now move your furry 'okole!" he said. "You're blocking my way!"

'Ilima sniffed, turned her head away, and laid down, blocking the entire trail.

Uncle Kahana glared at her and crossed his arms.

She closed her eyes and pretended to sleep.

He stomped around in a circle.

She ignored him.

Finally, he roared. "Fine, then! You and I will meet the kids at the bottom of the slide! Happy?"

'Ilima's ears perked. She opened her eyes and wagged her tail, but didn't move off the trail.

"Uncle Kahana, you're not coming?" Jay asked.

"'Ilima and I have already been there, done that. Your turn now. Here, give me your umbrella, Z-boy. It's not going to rain."

He checked the sky.

"Not today."

He motioned Char Siu and Jay closer.

"You guys stick to the trail. You'll see the top of the slide a little bit to the left of a big koa tree. On the way up, each of you pick some ti leaves. But don't pick too many from the same plant. Have respect for the 'aina."

I glanced around, easily spotting several ti plants with leaves wider than my palm and longer than my arm. Bushy at the top with long spindly stalks, ti plants always reminded me of the tops of coconut trees or pineapples. I reached out and brushed a finger along the edge of one leaf before breaking it off.

Once in a Lua lesson, Uncle Kahana taught us that ancient Polynesians used ti leaves for everything from bandages to raincoats. Planted in rows, circles, or squares, ti plants marked ancient burials and kapu places and were a warning to stay away. We had a ton of them planted around our house for luck and protection—but what they protected us from, I didn't know.

"What're we doing with ti leaves?" Jay asked.

"You're weaving a mat for the Menehune chief to sleep on! What do you think, babooze? You're going to sit on 'em. That's your sled, old-time Hawaiian style."

I looked at the five or six ti leaves in my hand. I didn't know what this had to do with surfing, but I was willing to find out.

"I'll go first," I said, moving up the trail. "Excuse me, 'Ilima."

She snorted, but didn't move.

"Can, 'Ilima?" Char Siu mimed stepping over her.

'Ilima raised her eyebrows and sighed.

"*May* we?" Char Siu asked.

'Ilima thumped her tail.

Guess we may.

Jay, Char Siu, and I carefully stepped over her.

But when Uncle Kahana approached, I swear I heard her growl. Uncle Kahana glared, but 'Ilima wasn't moving.

"Really?" he said. "You used to love to mudslide."

'Ilima closed her eyes and started to snore.

"Go," he told us, throwing up his hands. "What're you waiting, Christmas?"

We hadn't gone very far up the trail when we heard Uncle Kahana smack a mosquito against his neck.

"They're sliding, and we're down here walking around the hill like a couple of old futs too makule to have fun. If you ask me, I'm not the one getting old, 'Ilima. I saw yesterday when you tried to—"

'Ilima sneezed.

Uncle Kahana stopped swatting mosquitoes and tipped his head up to see us standing on the trail above him.

"You talking to us, Uncle Kahana?" Jay asked.

"Uncle, you okay?" Char Siu asked.

"I'm fine! Why is everybody so concerned that I'm going to drop make-die-dead? Do I look like I'm going to keel over?"

Uh, yeah. Usually I see that color on a banana peel, not skin.

"You sure you're okay?" Char Siu asked.

He shooed us up the trail.

"I'm not dead yet! 'Ilima and I will meet you at the end of the slide. Go!"

Hearing the resignation in Uncle Kahana's voice when he said the words *end* and *slide*, 'Ilima stood up, stretched, and sauntered away from the trail. I don't think Jay or Char Siu heard Uncle Kahana's second attack on 'Ilima a few minutes later.

"Seriously? You think climbing this tiny hill is going to give me a heart attack? I'm not that old."

'Ilima chuffed and wheezed.

"An'den," Uncle Kahana continued, "you don't want *me* telling the kids about Morgan's Corner, but *you* can be a wolf at full-moon? No act, 'Ilima."

A small speck far below me, I saw 'Ilima look over her shoulder and flash her doggy grin as she continued on the trail around the hill, tail high in the air.

12

LAND SURFING

Pupule
Insane; reckless; wild; crazy.

When I finally stood at the top of the mudslide, breathless and holding a bunch of ti leaves between my legs, it occurred to me that maybe Uncle Kahana was a little pupule.

He didn't have a job and walked around in hammajang shorts and a ratty t-shirt all the time, unless it was a dress-up occasion like a baby lu'au. Then he'd bust out spotless white trousers and a freshly ironed aloha shirt that made him look like a parking valet or musician for an upscale Waikiki hotel. Where these clothes disappeared to in between weddings and graduation parties, I had no idea.

Uncle Kahana spent his mornings at the beach, fishing or just watching the waves. He talked to 'Ilima like she was a person, not so odd, perhaps, except he talked to her like she *answered*. In fact, as I thought about it, Uncle Kahana talked to most things like they answered, including rocks, coconut trees, and the occasional gecko. He even scolded me once for waking him from a nap on the reef at Piko

Point by telling me I shouldn't interrupt my elders' conversations and then apologized to the weird stone he was leaning against for *my* rudeness.

Pupule.

Not the most confidence inspiring thoughts to be thinking while standing on the edge of a cliff with nothing but a wad of ti leaves between your alas and who-knows-what at the bottom.

Is this what Jay feels when he's catching a wave?

"Eh, Zader! What you waiting for? Christmas?" Char Siu snickered, standing next to the koa tree. She was smoothing the stems of her ti leaves and showing off by braiding them into a handle.

"Cool your jets, Char Siu!" I said.

I looked down the slide, waving a hand in front of my face.

"Ho, choke mosquitoes around here. I think they're eating me alive."

"No act, Z. You never get bit," Jay said.

He flattened a juicy one and casually flicked it off his arm.

"Every time there's a mosquito in our room, it sucks me dry and leaves you alone! Wonder why?"

"'Cause he tastes junk, that's why," Char Siu chortled.

Jay smirked.

Traitor.

"Eh, Zader! You scared?" she mocked, pointing to her scabby face. "You want me to go first? *Again?*"

"I said cool your jets, Char Siu. I got this."

I'm going to do it.

I'm sliding down the hill all the way to the bottom.

I think.

"Need help, Zader? It's like this: You put your 'okole on the ti leaves and jump. That's it. Want me to write 'em down for you?" Char Siu sang.

"Char Siu, back off," Jay nudged. "Think for a moment. What makes mud? Water and dirt!"

"So?" Char Siu said, annoyed Jay was spoiling her fun.

"So maybe it's not so simple, yeah? Blisters!" Jay whispered.

"Oh!"

Char Siu's eyes bugged wide. She tugged at my arm.

"Zader, I changed my mind. I want to go first! You said I could have the first ride!"

"That was on cardboard," I said. "This is different."

"That's right; there's no water in the ravine. We don't know about the trail. Let me check it out for you," she said.

"It hasn't rained in a week."

"Zader!" yelled Uncle Kahana from the rainforest miles below. "Don't be scared! 'Ilima and I are right here. Chance 'em, brah!"

Easy for you to say, Uncle Kahana. It's not your eggs in the blender.

"I don't mind going first, Zader," Char Siu said.

I do.

Why am I such a panty?

I jumped.

The sticky mudslide was greased lightning under the ti leaves. I swooped down, bobbing and weaving through ginger, heliconia, and laua'e ferns, their trailing sweetness lingering in the heavy air as I dashed by.

No wonder Jay loves to surf!

Faster and faster, everything blurring to slashes of green, white, and brown, making my head spin and my eyes tear. I closed my eyes and clung to the fragile ti leaf sled, praying.

Please don't let me scream like a girl if I crash!

I heard 'Ilima bark, bark, barking.

"Left! Zader! Go left!" shouted Uncle Kahana.

"What?!" I screamed, my eyes screwed tight.

Bark, bark, BARK, BARK!

"LEFT!"

"Aieeeeeeeee!" I squealed.

Oh, no, I sound like a girl!

Airborne, the cold mud no longer slick beneath the ti leaf sled, I had a moment of achingly beautiful perfection, gracefully rising over the ferns and wild orchids, a boy in flight without wings—until I plummeted, landing face first, tumbling through a muddy bog.

"ZADER!" shouted Jay as he flung himself down the slide.

I lay there in the muck and rotting leaves, not moving.

Mud.

Equals.

Dirt.

Plus.

Water.

Suddenly, I exploded, erupting out of the bog like Pele from Halema'uma'u, mud flying like lava over the cool green rainforest.

"Woof!" snorted 'Ilima, backpedaling away from the bog monster sloughing toward the bank.

Uncle Kahana reached down and helped me up. Mud was in my nose, eyes, ears—even my teeth. I sneezed three times in a row and collapsed. The stench of rotting ugi things on my skin was enough to gag me.

Just don't barf. Not on top of all this, I prayed.

"Eh, Z-boy, you okay?" Uncle Kahana asked, prodding my arms, chest, back. "You're not bleeding? Nothing broken?"

I shook my head no, not daring to open my mouth.

"Good, good. How many fingers?" asked Uncle Kahana.

Jay dragged his feet to slow as he slid into a stop. "What happened?"

Uncle Kahana shrugged. "I said go left; he didn't and landed in the big mud puddle over there."

'Ilima whined and pressed her nose under my arm. I patted her with my elbow since my hand was still clutching the ti leaf sled and absently wiped the muck out of my eyes with my free hand.

I rolled my tongue around my mouth and grimaced.

Yuck! J'like old sweat socks.

I spit into the bushes, pretty sure I wouldn't barf.

"Zader? The blisters! How bad?" asked Jay, putting his arm around my shoulders.

Blisters?

I paused and looked at my hands. I patted my stomach and checked my arms and legs.

"Not," I said in amazement; "There aren't any!"

"Does it hurt?"

I shook my head. "It just feels cold."

I checked myself again.

"Uncle Kahana, how come I don't have blisters from the water?"

THE SCIENCE GUY

Ugi

Beyond disgusting; total gross-out.

"Yeah, Uncle Kahana, why doesn't Zader have blisters?" Jay asked.

Before Uncle Kahana could answer, Char Siu slithered to a stop behind Jay.

"That was awesome!"

She looked at me.

"But Zader you look like you lost a fight with the Creature from the Black Lagoon!"

"Char Siu!" Uncle Kahana scolded.

He tilted his head thoughtfully.

"Maybe you're older, Zader. Less sensitive. Aunty Lei had the same kine allergies as you, and I remember her walking in a light rain and through puddles." He wiggled his hand. "Maybe same-same."

Bet she never fell into a swamp.

Bet she never tried to go surfing down a mudslide.

Bet she never had a crazy brother or an Uncle Kahana.

"Zader, remember last week," Jay said, "when we were picking ti leaves and ferns for Aunty Amy. You didn't blister then."

"Yeah, but it was barely sprinkling that day. We thought I didn't blister because I'd just had a coconut oil and raw sugar bath. We thought the oil was beading the water on my skin."

Uncle Kahana frowned. "You were out in the rain without your umbrella? Why didn't you tell me?"

"Chee, you fo'real, Uncle Kahana?" asked Char Siu. "Zader didn't want lickin's, that's why."

Uncle Kahana harrumphed. "I need to know about these kinds of things, Zader!"

Uh, no you don't.

I kept my eyes on the mud.

"Zader?"

I'm not saying a word.

"We're through sledding today," Uncle Kahana declared.

'Ilima jumped up, ready to head to the car.

"Ahhh!" complained Char Siu.

Uncle Kahana gave Char Siu his meanest stink-eye. "I said pau!"

He pointed to Jay and Char Siu. "You two, go wash the mud off your feet and legs in the stream. And you," he looked at me and scratched at a mosquito bite on his cheek. "You, Mr.-I-Don't-Need-An-Umbrella, come stand on the bank. We're going to do a little water experiment."

I struggled to my feet, flinging mud off my arms and onto the bushes. In a panic, I checked my pocket and felt the outline of my knife.

Still there!

Relief rush through me.

If I lost it, I wouldn't know what to do.

I could still taste the mud in my teeth and felt it itching in my nose and deep in my ears.

Ugi!

I pulled the cleanest ti leaf from the bunch still clutched in my hand and tried to wipe my face. It didn't work. Looking at all smears of putrid mango, smashed guava pulp, dead leaves, and grime on my skin, I cringed.

I'll never be clean again, not even if I had an Olympic-sized pool of coconut oil and a million tons of raw sugar for scrubbing.

I wanted to cry, but that would only make things worse.

How ridiculous is it that my biggest fear is a shower?

Only a freak is afraid of water and soap.

I followed Uncle Kahana to the water's edge, swallowing hard and remembering the last time I was surrounded by water. Something strange happened that day at Piko Point, something I didn't understand and didn't like to think about.

When 'Alika punched me, and I fell on the reef, the saltwater touched my skin. There was pain, that's sure, but it was different than when I accidently stepped in a rain puddle or on wet grass. I don't think I'd ever touched the ocean before.

It seared and sizzled, burning like Pele's own fire, but angry at 'Alika's bullying, I ignored it, and thought instead about how much I hated being his victim. That's when something dangerous and powerful surged through me like lightning, snapping and buzzing through my blood like a live wire.

I stood up to 'Alika and gave him a reason to leave me alone.

The seawater changed me in scary and thrilling ways.

But I haven't dared try it again. Since that day, I haven't gone anywhere near the reef without all my protective gear on.

I hope Uncle Kahana knows what he's doing.

As Uncle Kahana fiddled with something, I watched Jay and Char Siu tiptoe across moss covered rocks until they were perched mid-stream.

"You first," said Jay.

"Chicken?" taunted Char Siu.

"Yeah," Jay said, "So?"

"Fo'reals?"

"The water's freezing," Jay said, "bumbai my alas going crawl up my throat."

"Bulai."

"Not. Hard to talk with your alas in your throat, you know."

Char Siu snorted. "It's your turn to go first."

"What if I drown?"

"Wave your arms," Char Siu said. "I'll call a life guard."

She shoved him, trying to push him off his rock and laughing as he started to windmill his arms, but Jay was quicker and tangled his arms in hers. Her laugh turned to a shriek as they splashed into the stream.

'Ilima barked as the cold, clear water splattered back on the bank at her feet.

"That's right, 'Ilima, you tell them buggers!" scolded Uncle Kahana. "You kids are lucky you never cracked your heads like watermelon!"

"Aieeeeeeeee!" squealed Char Siu.

"Cccccccold!" gasped Jay.

"Eh, only your legs and 'okoles were muddy! How come you guys jumped? Now you two lolo-paloozas gotta dry off before we leave. Never thought of that, did you?" Uncle Kahana shook his head.

Jay turned toward the bank, holding his arms out from his body.

"Jay! Where do you think you're going? Get back in the water and get all the mud off! I don't want any in my car!"

"Why?" Jay shot back. "Because mud would ruin the duct-taped seats?"

"It's a classic, brah. You don't mess with a classic."

"Classic? Junkalunka is more like it!" Jay said.

"It's a long walk back to Lauele, J-boy," Uncle Kahana said. "Better start now if you want to get home in time for breakfast."

Jay laughed, stopping at the edge of the stream to wash the mud off his legs. Char Siu stood thigh-deep in the water, twisting the front of her t-shirt and wringing it out.

On the bank I stood by 'Ilima, watching Jay and Char Siu laugh and tease as they shivered in the mountain stream.

What would it be like to touch water without getting hurt?

'Ilima looked up at me and whined.

I knelt down and whispered in her ear, "Do you think it's possible, 'Ilima? No more umbrellas? I can swim?"

'Ilima whined again, stood, and shook her coat. She took a step toward the water.

Uncle Kahana eyed 'Ilima.

"No getting ideas, 'Ilima. I got enough to handle with these kids. I don't need a wet dog, too."

'Ilima bowed her head and sat back down, ears and shoulders slumped.

I looked at 'Ilima's sad face and felt one thousand sand crabs scrambling in my throat.

"Uncle Kahana? I'm not too sure about this."

"Relax, Zader. We'll do this step by step. It's an experiment, just like the science guy on TV, what's his name—Bull Lye."

"Bill Nye."

"Hah?" Uncle Kahana asked.

"His name is Bill Nye, not Bull Lye."

"What? You sure?"

"Yeah," I said. "Are you?"

"Bill Nye. Huh."

"Uncle Kahana," called Jay, "How are we going to experiment?"

"I thought we could have Zader start with one toe at a time. See how it goes."

"Or we could just splash him!" Char Siu giggled. "Marco!" she said, flinging water at me.

Little fiery needles stabbed, burning like Pele's sparks, blistering angry red wherever the water dropped on bare, tender skin. My face, neck, arms, legs, and feet were dotted and swelling. The wind rushed out of me; I couldn't gather enough air to scream. Frightened, I stumbled and fell, but 'Ilima cushioned my fall and kept me from going into the stream.

"Zader!" shouted Jay.

Uncle Kahana was closest; he ripped a ti leaf from a nearby plant and started blotting the blisters, crooning, "It's okay, Zader, it's okay. This will help take the fire away. Let the ti leaf cool the burning. It's okay."

I trembled and moaned, holding my hands and arms away from my fire-scorching wet shirt.

"Jay! Get more ti leaves," called Uncle Kahana as he stripped my muddy shirt off over my head.

Through the misery I caught a glimpse of Char Siu standing in the steam, eyes round and face pale, not moving, not breathing.

I wanted it so bad, too, Char Siu. Not your fault.

Slowly, slowly the blisters began to fade as more cooling ti leaves wrapped my aching body, drawing out the heat and taming the redness.

Uncle Kahana sighed. "See? What I said? You're going to be okay."

"What . . . what happened?" Char Siu asked, dazed. "You said it was over. I heard you. He was older now; water wouldn't hurt him."

"I said we were going to *experiment*," Uncle Kahana said.

"Jay! You said the rain—" faltered Char Siu.

"I did. I thought—"

"This is not how you experiment!" thundered Uncle Kahana.

Quickly, I said, "It's okay. I'm okay."

I eased back on my feet and patted 'Ilima for her help. The blisters were almost gone now. I could see tiny islands of clean in the ocean of mud that covered my arms and body.

"Why didn't it work, Uncle Kahana? Why blister now with just a few splashes and not in the muddy bog or rain? Water is water, right?" I asked.

"Maybe, maybe not. Maybe this water is too cold—colder than the mud puddle or rain."

"Maybe," I said.

It didn't feel right.

"I dunno. I gotta think about it some more," Uncle Kahana said.

"More experiments?" asked Jay.

"Not here. I don't wanna take the chance. Zader, grab some leaves and wipe the mud off best you can. I have an old towel in the trunk. You can sit on 'em on the way home."

"What about us?" Jay asked.

"You two can ride in the trunk."

1 4

WAITING

Hoʻokaumaha
To worry.

Liz, Zader and Jay's mom, closed her eyes as she listened to Amy, Char Siu's mom, on the phone.

"I don't know, Amy. I haven't been home all day. It makes sense that Charlene is with the boys, and they're with Uncle Kahana. They're probably stealing mangoes or exploring the ravine or rescuing a mongoose. Never know with Kahana."

Pause.

"I'll send her home when I see her. Don't worry, they're fine. Okay. Take care."

Liz hung up the kitchen phone.

"Char Siu's missing, too?" asked Paul, Zader and Jay's dad.

He looked up from the kitchen table where he was reading the paper and sipping a glass of juice.

"That settles it. For sure they're goofing off somewhere with Uncle Kahana."

"Where?" Liz paced in the kitchen. "It's past dark! They know they're supposed to be home before sunset."

"Liz, relax. I'm sure Uncle Kahana took them somewhere fun, and they forgot the time."

"Yeah, like that old man even has a watch!"

"You want something to drink?" Paul said. "Let me get you a drink. A soda, juice, ice water—"

"I don't need something to do with my hands, Paul, and neither do you. I just need them to come home."

Lili walked into the kitchen.

"They're okay, Mom. They're together. They're fine."

"I should have made it clear they had to stay home!"

Lili blinked. "Mom, you don't really think something's happened to them?"

"I don't know." Liz bit her thumbnail, tearing it off in one long strip. "I hope not, but it's getting late."

"But the sirens never—"

"Ah, Lili, why don't you get the flyer with Koko's pizza specials," Paul interrupted. "I'm sure by the time we bring the pizza home they'll be back."

"I'm just saying that if it was an accident, we'd hear—" Lili sputtered as Paul pushed her out the door.

"Just get in the car, Lili. We don't need to talk about sirens and accidents."

"Oh. Right, Dad," Lili said, giving Liz side-eye.

Paul grabbed the keys off the hook.

"We'll be back soon, Liz."

He looked at her standing next to the sink, her arms wrapped around her middle.

"Or do you want me to wait with you?"

"No. Lili's right. If they were in trouble, we'd hear it. Go get the pizza. I'll stay here."

Paul kissed Liz's forehead.

"Love you."

"Love you, too."

Ten minutes after Paul and Lili left, Liz heard Uncle Kahana's junkalunka car rattling up the driveway.

Finally!

She rushed out the front door and down the stairs.

COMING HOME

Lickin's
Another use for slippahs.

Striding to the car with the righteous indignation of an avenging angel, the lights from the lanai like a halo behind her, Mom thundered, "Where were you?!"

In the shadowy anonymity of the backseat, Jay and I cringed.

This was bad. Mom was already mad, and she hadn't even seen the mud yet.

'Ilima jumped out the shotgun window, trotted up to Mom, and licked her hand.

"Not now, 'Ilima," Mom said, wiping her hand on her shorts. "You guys better start explaining."

'Ilima ducked her head and slunk under the lanai stairs where it was safe.

Uncle Kahana opened his door. He slowly swung his legs out and stood up, moaning a little as he rubbed his lower back. He stretched, yawned, then pretended to be surprised to see Mom standing by the car.

"Eh, howzit, Liz! How was your day?"

"Don't you 'howzit' me like nothing's wrong."

"Hi Aunty Liz," Char Siu said, climbing out the backdoor with Jay on her heels.

Uncle Kahana didn't make Jay and Char Siu sit in the trunk, but it was a close thing.

"You! Your mother's looking for you, Charlene! She's plenny huhu."

"Sorry we're so late, Mom," Jay said, standing in the yard and shifting his weight from foot to foot.

"What's the matter? You gotta 5-4-4?" Mom said.

"Uh, no."

"Then why are you dancing?"

Jay stilled. "I'm not."

Mom rolled her eyes. "So, where were you?"

"Uncle Kahana took us mud sliding up Nu'uanu," Jay said.

"What? Nu'uanu? Let me see your hands."

Mom grabbed Jay's hand, then Char Siu's, turning them over and over.

"Wiggle your fingers. Good. Not broken."

She glared at both of them.

"So why didn't you guys leave me a note?"

Ashamed, they looked at their feet.

"Hah? Nothing? Nothing to say?"

She jerked her head at Uncle Kahana.

"I doubt he knows how to write—"

"—aw, Liz, no act—" Uncle Kahana protested.

"—but you two should've known better," she said.

"Sorry, Mom."

"Sorry, Aunty."

"And where's your brother? He's missing his share of the scoldings."

"Here, Mom," I said, getting out of the car.

Mom gasped. "Holy . . . "

The mud had dried in streaks and swirls on the way home. It matted my hair and clung to my clothes; it was wedged under fingernails and stiff in the creases of my neck; it was even caught in the cracks and corners of my lips and eyes.

Mom reached out and touched my hair, rolling it between her fingers. A shower of fine dust fell, snapping her out of her shock.

"Never," she whispered. "Never. You'll never be clean again. No way coconut oil's gonna make this mess all better. There's not enough coconut oil and raw sugar in all of Hawai'i nei to get you clean."

She turned to Uncle Kahana. "How," she growled, "how did you let this happen?"

"I said go left." Uncle Kahana shrugged. "He never."

Mom blinked, shook her head, and blinked again. She rubbed her forehead.

"What are we going to do? Zader can't stay like this!" she said.

Uncle Kahana bowed his head. He tapped the roof of his car with his fingers and chewed on his cheek. He paused for a moment, cocked his head to the right, and then slapped the roof hard.

"Get tea?" he asked.

16

ONE LUMP OR TWO

Auwi
What you say when it hurts.

"What?" Mom asked.

"Tea? Do you have tea? Mint, chamomile, lemon—any kine?"

"Mint. I'll get it," Jay said. "I know which cupboard."

"Good, good!" said Uncle Kahana. "Brew a big pot! Make 'em strong, yeah? And Char Siu—"

"Yes, Uncle?"

"Find the big fishing cooler in the garage and drag it out here. We're going to fill it with water from the hose and add some stuffs to it."

She took off.

"What's going on in that pupule head of yours, old man?" Mom asked.

"Liz, think about it! What's mud?—Water and dirt. Look!" Uncle Kahana held out my arm. "Zader fell in a mud puddle and didn't blister. You're so busy worrying about how he's going to get clean that you never asked the right question!"

"No blisters?"

She grabbed my other hand and felt along my arm.

"None, Mom."

"And last week, he didn't blister when the rain beaded off the coconut oil—" Uncle Kahana started.

"Rain? What rain?" Mom's eyes narrowed.

"Ah, nothing. Not important," hurried Uncle Kahana. "But I'm thinking maybe his allergies are weakening, and he can handle some water now. He drinks juice, right?"

"Rarely."

"Cold?"

"No. He doesn't like ice."

"Warm juice, then. Room temperature. And what is juice? Water and fruit! So I thought: what's like water and fruit, but not sticky?"

"Tea," breathed Mom. "You think we can give him a tea bath?"

"Tea's not pure water," Uncle Kahana said. "It's like juice. What if we made it room temperature?"

"Not like cold Nu'uanu stream!" Char Siu said, dragging the big fishing cooler down the driveway. "Lukewarm tea's like muddy puddle water! Zader, you can take a tea bath standing in the cooler! You can wash the mud right off!"

Uncle Kahana said, "Fill the cooler halfway, Char Siu. We'll mix the cold water from the hose with Jay's hot tea."

Char Siu unwound the hose and turned it on. The water rushed into the cooler, splashing up the sides before getting down to business.

"Uncle Kahana, you really think this will work?" Char Siu asked.

"Can't hurt to try," Uncle Kahana said.

"Speak for yourself," I mumbled.

"What? Wait. I thought you said you didn't get hurt?" Mom asked.

She touched my shoulder, turning me toward her.

"Uncle Kahana's experiment," I said, biting my lip.

"Experiment? You tried this before?"

Mom shot me a worried look.

I ground my teeth and looked away.

"That was my fault, Aunty Liz," Char Siu said. "Uncle Kahana wanted to test the water in Nu'uanu stream. I splashed Zader before he was ready. He blistered and burned."

"How bad?" Mom asked.

I pointed to the clean spots and grimaced.

"I don't know about this," Mom said.

"This time you're in control, Zader," Uncle Kahana said.

Mom lifted my chin.

"You don't have to do this, Zader," she said. "We'll find another way."

"One finger, brah. That's all." Uncle Kahana said, but I didn't want to meet his eyes. "Think of it, Z-boy! If works, we can make you an outdoor tea shower, j'like the ones the military guys use in the field. You can 'au'au every day!"

The screen door banged. "Here's the tea," Jay said, carrying the big glass mixing bowl wrapped in a towel. "It barely fit in the microwave."

Under the mud, I blanched.

"Don't let fear hold you back, Zader. You can handle this!" Uncle Kahana said. "Pain goes away. Just try one finger tip."

"You don't have to," Mom said.

I looked in the steaming bowl and saw tea bags floating in pale green liquid; it hadn't been brewing long. The sharp smell of mint tickled my nose.

Mom put her arm around my shoulders and squeezed.

"I don't know what's going on, but I'm behind you. Whatever you want. It's up to you, honey."

I stuck my index finger out.

One finger, just the very tip.

Jay looked confused. "What's up to him?" he asked as I reached into the bowl.

"Auwi-eeeeeeeeee!" I shrieked, snatching my hand back.

"Let me see, let me see!"

Mom grabbed my wrist. She turned my finger toward the light from the garage. There, on the very tip of my index finger, an angry red blister swelled.

"Quick," Uncle Kahana urged, "by the stairs, Char Siu, grab ti leaf or aloe."

Char Siu ripped a ti leaf from its stalk and wrapped it around my finger.

"Here," she said. "Better?"

I nodded, holding my eyes open wide so the tears wouldn't drip down my cheeks.

Again!

I fell for his pupule ideas, again!

When am I going to learn?

I'm doomed to sitting on the beach wearing waders and a diving helmet.

Jay surfs; I draw.

I'm the weird one with the umbrella.

I wish everybody would just leave me alone.

"Why did you think this would work, Uncle Kahana?" I moaned. "I'm cursed with allergies that don't make sense. They don't have to. Stop trying to make things better!"

Still holding the ti leaf on my finger, Char Siu turned to Uncle Kahana.

"Maybe the tea's not strong enough," she said.

"Maybe. I dunno." Uncle Kahana rubbed his chin. "Something's still off. There's an answer, but we're just not seeing it."

"Want me to go make a different kind?" Jay asked. "There's chamomile. We can try again."

"I don't think that's it, Jay," Uncle Kahana said.

Nobody's listening.

Again.

Mom reached for my burning finger.

"Here, let me look."

"It's okay, Mom; it doesn't hurt anymore," I said. "It was just the very tip."

"Let me see anyway," Mom said.

"Guys, what do you want me to do with this? It's kinda hot."

Jay looked for a place to set the bowl down.

Uncle Kahana snapped his fingers. "That's it!" he said.

"What?" said Mom.

"This!" said Uncle Kahana.

He plucked the ti leaf out of Mom's hand, wrapped it around my wrist, and plunged my whole hand into the bowl of hot tea.

17

ALOHA, MARY POPPINS

Pau
Finished; complete; done.

"Auwi-eeeeeeeeee!" I shrieked again, the pain engulfing my hand like lava as I ripped it out of Uncle Kahana's grasp and away from the tea.

I flick, flick, flicked my wrist, sending scalding tea drops into the night.

This was getting old.

"Are you crazy?" Mom gasped, shoving Uncle Kahana away. "Are you trying to kill him?"

Char Siu reached out and caught my flailing wrist, holding it out to a yard light.

"Let go!" I howled.

"No!" she said, "Look! Aunty Liz, look!"

"What?" Mom said.

"No blisters, Aunty Liz! It's just a little red!" Char Siu said.

Stupid Char Siu!

Let me be alone in my pain!

"Let go!" I hissed.

"Just look!" she shouted.

"Let me see," Mom said, holding my hand steady in hers.

She pulled me closer to the light, turning it over and over. "Char Siu's right! No blisters!

"But it hurts!" I whined. "It's all red!"

"Of course, stupid head," Jay laughed. "I didn't make *iced tea*! Your hand's just a little red from the heat, you panty."

"Ti leaf," Uncle Kahana said, sucking his teeth in pride. "When you fell into the mud bog, you were holding ti leaves."

Like he's Sherlock Holmes.

All he needs is a pipe.

"And when it rained you were carrying ti leaves!" Jay said.

Watson.

"But not when I splashed you! Or when you first put your finger in the tea!" Char Siu grinned.

Nancy Drew.

Everyone stood around with big, goofy grins on their faces.

All I wanted to do was run and hide.

But the last time I did that I ended up at Piko Point.

I shivered.

I looked at the soggy ti leaf still wrapped around my wrist.

Ti leaves.

All this time it was ti leaves!

That's what Maka meant when she tossed me her ti leaf lei!

"I think—" I walked to the fish cooler, the forgotten water now overflowing onto the grass.

I held onto the ti leaf and plunged my whole hand into the water.

I heard my Mom's shocked gasp and Uncle Kahana's stifled, "Wait," but then—

Chilly.

Like walking into a movie theater or that first moment when you slide between the sheets at night. No pain, but a faint tingle buzzed along the surface of my skin, like the time Jay put one of Lili's country music CDs in the microwave to see what would happen. Through the microwave window, we watched lightning sizzling along the CD's edges, cracking and crazing like the chicken skin it raised on our arms.

My skin *hummed*.

Underwater, I wiggled my fingers, and the light from the lanai danced along the surface, blurring as flecks of dirt leaped from my skin like fleas abandoning a dog. I pulled my hand out of the cooler and held it out. It was spotless from my nails to my wrist, the skin shiny and bright and new.

I'd never been this clean.

I turned to Uncle Kahana. "Look!"

"No blisters!" Mom breathed, reaching for my hand. "No pain! It's a miracle! Oh, Alexander Kaonakai Westin!"

Her hands massaged each ridge and joint, assuring herself there were no blisters or pain.

"Does this mean I'm cured? I'm normal?" I almost couldn't say the words.

Jay opened his mouth. I heard the words *'Normal? Never!'* form in his mind, but he was grinning too big to say it.

So, Char Siu did. "Normal, Zader? You? Never!"

"With a ti leaf, I'm as normal as you are, Char Siu!"

I was smiling so big, my cheeks hurt.

"Eh, Zader, you know what this means?" nudged Jay. "No more umbrella-boy!"

"Aloha, Mary Poppins!" Char Siu high-fived me.

I couldn't wrap my head around it.

No more umbrella.

No more long sleeves and pants.

No more fear of sprinklers coming on in the middle of a soccer game.

No more watching each cloud in the sky.

No more shoes; I could wear slippahs like everyone else.

"Instead of an umbrella, I'll carry a ti leaf!" I said.

"Easier," Jay laughed.

Uncle Kahana's hand clasped my shoulder with a little squeeze and a shake.

"You won't have to carry a ti leaf, Zader. You can wear it. We'll make you a simple ti leaf lei you can wear next to your skin," he said.

He shook my shoulder again. "Looks like we don't need the tea after all, Jay. Zader can shower in regular water. First time ever."

Jay dumped the tea out on the grass, set the bowl on the stairs, and tossed me the dish towel.

"To dry off," he smirked, giving me a brotherly punch in the arm. "You gotta learn how."

"Zader's got plenny new things to learn," Char Siu said. "Swimming!"

My mind reeled.

Swimming!

"Jay, you can teach me to surf!"

"Shoots! We'll—"

Bark, bark, bark!

'Ilima rushed out from under the stairs and jammed her cold, wet nose on my leg.

"Aiyah!" I yelped. "That's ugi, 'Ilima! Get your snotty nose off my leg!"

She spun away to dash twice around Uncle Kahana's legs and then back to me. She barked some more as she swiveled her head between us.

"I get it. I get it. Timmy's in the well," Uncle Kahana muttered. "Kulikuli, 'Ilima!"

'Ilima's ears drooped.

She stopped barking, but her eyes narrowed, never leaving Uncle Kahana's face.

"What's up with 'Ilima?" Char Siu asked.

"What? Never heard a dog bark before? Don't most dogs run around the yard?" he asked.

Uncle Kahana raised an eyebrow at 'Ilima.

'Ilima blinked, then snapped her nose to the ground and started sniffing my toes and the fish cooler.

"'Ilima," I said.

She ignored me as she slurped some water, smacking and yawning like the only thing she was thinking about was taking a nap.

When her mouth stretched wide, I swear I saw little flickers of light surrounding her head for a second like Tinkerbelle's tiniest friends. She sneezed, and they were gone.

"Did you see—" I began, but Uncle Kahana gripped my shoulder, cutting me off.

"Zader, I know you want to surf with Jay," he said, his eyes scanning me from head to mud-covered toes. "But easy, yeah? Don't go so fast! If you're wearing a ti leaf lei, I think maybe you can handle fresh water for a short time, like getting caught in the rain or stepping into a puddle or even taking a shower. I dunno about swimming, especially in the ocean. The ocean's a whole other thing."

"Water's water, right?" I asked.

"No."

He tried to look me in the eyes, but I kept my eyes on 'Ilima as she yawned again. No sparkles, no fairy dust. She reached back and nibbled a spot on her leg, then scratched her ear.

(Just a dog. I'm just a dog. But no way am I licking my butt!)

What?! That wasn't MY thought!

"Zader, focus," Uncle Kahana said. "Salt makes your mouth tingle, right?"

"Yeah. A little bit. But I've never eaten salty stuff wearing a ti leaf," I said. "Things are different now."

"We need to do this slow, Z-boy. Remember our first experiments? We don't know the consequences of our actions—we only think we do. Promise me you won't do something crazy like jump in the ocean after Jay."

Jay chimed in, "But I can teach Zader to surf, Uncle Kahana, I know I can, just like Nili-boy and you taught me. Don't worry, Uncle; Zader's safe with me!"

"He's not the one I'm worried about," Uncle Kahana snapped.

Jay stepped back, confused. We knew Uncle Kahana was mad, but not why.

Isn't this a good thing?

Jay wants to teach me to surf.

I want to go.

Isn't this what we were all hoping for?

"Why?" I pushed, "Why can't Jay teach me to surf."

"Are you listening, Zader? We don't even know if you can go in the ocean without sizzling like a steak on a grill, and already you're planning to go surfing with Jay." Uncle Kahana frowned.

"So let's find out," I said. "The beach isn't far."

Uncle Kahana sighed. Jay looked at his toes, miserable. Char Siu picked at a scab, and 'Ilima nudged my hand with her nose.

I waited, but no one would look at me.

Invisible.

Mom crossed her arms. "No, Zader," she said. "Uncle Kahana's right. We don't know what could happen. It's late; it's dark. I don't care who you are, nobody should get in the ocean at night."

I knew my mother; she wasn't moving on this. It was all too much, too fast, and she didn't like making decisions when she couldn't see the road. If I continued to beg about going to the beach right now, she'd say it I didn't understand the risks. Out of love and a fierce sense of protection, she'd forbid me from surfing forever.

I didn't want that.

There was something about the ocean that called to me. I wanted to jump through the waves, feel the currents as I floated, and taste the salt in the back of my throat. I remembered the brief moment of perfection I felt mud sliding, the adrenaline rush of speeding into the unknown. If that was even the tiniest bit like surfing, I wanted it. But more than that, I wanted what Jay and Char Siu had; I wanted to be an island kid.

Tonight I'd have to settle for being able to run in the rain and take a shower. Losing the umbrella was huge. It was enough.

For now.

18

EYES ON THE BACK OF YOUR NECK

Tsunami

A series of massive ocean waves caused by earthquakes.

Standing in the front yard, the yard lights glowing like islands in the vastness of the ocean's dark, I felt tiredness sweep over me like a tsunami.

My limbs felt too heavy to move. For the first time in my life, I didn't want to eat dinner. I didn't care that the mud was itchy or that I could simply wash it all down the shower drain instead of oiling and scraping. I just wanted to curl up on the grass next to 'Ilima and go to sleep.

Can't this just be over.

"Okay, Mom," I said, swaying a little as the second wave of tiredness hit. "I understand. We're not going to the beach tonight."

"But we don't need to go to the beach to do another experiment!" Char Siu said, "We just need salt!"

She pivoted and flew up the stairs to the house.

"You're right, Char Siu!" Jay perked up, following her train of thought. "Grab something to mix it in!" he shouted.

"What's going on?" I slurred.

Can I do it lying down?

Jay ran to a ti plant near the house and stripped a few leaves.

"I'll make a lei," he said. "Char Siu's making saltwater. We'll prove to Uncle Kahana and Mom that you can go surfing."

"Whoa, Jay. If Zader's going to wear a lei to protect himself from water, it needs to last longer than fifteen seconds. I'll make it," Uncle Kahana said. "Take the leaves, wrap them in damp paper towels, and microwave them a little. They'll be easier to work with. "

More experiments.

I yawned, then bounced a little on my toes.

Got to wake up!

Char Siu came flying back down the steps and held out the salt shaker to Uncle Kahana.

"Here," she said.

'Ilima's head suddenly snapped toward the driveway, leaning forward as she peered into the darkness. I could feel her grumble, a sound low in her throat that was almost a growl. The hair stood up on the back of my neck and chicken skin prickled along my arms. I felt exposed, vulnerable.

Something's wrong.

Like a crab caught by a flashlight, Uncle Kahana froze, his hand held out for the salt.

"I know, 'Ilima," he whispered. "Now kulikuli. Don't draw attention. Don't make waves."

'Ilima lowered her head. I could see her twitch and quiver, trying to keep her sounds to herself.

"Chill, 'Ilima." Uncle Kahana's lips barely moved. "Don't give him a reason to look closer."

"What, Uncle?" Char Siu asked.

"I said thanks, Char Siu." Uncle Kahana absently patted her shoulder and took the salt.

A spot on the back of my neck twitched. I wanted to turn around and look behind me, but somehow, I knew that wasn't a good idea.

It's just a cat. The Chock's orange tabby, slinking around the bushes.

"Charlene, you better run home and let your mother know you're back," Mom said.

"And miss all this? No way!"

"Go call her at least," Mom said.

"Call who?" said a voice from the shadows.

"Mom!" Char Siu said.

Aunty Amy.

That's what's causing the hair to stand up on the back of my neck. She must have been watching us from across the street.

"Oh, so now you remember me, hah?"

Aunty Amy's slippahs slap, slap, slapped the driveway as she stepped into the light.

"I was just going to call you!" Char Siu said.

"Sure, sure," said Aunty Amy. "And I was just going to win the Miss America Pageant. Had my speech all ready and everything."

"Hi, Amy. As you can see, they're safe and sound," Mom said.

"Yeah, I see. I can see from my house. Good thing, too, or I would still be worried they were make-die-dead on the highway somewhere."

"Eh, howzit, Amy," Uncle Kahana said, clearing his throat. "Nice night, yeah?"

"You," she shook her finger. "You I'm going to deal with later."

"We went sliding down Nu'uanu," said Char Siu. "Zader fell in the mud."

Aunty Amy turned and really looked at me. "Aiyah! What happened to you? You look like you've been wrestling pigs! Is that rotten mango on your shirt, Zader?"

I sighed.

"I said turn left; he never. What can you do?" Uncle Kahana shot me side-eye.

"Mom! Zader doesn't have to worry about water anymore! All he has to do is wear a ti leaf!"

Aunty Amy looked between us. "You guys are pulling my leg. I've seen what water does to Zader."

"No joke! Fresh water is fine," Char Siu said, holding out the salt shaker. "We're testing saltwater now."

"Aunty Amy, maybe I can surf!" I said.

"Liz?" Aunty Amy asked.

"I don't know. I can't explain it, but it seems to work."

Aunty Amy exhaled sharply and crossed her arms.

She doesn't believe us.

Jay came back, waving the nuked ti leaves to cool them.

"Hi, Aunty Amy," he said. "No way, yeah? A miracle!"

"Jay, give me those leaves," said Uncle Kahana.

He stripped the center stems and deftly braided them into a lei that he tied around my left wrist.

"Keep it on all the time, Zader. Wear it tight, so it touches your skin all the way around."

We all stood in a circle, admiring my new lei.

"Now what?" I asked.

Mom turned to Uncle Kahana. "How is this even possible? How can wearing a ti leaf lei cure an allergy to water?"

Uncle Kahana shrugged. "What's a water allergy?"

"You told me when you brought him to me as a newborn baby it was an allergy," Mom said.

What?

Now I was wide awake, adrenaline squishing into my blood.

"You've seen the blisters, Liz. What do doctors say?"

"He obviously has a violent reaction to water, but only if it touches his skin. Nobody's heard of an allergy like this before, but doctors admit they don't know everything. Because you told me water would kill him, we've been keeping him from it since he was born." Mom bit her lip

She's forgetting that finding out about ti leaves was a good thing!

"But Mom, look!" I said, shaking my clean hand in her face.

"I see it, Zader. I'm just not sure I believe it."

19

SALTING THE WOUND

Pono
Goodness; proper; uprightness; well-being; in perfect order; balanced.

Uncle Kahana shrugged. "I dunno why, Liz. Like you always say, I'm just one broke 'okole old man. But does it really matter?"

"Yes. No."

She thought about it.

"I don't know. I just want Zader to be happy and safe."

Uncle Kahana said, "Zader's allergies came from Aunty Lei's side of the family. Maybe Aunty Lei wore ti leaf leis too. Hard to know. Everybody wore ti leaf leis back then."

"If ti leaves are the miracle cure why don't people know about this?" Mom asked.

"How many people do you know with water allergies, hah?" Uncle Kahana cleared his throat. "Maybe a long time ago people knew, but forgot."

"I've never heard of anything like this," Aunty Amy said. "Painting a ti leaf lei on the bottom of Jay's surfboard cured him of his fear of sharks; now wearing a ti leaf lei cures Zader of his water allergy? What's next, cancer? The common cold?"

"The old folks knew a lot, Amy. Anytime anybody was sick or traveling, they wore a ti leaf lei."

He stared at the moon, looking for inspiration.

"I'm not saying ti leaves cure anything—not really. People also used them for everyday things like wrapping food. I don't think it's the ti leaf itself; Hawaiians are all about symbols. It could be that wearing a ti leaf lei announces to the world that here is a civilized, respectful human being—what my father called pono. He always said 'aumakua or gods or spirits go out of their way to help and protect those who are pono."

"So spirits or whatever are blocking the water? That's what's helping Zader?" Char Siu asked.

Uncle Kahana sighed. "I really don't know. I'm sure my father knew, but I was too stubborn to learn."

"Why don't I know any of this?" Liz asked. "You're my uncle. I danced hula. I memorized chants. I learned about the healing properties of plants!"

"As a kid it was all around you, but you never learned how to listen. Your mother's fault. She was too modern. Me, too."

Mom drew breath to answer, but Jay was impatient.

"If it works who cares why? Let's do it!" he said.

"Zader," Char Siu nudged me, "try the salt."

"Straight or in the water?" I asked.

"Try 'em straight," Uncle Kahana said.

"Straight," Jay repeated.

"Okay, straight."

I held the salt up in the light and shook a few grains out onto my dry, clean palm.

"Well?" Char Siu asked.

Nothing.

This is good.

"It . . . stings, a little, maybe, but it doesn't hurt."

I licked off the salt, rolling it around my tongue.

"Same as always. It prickles a little. Kinda buzzes."

'Ilima rumbled again, but Uncle Kahana flicked his wrist and she stopped. She kept her eyes focused on something just out of the yard lights.

I looked, but didn't see a cat.

"The salt buzzes?" Uncle Kahana asked.

"Fizzes, maybe. Kinda like strawberry soda."

"Aw, no biggie! Salt does that to me, too!" Char Siu said.

Taking the salt, Uncle Kahana unscrewed the lid and poured a third of it into the glass of water.

"Ocean water is really salty." He swirled it around as it dissolved. "It's different than this. Sea salt isn't just salt; that's why it tastes better. I don't know what's in this salt or where it comes from, but we're going to try it anyway."

He handed the glass to me.

Let's get this over with so I can go to the beach in the morning!

I started to tip the glass, intending to pour it gushing over my hand.

"Remember Bull Lye, Zader," Uncle Kahana warned.

"Bill Nye," Char Siu said.

"Whatever. It's an experiment. Go slow."

I looked at Uncle Kahana, then used my index finger to barely brush the salty water's surface.

"Auwi-eeeeeeeeee!" I squealed, yanking my hand out of the glass and flicking the drop of saltwater from my finger.

Mom snatched my hand. "It's blistering and turning gray," she said.

Uncle Kahana handed Mom a ti leaf scrap. "Here, put this on it."

The ti leaf cooled the fire and the pain eased. "Better, it's feeling better," I said.

"I thought we had this all figured out!" Jay groaned.

Uncle Kahana punched my shoulder. "No surfing, Zader. Not yet. Promise me."

I nodded, my eyes on my finger.

A glass of Morton's salt in a cup is not the ocean.

Sensing my thoughts, Uncle Kahana held my chin, forcing me to look at him.

"You wear your waterproof gear on the reef. You understand?"

"Yes."

"No chance 'em. I mean it." Uncle Kahana glared at me. "Tell me, 'ae, Kumu."

"'Ae, Kumu," I repeated.

"And you two! No teasing or daring Zader to break his word! No experiments on your own."

"'Ae, Kumu," parroted Jay and Char Siu.

We heard the steel in Uncle Kahana's voice and knew he meant every word. Only fools crossed their fingers on a promise to their Lua instructor. In the old days it meant death, and while we didn't think he'd actually kill us, we feared there were worse things he could do.

"But the ti leaf lei works with fresh water, right?" Char Siu asked. "That's more than he had, yeah?"

I rubbed a finger along my lei, feeling the braid against my wrist.

Life was changing and I was tired, too tired to think about it. I felt tears start to well, but this time I didn't have to fight to keep them from spilling down my cheeks.

"Z?" Jay said.

Mom reached out and pulled me close, not caring that I was muddy or my nose was running.

"It's okay," she whispered. "It's a good thing. We'll figure this out."

"Now what?" I asked.

"Hose," said Mom, tugging at the collar of my shirt. "Backyard so you don't track mud through the house. Then we're going to introduce you to a hot shower and his best friend, soap!"

"Great," I mumbled into her shoulder. "Now I won't smell like a macaroon anymore."

She laughed. "No, you'll smell like flowers like everyone else."

Mom put her other arm around Jay.

"Come on you two. We've put on enough of a show for tonight," she said. "Good night, everyone."

"Aloha po, Liz," said Aunty Amy.

"Laters, Jay and Zader," called Char Siu.

"Man, is Lili going to be bummed," said Jay, punching my arm. "Now she'll have to fight two brothers for the shower!"

20

CONFESSION IS GOOD FOR
THE SOUL

Kapu
Taboo; prohibited; sacredness; consecrated; to keep out.

"Charlene Suzette, go home now. There's chili on the stove and rice in the cooker. Make a plate. I'll be there in a minute," Amy said.

"Okay, Mom."

Char Siu scuffed her slippahs down the lawn and out into the street.

"This was a good day!" she said.

Kahana and Amy stood in the driveway, listening to the squeals and shrieks coming from the backyard as cold water washed the mud from Zader's body.

A first, Kahana thought. *Wonder how many more are coming?*

Leaning against the hood of his car in the darkness, Kahana waited. Instead of jumping in the car when the boys went to the backyard, 'Ilima jogged up the stairs and curled up on the lanai, making a point of ignoring Kahana.

Great, Kahana thought. *I have two wahines huhu with me, and I don't know which one will bite first.*

He looked at the moon and sighed.

"Come, 'Ilima, we go."

He opened the car door and motioned to her.

'Ilima settled her head onto her paws.

"Kahana," Amy said.

He turned towards her, his face half hidden in the shadows.

"What happened to Char Siu?"

He shut the door.

"The kids built a cardboard sled. She went down the hillside near the ravine and landed on kukus. She's okay."

Amy nodded. "Jay's nose?"

"Char Siu's fist."

Amy blinked.

Uncle Kahana wiped his face.

"He deserved it. They worked it out."

When Amy didn't reply, he opened the door again, and whistled for 'Ilima. She tucked her nose under her tail and settled deeper into the lanai.

"Kahana, look at me," Amy said. "No allergies have ever been cured by a ti leaf."

"How do you know, hah?" he blustered. "Old days everybody wore ti leaves. Maybe nobody had allergies then."

"You are so full of shibai," Amy said, "I gotta wear taller slippahs around you."

Kahana tsked and hung his head. He met her eyes and nodded.

They stood there together in the fullness of the night, listening. In the distance, Kahana heard the sound of the waves brushing against the sand and the wind in the ironwood trees. Moths fluttered around the garage light, ready to be snatched up by bats or slurped up by geckos.

It was all the same in the end.

"Niuhi," Amy said.

"Niuhi only stories."

She nodded. "Stories to keep kids home at night, out of the ocean, and out of trouble. Stories that taught about respect for the old ways. Stories about kapu."

Kahana said, "The kapus managed natural resources. No area over-fished. No food source overharvested. Kapus ensured respect for chiefs and priests, keeping us all in line. Just ask any anthropologist. They know our past best."

Kahana tried to open his car door wider, but Amy blocked it with her hip.

Amy said, "I know what all the guys with lots of letters after their names say about our culture. I also know that a lot of the things they claim are true are really based on bulai stories told by old time Hawaiians playing Look-What-I-Made-a-Haole Believe."

"Tsk," said Kahana.

"Don't give me that," said Amy. "How many times have I heard you tell tourists that the hala tree at the pavilion is a pineapple tree?"

"Not my fault if they don't know the difference."

"Well, I do. You Kaulupalis are not the only old Hawaiian family from around here. I was a Kawena before I married," she said.

"Kaulupali. Kawena. Ho'opo'i. Kaneakoa," Kahana said. "I know the old families. We're all related."

"Niuhi," repeated Amy. "My grandmother knew your Aunty Lei."

"Ah."

"My Kawena kupuna told us kids stories about Ka-Pua-O-Ke-Kai and Ka-Lei-O-Mano and the reason the Niuhi sharks moved to Hohonukai. Liz never heard the stories?"

"No. My sister Beth, Liz's grandmother, wanted . . . something different. She never taught her daughter Becca, so Liz's mother never taught her. I was hard-headed, too. I had to lose everything before I learned to listen."

"Ka-Pua-O-Ke-Kai—"

"Zader's birth mother."

"Niuhi. I never thought I'd see the day. All these years! He doesn't know?"

"I thought it safer."

Amy's head rocked back. "For who? Him? Us?"

Kahana sighed. "Everybody."

"What're you going do?" she asked.

Kahana sighed again, looking to the stars. "According to Pohaku, it's up to kupuna to teach these kids," he said. "My kuleana, yeah?"

"As Kahuna Niuhi you bet it's your responsibility. Don't wait too long," Amy said. "Think of Nana'ue."

"We're fine. Zader is nothing like Nana'ue."

"What if one day Zader can't stand it and jumps into the ocean? What then?"

"He won't. He's been conditioned since birth to fear water," Uncle Kahana said. "Blistering is enough to convince anybody it hurts. If you think it hurts, it hurts."

"He's in the shower as we speak! I think he's past the fear of pain."

"Saltwater's different."

"I've seen him on the lava flow at Piko Point," Amy said.

"Covered from head to toe."

"And what other teen would spend so much time in that ridiculous outfit? He's there because he's fascinated by the ocean and reef. You can tell yourself he's out there to be close to Jay and the other surfers, but you know it's more than that. Every day you don't tell him, you're playing with fire, Kahana," Amy said. "And we're the ones gonna get burned. Nana'ue—"

Kahana slammed his hand on the top of his car. "Zader is NOT Nana'ue! I won't let him be!"

Amy threw her head back and filled her lungs.

Hands on her hips, she rounded on him.

Beep-beep!

Paul and Lili pulled up and parked on the grass next to Kahana's car.

"Hey, you guys are back!" Paul said.

He reached over and flicked off the radio.

"Howzit, Uncle Kahana, Aunty Amy! You guys want some pizza? We brought home plenny!" Lili said, holding up the boxes. "Dad always buys too much!"

Paul walked around the car and opened the door for Lili.

"Liz is such a worrier!" he said. "I told her nothing happened!"

Nothing happened! Kahana thought.

He thinks nothing happened.

Don't look at Amy.

You'll lose it.

Amy caught his eye.

Don't.

It was no use.

They cracked up.

"Bwahahahaha!"

Kahana doubled over. 'Ilima barked, jumped off the porch, and ran in a circle around the cars. Amy's whole body shook as she wiped her eyes.

"What? What'd I miss?" Lili asked.

Kahana and Amy fell against his car, holding their stomachs.

'Ilima bark, bark, barked, thumping her tail against their legs.

"I'm guessing it was something big, Lili," Paul said. "You guys wanna tell us over pizza?"

Kahana wiped his eyes and nodded.

"Better—better—" he gasped, "plant plenny ti leaf, Paul. You're gonna need 'em."

"Cheaper than umbrellas," wheezed Amy, "when it comes to showers."

"I think Zader's pau 'au'au for now," Kahana sputtered.

Amy whooped louder, 'Ilima dancing at her feet.

"Let's go, Dad," Lili said, shaking her head. "They're gonna be like this all night."

Lili walked up the stairs with the pizzas.

"Daddy," she said, "how come we always miss the good stuff?"

21

COMING CLEAN

Hoʻohuli
To cause or induce change.

I washed the last of the mud off my body, sending it swirling down the drain with the soap bubbles and shampoo.

I was warm clear to my core, the heat from the shower seeping through my pores to stoke an internal flame I didn't know needed fuel. I'd never been this warm before, not even sitting on the beach in the sun.

Is this what it's like to have a fever?

I watched my skin turn pink and red in the hot water, the steam rising like smoke from a campfire or Pele's breath from a lava vent.

The skin on my shoulders, back, and chest felt tight and swollen. My body felt plump, like a too-ripe mango falling from the tree. The buzzing in my blood and brain was low and steady, a low-voltage echo of the electricity that had snapped along my nerves and sinews months ago, the power releasing like lightning through my body at Piko Point.

Surrounded by ocean and pock-marked by saltwater splashes—no place to run, no place to hide—it was the moment I decided to stop acting like prey and turned the hunt on the hunter, breaking 'Alika Kanahele's nose along with his reign of terror.

Things were changing too fast. Just when I was ready to face next year's school without Jay, I found out I'd be going to Ridgemont with him and Char Siu. Just when I was resigned to carrying an umbrella and eating over-done steak for the rest of my life, I discovered the secret Maka was trying to tell me when she tossed her ti leaf lei at me.

What else had she been trying to say?

I haven't seen Maka since the night we spoke in my dream that wasn't just a dream. I wore my shark tooth necklace to bed most nights, but nothing's happened. Even when I fall asleep holding its sharp edges so tight in my palm that there are drops of blood on the sheets in the morning, nothing's happened.

Last week, when I carried the raw hamburgers to the barbecue, I had a strange compulsion. I needed to take a bite, or better, a whole patty, and slide it down my throat in one long greasy gulp.

Repulsed, I pushed that thought away, handed Dad the tray, and stood next to him as he dusted salt and pepper on the burgers and chucked them on the grill.

I stayed, fighting the urge to snatch one that was seared, but still bloody in the middle, and devour it right there.

In my mind, I saw myself satisfied and blowing on fingers burnt just a little bit.

Totally worth it.

More afraid of that thought than anything else, I turned and fled to my room, leaving Dad holding the bloody platter.

Later, I did sneak a piece that was still pink in the middle, wolfing it down in the kitchen.

That night I couldn't sleep and paced a circle from my bed to the living room to the refrigerator and back. I ended up sitting on the front lanai listening to the ocean until near dawn, and then slept too deeply to dream.

In the shower, my stomach growled.

The image of an uncooked chicken breast popped into my head, making me shudder, but I didn't know if it was hunger or revulsion that left me breathless and shaking.

Get a grip!

Raw chicken? You're crazy!

Nobody eats chicken raw!

I smelled the smoke from kiawe coals and heard a sizzle as the cold chicken's skin melted against the hot grill. My mouth flooded with the imaginary flavor of salty-gingery hulihuli chicken. I felt my teeth slicing through crisp skin to tender meat, a torrent of juice on my tongue.

No charcoal, no crunch.

Can't give that up.

Whaaaat?

Each thought whirled and blended, chasing faster than schools of fish on a reef.

I shook my head to clear it.

I leaned back into the water spray and rolled my shoulders as I tried to ease the tension I felt building inside me.

How can people do this every day?

Do showers unhinge everyone's brain or just mine?

As the water coursed down my spine, I felt like I was standing on the edge of a cliff, ready for the next step into nothingness. Like a fledgling, I was ready for flight. A fierce joy beat in my heart, drumming a rhythm that said my life was finally beginning. I was done huddling under umbrellas and jackets, afraid of every cloud and sprinkler.

No more hiding in the shallows.

I had three ti leaf leis—triple protection Mom insisted I wear—one around my neck that lay under my shirt and next to my skin, another around my right ankle, and the last one on my left wrist—left because it freed my right hand to draw and paint and pick my nose.

Mom made the neck and ankle leis from six strands; they were stout and unlikely to snag or rip. Woven with a simple tight twist, Uncle Kahana's lei on my wrist looked like a thin piece of green twine, a little thicker than a friendship bracelet with its ends newly secured by some floral wire Mom pulled out of the junk drawer. Anyone seeing it wouldn't think twice.

Perfect.

Hidden in a box under my bed, Maka's lei was fluffier, more girly, more like the ti leaf leis hula dancers wore to show off the precision of their moves.

My wrist lei was more like the one I'd painted on the bottom of Jay's surfboard, the one Uncle Kahana and Nili-boy said reminded Niuhi sharks of their manners.

I promised Uncle Kahana I wouldn't go on the reef without my head to toe waterproof gear, and I won't.

Not yet.

2 2

PIQUED

Ho'opihoihoi
To excite; to disturb; to upset; to alarm.

I t was late, the sun just a couple of hours away from cresting the
pali cliffs at dawn, when Kalei circled back to the house. Earlier
in the evening, Kahana and 'Ilima had stood in the yard talking
story with the people who lived there. Even to Kalei's eyes there had
been something odd about the gathering: lots of banging up and down
the steps, in and out of the house, and most of the attention focused on
a mud-covered boy.

'Ilima and Kahana knew I was there, Kalei thought, *and so did the boy
covered in mud, but how?*

He ran his tongue along his too many teeth.

This needed looking into.

23

THE GAME

Konane
Ancient Hawaiian board game similar to checkers played with black lava and white coral pebbles.

U nder the moon, Pua and Maka sat on the lava flow at Piko Point, a konane board between them.

"Pohaku, what's my next move?" Maka asked.

Waves of gentle laughter washed through Pua and Maka's minds. As a stone, Pohaku had a special interest in konane.

"Pohaku, stop helping! Maka needs to figure this out on her own," Pua said.

Pua brushed her hair back from her face and stretched, pulling each wrist high over her head. The kukui nut candle smoked a little in its coconut shell bowl, but the light it cast was more than enough for Pua and Maka to see the board. Maka had two, perhaps three moves before Pua won, but Maka didn't see it yet.

Strategy is her weakness, Pua thought. *She needs to think ten, twenty moves ahead. She's always not reacting, not anticipating. My daughter still thinks this is a game.*

"I'm going to win this time, Mom," Maka said.

It was their fifth konane game of the night.

Pohaku knew whatever Maka did, it wouldn't matter. When fate was cast, all an 'aumakua could do was give you a safe harbor to rest for the moment, then guide you to the next realm when the end came. He was a stone, a memory, and a go-between, not a miracle worker. In the old days when the beach pavilion was still a minor chief's taro and sweet potato fields, and Pohaku lived on the hillcrest above it, the people knew that.

He thought back to his first memory as an 'aumakua—watching a banana tree grow. While he could no longer remember the human face that once looked back in a calabash of water, he knew he was connected to this land and people in ways both profound and mundane, a matter of blood more than belief.

Change, like the ocean tide, is inevitable.

Sometimes it takes a stone to see it.

When the terrible day came, the day angry voices pushed aside his priest, and Pohaku was hewn from his altar and rolled down the ravine; the day when all the gods and 'aumakua were swept away in tidal waves of fear and confusion; the day the kapu laws were forever broken by the young Hawaiian king who dared to eat with women, Pohaku didn't waste time grieving. He rested and waited, watching clouds and seasons pass until finally, he was lifted out of the mud.

Washing away the dirt, Kahana offered him a new calling out on the reef. The Niuhi shark Pua had left her newborn son at Piko Point for Kahana to find, the baby the Westins called Zader. A go-between was needed to carry messages between Kahana and Pua.

There would be secrets, Kahana warned, and the Niuhi shark Kalei must never know.

Pohaku beamed; a child raised in secret was just like the old days.

But he didn't know until Pua laid the first birthday gift wrapped in banana leaves on the reef next to him that like Kalei, Zader had a twin sister, too.

Custom.

Destiny.

Tradition.

It was the same for Niuhi as 'ali'i.

It was enough to make a stone weep.

Maka studied the board. She reached to move a stone.

(NO,) Pohaku bubbled in her mind, (LOOK TO YOUR MOTHER.)

Pua was sitting relaxed and easy, a faint smile on her lips.

Maka withdrew her hand. She edged her fingers toward another, but her mother gave nothing away.

A splash at the big saltwater pool was the only warning before Kalei appeared, squatting next to his niece.

"You have no move," he said. "You're trapped. Might as well give up."

"Kalei, hush. Let her figure it out," Pua said.

"Even Pohaku can see she's lost." He patted Maka's shoulder. "Don't feel too bad; your mother has beaten me more than once."

"I give up," Maka said. "You win, Mother."

"Again, Maka," Pua said.

Maka sighed and reset the pieces.

To Pua, konane was serious business. Unless Maka came within three moves of beating her, Pua wouldn't leave Piko Point until dawn peeked over the mountain tops. The best she'd managed tonight was seven.

Kalei nudged Maka over.

"Let me," he said. "Maybe I can teach you something about strategy."

Pua's teeth gleamed in the moonlight.

"Accepted," she said. "White or black."

"Black."

Pua reached out and removed one white stone near the center of the board.

"Your move."

The pieces fell from the board faster than Maka could follow—ten moves, five moves, three moves, then the last move leaving Kalei's lone black lava rock with no white stone to capture, adrift alone on a konane sea.

"You beat me, Pua."

"Don't sound so surprised."

"You never used to beat me so easily when we were kids."

"Maka and I play nearly every day," Pua said, picking up the stones and resetting the board.

"Yes, Maka has you for a playmate." He tilted his head. "But that's not our way, is it? Do you ever wonder what it would've been like for Maka not to be alone?" he asked. "To have a twin to play with, to grow with?"

"She had a twin. Her sister died. You saw."

"I saw," he echoed. "I saw you grieve, but I never saw the birth. What I remember most is poor little Maka, so lost and all alone. Companionless."

"She's not alone," Pua said. "She has me."

"Our mother wasn't nearly as devoted," Kalei said.

"You and I had each other. We didn't need her."

"We had each other," he acknowledged. "But poor Maka has no one but you to play games with."

He toyed with the markers.

"You were never this good at konane as a child, Pua. I remember when you couldn't think two moves ahead let alone a whole game."

"I've brushed up on my strategy. I've had a lot of time on my hands."

"And I have had none."

Kalei flicked a hermit crab back into the water. He didn't like losing.

"Father keeping you busy chasing 'ahi?"

"No."

He picked up another crab and slipped it between his lips.

Bored Kalei is bad, Pua thought. *Too much time to notice what's best unseen.*

"I'm glad you're here," he said. "I've been meaning to talk to you. There's another Niuhi around."

No!

"Here?" Pua managed.

"Here."

Pua leaned back against Pohaku.

"That's impossible," she said. "You know we're the only Niuhi who dare to come to Lauele. Father's kapu was clear."

Eyes wide with terror, Maka took a breath as if to speak.

Pua quickly pulled Maka's head to her shoulder, smothering her words into a cough.

"What did I say about breathing from the top of your lungs?" she chided.

The stakes are too high. If Kalei sees Maka's face, he'll know!

In the hollow of her mother's shoulder, Maka hid behind her hair and tried not to shake.

"You've seen no one?" Kalei asked.

Pua shrugged. "The only Niuhi that come here are me, you, and Maka. Not even Father comes around anymore."

"You're certain?"

"Yes! Really, Kalei, you're obsessing. Are you afraid someone's going to steal your precious table at Hari's? I doubt any Niuhi cares about sumo like you. And if Father finds out—"

"He won't," Kalei said, "at least not from me. Just like he won't find out about your plans for Maka this fall."

"We went to school," Pua said.

"The old chief's school. That was different."

"So's this. Maka's going."

Maka twitched. Pua stroked her hair, soothing her.

Kalei brooded.

Finally, he spoke. "It might not be safe. I found blood."

He pointed at the edge of the big saltwater pool.

Pua turned her gasp into a yawn.

"So? Someone's lunch? Fishing bait, perhaps?"

"Niuhi blood, Pua. Not yours, not mine. Young."

Maka shivered and tried to disappear.

"Young? It must have been Maka's then. Darling, did you fall and scrape your knee? Breathing and walking, you know how it is," Pua laughed. "She just needs more practice."

"I know Maka's blood. It was similar, but not hers. A young male."

"There are no young males. You've made certain, Kalei."

Pua's eyes narrowed.

Maka moaned.

"Cough it up, sweetheart, you'll feel better." Pua rubbed her back in slow circles.

"I'll not have another Nana'ue, Pua. You know that. Once was enough," said Kalei.

"You act like I'm arguing," Pua said. "Your *son* was more than enough."

She ran her fingers through Maka's hair, coiling it into a bun.

"Besides," she continued, "no one's gone missing, at least not anyone who will be missed. There haven't been bounties on sharks in a generation or more—one of the benefits of the humans' greener living."

She tucked a flyaway strand behind Maka's ear.

Hair is such a bother, she thought.

"There're no young male Niuhi around here to devour your sashimi, Kalei. You're mistaken."

Pua smiled, showing all of her teeth.

"I smelled the blood, Pua. Niuhi blood," he said.

"A lot?"

"A ghost of a drop. Less. Not enough to track or follow. There was other blood here, 'ahi and human."

"Ah, don't you see? The 'ahi blood was from Hari's—somebody's sashimi lunch enjoyed at the beach. Really, Kalei, I don't see the attraction of Hari's; why do you insist on sitting in the dark eating stale, chilled fish drizzled with salty green fire and watching TV? You're as bad as the Menehune."

Kalei didn't like being compared to some of Hari's other night guests, although he knew they used his table, too. As he opened his mouth to argue that he'd seen the shows Menehune watched, and they were nothing like the thrill of sumo with its display of plump human meat slam, slam, slamming in slow motion, it occurred to him that this wasn't the point.

He's not taking the bait, Pua thought. *I've got to come up with another distraction.*

Kalei let the Menehune jibe pass.

"I know what I smelled, Pua, not wasabi and not Maka's skinned knee."

He sucked the last bit of crab out of its shell and spat it out.

"There's something strange going on. I've been watching a boy."

Pua pressed Maka's face deeper into her shoulder.

"Whatever for? Surely you can find something more exciting to do."

"He's a Kaulupali."

"The surfer, Jay. The one with the ti leaf lei on his board. I've seen him; he's good," Pua said.

"Not him."

"The older one they call Nili-boy? Though he's hardly a boy now."

"Not Nili-boy—although that's a good idea. I'll seek him out; he's helped me before."

"You talked with him?"

Kalei waved his hand. "Years ago."

"And you lecture me about being careful."

"This boy I'm watching lives with Jay—they are the same age, though not twins. He must be hanai. He must not like the ocean—I've never seen him in the water. I can't put my finger on it; there's something strange about him. He's aware," Kalei mused. "I think he sensed me tonight."

"He's a Kaulupali, you said? Runs in the family. He's probably fostering as Kahana's apprentice."

"No." Kalei picked up another crab. "There's an older girl. She would be the apprentice for this generation, I think. She would be the one to inherit Kahana's responsibilities as the go-between humans and Niuhi."

"A new Kahuna Niuhi?"

"Yes."

Kalei's still curious. Time to remind him of our obsolescence.

"There was another Kaulupali girl—Kahana's older sister—who was supposed to be the Kahuna Niuhi. She was well-trained, but she died, leaving Kahana to muddle through. The old ways are lost, Kalei. People do the best they can," Pua said, shifting her weight. "You can't blame them when their lives are so short, and they've forgotten how to ask the old ones for knowledge and memories." She patted Pohaku. "Think of our dear friend, Pohaku! He lives on the reef now and gets foolish fish offerings like some minor ocean god—you don't hear him complain."

"It's not the same," Kalei said.

"You want offerings—a priest dropping bundles of poi into your mouth as you swim by? Is that it?"

"I don't need offerings, Pua."

"Good thing."

"It's just this boy. There's something strange about him. If the old ways are lost, why hanai a child to apprentice these days?"

Pua shrugged. "Kahana wasn't the eldest and didn't complete the Kahuna Niuhi training, but he *is* the Kaulupali Kahuna Niuhi. Maybe shirttail relatives sent this boy to him to learn the old ways."

"He doesn't live with Kahana," Kalei said. "Kahana is involved, I'm certain, and 'Ilima, too. How anyone can believe she's a dog is beyond me."

"People see what they expect to see," Pua said. "You should know that better than anyone else."

"Those Kaulupalis are dangerous."

"They are 'ohana."

"Hmmmm," Kalei said. He stood up. "The boy bears watching."

"Boring," Pua yawned.

"I'm curious," Kalei said.

Maka whimpered, and Pua held her tight.

"Shhhhh," she soothed, "it's too much for you tonight. Let's get back into the water."

Pohaku hoped Kahana would visit him soon.

They had a lot to talk about.

24

A KNIFE THAT KNOWS YOUR HAND

Hae
Wild; fierce; savage; ferocious.

After our Lua lesson in Uncle Kahana's apartment, we'd stacked the practice mats in the corner, and Jay and Char Siu were putting back the dining room chairs, when I reached into my pocket and pulled out my pocket knife.

I snapped it open and tested the blade.

Still sharp.

The light through the sliding doors was warm; the sun would be setting soon, and I liked the way it played along the edge. I twisted my knife this way and that, carving the air and thinking of dragons fighting in flight.

"You like the blade."

I blinked.

In the dining room, Jay and Char Siu were frozen like statues, chairs held still in the air. Under the table, 'Ilima's ears were perked, and her tail was raised in warning. Uncle Kahana tried to look relaxed as he leaned against the kitchen counter, but anyone could see he really wasn't. His weight was evenly balanced, and I could tell he was ready to Lua strike in any direction—hands, feet, body, or head.

All eyes were on me.

I swallowed and straightened, fighting air dragons forgotten.

The way everyone was watching my hand made it feel dangerous, like they expected my knife to fly and cut somebody's throat. They didn't like my knife in my hand, but I didn't know why.

We were wiped out; Uncle Kahana had worked us hard for an hour, stretching and building strength, and then we'd practiced a new lua 'ai form for another hour, throwing and being thrown.

My body ached all over, but I knew better than to complain. Jay tried that once. Uncle Kahana apologized by saying it was his fault we weren't conditioned enough, then he worked us triple hard for a month.

Nobody ever complained again.

I looked at the knife in my hand.

"It's just my carving knife," I said.

Jay and Char Siu put the chairs down and stood awkwardly shifting their weight. For some reason Char Siu lifted her hair into a ponytail and twisted it up into a bun, like she did when we got ready to spar. Jay's fingers twitched. Uncle Kahana's eyes never left my face.

"Do you carry it everywhere?" he asked, like he was asking if it was raining outside.

Yeah, I thought.

"Sometimes," I said.

"Even when you're not working on a new carving?"

I shrugged.

"Let me see." He held out his palm.

No! Mine!

Thoughts pure and unbidden surged like adrenaline in my blood. I gripped the handle tighter.

Wait!

What am I doing?

I paused, confused.

Uncle Kahana saw it all as clearly as if I'd said it aloud, and I saw the thousand year stare of an 'olohe lua, a master warrior, looking back at me. He no longer pretended to relax against the counter.

I looked down, troubled.

I snapped the blade closed, walked over to him, and placed my knife in his hand.

I looked at my feet.

"Mahalo, Zader," he said mildly, like I'd handed him a soda or the TV remote.

I felt Jay and Char Siu breathe out as the tension left the room. Char Siu shook her hair loose while Jay straightened the last chair.

Uncle Kahana raised his voice slightly. "Kids, I think it's time to make a few changes to our training. We'll still meet all together once a week for conditioning and practice, but I want to meet twice a week with Zader alone and Char Siu and Jay together. You guys have different talents and gifts, and I need to work with you individually."

"How come I gotta train with Char Siu?" Jay asked.

"'Cause I need a tackle dummy for throwing," sniped Char Siu.

"Shut up!"

"You shut up!"

"Enough," said Uncle Kahana. "Because I said so. Because there are some lua 'ai I want to teach that takes two to learn. Maybe later I'll split you guys up, but for now, Char Siu and Jay, you will train together."

If some lua 'ai takes two people to learn, how does that work for me?

"What about Zader?" Jay asked. "Who's he going to train with?"

Good question!

Uncle Kahana bounced my knife in his hand, hefting it and watching me. I kept my eyes down.

"You two go get a soda from Hari's. Tell him it's on my tab. Z-boy, stay a little longer. I want to talk with you. You guys can wait for Zader downstairs."

"'Ae, Kumu," they murmured.

They slipped on their slippahs and shuffled out the door.

The silence was loud when they left.

Uncle Kahana put my knife on the kitchen counter and turned to the fridge.

"You thirsty? Want a drink?"

"No, thanks," I said, my eyes still on my knife.

He opened the fridge and pulled out a Diamond Head soda.

"Sure? Get orange."

"No. Jay will get me one from Hari's."

Uncle Kahana nodded and shut the door. He flicked open the can.

"Jay's good like that."

"Yeah," I said.

He chugged half the can, then put it down. When he picked up my knife again, I flinched. Even though his eyes weren't directly on me, I know he saw that. I could feel him assessing me, watching my reactions. I steadied myself, ready for his next move.

He flipped my knife over in his palm and flicked it open, kissing the edge with his thumb.

"Ho. That's wicked sharp. You do 'em yourself?"

"I have a stone in my nightstand."

"Every night?"

Yeah, I thought.

"Sometimes," I said.

"Since when do you carry a knife?"

Since the fight with 'Alika at Piko Point.

Since things have turned upside down.

Since I dreamed Maka threw me a ti leaf lei, and even though it's impossible, I have that dream lei in a box under my bed.

Since I've had chicken skin from eyes watching me in the darkness.

Since my compulsion to eat raw meat.

I shrugged.

He pinched the blade between two fingers and held the handle out to me.

"Take it," he said.

Nestled in my palm, my fingers automatically slid home; my knife in my hand was as familiar as a cell phone.

Uncle Kahana tilted his head, considering.

"Okay, Zader, I'm going to touch your hand and the knife. I want you to relax, but keep a grip on the knife. I'm going to turn your hand this way and that."

"Why are you telling me this?"

"Because I don't want you to react and cut me."

I almost dropped the knife.

"I wouldn't do that," I said, shocked to my core.

He caught my eye and held it.

"You would," he said, "if you thought I was trying to take it from you. You'd do it without thinking."

I don't want to believe him, but he might be right.

I remembered *no* and *mine* and shuddered.

"Okay. You can touch my hand."

Slowly, easily, he reached out and cupped my hand in his. He turned my wrist over and ran a light finger along the knife handle, reading how it fit in my hand. I had the blade down, like when I used it for carving.

He nodded and released me.

"I'm going to hold the blade. I want you to release your grip. I'm going to flip the knife over, and I want you to take the handle again."

"No need, Uncle Kahana. I can switch 'em."

I relaxed my grip, flicked my wrist, and the knife blade switched from pointing down to pointing up.

Uncle Kahana raised his eyebrows, but only said, "Let me check 'em again," and felt along the line of the handle in my palm.

"It's a knife that knows your hand," he mused.

"What?"

"Nothing." He waved it all away. "Show me what you were doing before. Carve the air."

I backed away from the counter.

"Like this?"

I flashed it right and left.

"No."

He frowned.

"What were you thinking of before?"

"Uh . . ."

"What?"

"Fighting flying dragons," I muttered.

"Flying dragons." He rolled his eyes. "Of course. Show me."

In my mind, I saw a red dragon with golden eyes and silver talons reaching down to strike at me from the ceiling.

"Aiyah!" I roared and counter-attacked, slicing the tip of its wing.

The dragon reared and thrust a claw at me.

I nipped it off and dove at its heart.

When at last the dragon was defeated, and I was breathing hard, I came to myself to find Uncle Kahana looking at me with his warrior's stare and steel in his eyes.

I quietly set my knife on the counter, and his body language eased.

"Kali," he said.

"Kali?"

"Kali. Filipino knife fighting. It's the best in the world. You are called to the blade, Zader. It speaks to you on a visceral level. That's not a knife in your hand. It's an extension of your mind and body."

"Kali."

My heart beat faster. I was going to keep my knife.

"Hari," he said.

"Hari?" I shook my head. "I thought you said Kali?"

"Hari is a Kali master. We trained combat soldiers together out at Bellows and Hickam."

Uncle Kahana saw my skepticism and laughed.

"Well, we were a lot younger then. Hari's the knife master. He's the one who should teach you."

"Hari?" I was beginning to feel like a parrot.

Hari was a slight man, smaller than Uncle Kahana. A chain smoker who hid his addiction behind a cupped hand and an easy grin, Hari was always accommodating, always had a card game going on in a back room, and always let Uncle Kahana use the store as his own personal pantry—I never saw Uncle Kahana pay for anything. Out of all the people I knew, Hari was the last person I'd suspect of being able to haul someone's trash.

Then again, Uncle Kahana didn't look like much either.

"Let me talk with him," Uncle Kahana said. "We'll set up a time this week and get started."

Knife fighting for real?

Awesome!

"But Zader." The steel was back in his voice. "Keep that knife in your pocket. I don't want you taking it out unless you're actually going to carve a piece of wood."

Limits.

More rules.

It's my knife.

I didn't like it.

I felt my shoulders tense and my fingers twitch, gripping my knife too tight.

"Can I sharpen it?" I asked.

He regarded me a moment. Not taking his eyes off me, he reached out to his soda, polished it off, and absentmindedly crushed the can flat.

Message received, Uncle Kahana.

"Yes," he said. "You can sharpen it. But you gotta be alone in your room when you do it. Jay can't be there. And only sharpen it in your room. Are we clear?"

"'Ae, Kumu."

"Good. Better head downstairs; Jay's waiting. By now the ice in your drink's melted. Get a new one if you like. Tell Jay and Char Siu refills are on me, too. I'll see you tomorrow."

I ran down the stairs and entered Hari's by the side door.

Jay and Char Siu were standing near the drink fountain, three giant sodas between them.

"So what? Are you in trouble?" Jay asked.

"No. Hari's going to teach me Kali."

"Kali?" Char Siu chirped. "You're going to learn to fight with a knife! Lucky!"

"But not us." Jay scuffed his slippahs on the cement. "Here," he said, as he handed me a drink.

"Thanks," I said.

It was easier now that I didn't have to wrap everything in layers of paper and plastic to protect myself from the condensation. Now that I could, I found I liked my drinks full of ice and very, very cold. I took a sip and let the sweet combination of fruit punch and Sprite sweep down my throat.

'Ono.

"Too much fruit punch?"

"No, it's perfect," I said. I took another huge gulp. "I don't know what Uncle Kahana's thinking. Maybe the three of us in one room with knives is too much."

"Seriously, Z, what's up with you and that knife? I've never seen anything like it," Jay said.

"Yeah. It kinda creeped me out how you were whipping it around," Char Siu said. "You were weaving it in and out, totally locked into whatever you were seeing. It was like—like—"

"Like we weren't there," Jay said.

"Yeah," said Char Siu. "I thought—I know this is going to sound crazy, but I thought—"

"Someone was going to get cut," Jay said. "Like there was going to be blood."

"That's it," Char Siu said.

"What?" I laughed. "I've used that knife a million times. I've never cut myself."

I saw Jay and Char Siu give each other side-eye.

Drop it, their eyes said.

"What?" I asked.

Jay shook his head. "Three of us in one room with knives could get crazy."

Char Siu shuddered. "I don't think I want to learn knife fighting anyway."

"Uncle Kahana said we all had different gifts and talents. He's going to teach you guys things without me, too, remember?"

"We'll just have to share. Teach each other what we learn," Jay said.

"Of course," said Char Siu. "But I think I want to skip the knife parts."

All the way home Jay and Char Siu bantered back and forth, arguing which weapons were best and over who would win if a Maori warrior took on a Shaolin monk. I listened and smiled, but my mind was far away.

My knife was heavy in my pocket, and my skin between my shoulder blades itched; I had the same feeling in the pit of my stomach I used to get just before 'Alika and Chad jumped me in the hallway at school.

There were eyes watching us in the darkness that I couldn't see.

I felt more like prey than ever before.

25

STALK

Chum
Blood and bits that fishermen use to get a shark's attention.

Kalei followed the three kids, trailing along in the shadows, not worrying if they passed out of sight for a moment or two. He knew their scents now and could track them at will. Kahana was teaching them Lua, and that made them interesting. Most interesting was the one called Zader, the one with the ti leaf leis. There was something about him, something familiar, but Kalei couldn't put a finger on it.

It was an itch he couldn't scratch.

26

K-POP DIVAS

K-Pop
Korean pop culture in all its forms, but especially music.

T wo days later, when I arrived for my appointment at the beach pavilion between Nalupuki and Keikikai beaches, Char Siu and some of the girls from her hula halau were already there, looking like shave ice samples in the window of a manapua truck.

Wearing electric pink, yellow, orange, and green high heels, short boxy jackets, and glitter bows, they were practicing what looked like a kapakahi version of the chicken dance to a wicked backbeat.

"No, no, no, no!" Lisa Ling bellowed over the blasting boom box, "Like this!"

On the downbeat she threw her hands in the air, bobbed left, right, swiveled her hips, and turned.

"Now you try!"

She re-cued the music.

Obediently Char Siu, Mele Kalima, and Becky Walters tried to mimic her moves.

"No," Lisa shouted, exasperated. "It's one, TWO, three, FOUR, swivel, turn, head shake, head shake! Remember the video! Krystal QT holds her hands like *this*," Lisa's hands pounced into cat claws, "and flicks her pinkie like *this* when she turns. You guys are off."

"Hi, Zader," Char Siu said.

She had raccoon eyes and yellow-tinged skin that was melting off her face and smearing on the collar of her bright orange and green jacket. It looked like the same jacket Aunty Amy wore to last year's Halloween party.

Now that I thought about it, they all looked a little Halloween-y to me.

Lisa whipped around. "You? What're YOU doing here?" she said.

I gave Char Siu-dem a howzit chin lift.

"Waiting for the Art in the Park guy. Why?"

Lisa threw her hands up in disgust. "That's today? You guys are painting the pavilion today?"

I nodded. "Getting started, at least."

"Codeesh! Now how are we gonna learn all the Krystal QT moves in time!" she wailed.

I didn't understand Krystal QT and the whole K-Pop diva-thing. The girls were obsessed with it, copying the hair, clothes, and make-up from their favorite performers. It all sounded like cats huffing helium to me, and the dance moves were jerky and fast, like anime on speed.

It made me twitch.

"We can do this, Lisa," Becky said.

"Not if we can't practice! Not before the first school dance!" Lisa said.

"Lisa, it's mid-June," I said.

"I know! We're running out of time! Ugh!"

She reached over to the boom box and twisted a knob, cutting off Krystal QT's screeching mid-screech.

Thank goodness, I thought. *My ears were starting to bleed.*

Between the music and the colors, K-Pop gave me headaches. I had to leave the room whenever Lili and Jay turned it on. Jay claimed he watched it to make fun of the K-Pop boy bands with their long droopy bangs and eyeliner, but I knew he was in love with Krystal QT.

I couldn't blame him; with her satin skin and cat eyes, Krystal QT was flawless—as long as she didn't open her mouth to sing or dance too fast.

"We can go to my house," Becky said. "My dad set it up so we can watch internet videos on our TV. As long as we keep it down, my mom won't mind."

A car door slammed in the parking lot. A guy in a baseball cap wearing an Art in the Park t-shirt headed toward his trunk.

"That's him," I said. "That's the Art Park guy I'm meeting. We're only painting the walls, so maybe you guys can still practice. I'll try not to watch."

"Ugh! Okay! We're going to Becky's house!" Lisa growled.

Everyone started gathering their stuff. Lisa opened her bag and dug around for a compact. She looked in the mirror and shrieked.

"Wait! Wait! Wait! We can't go anywhere looking like this! Lauele Girlz gotta glow with glam, not sweat! Quick! Everybody move! I'm dumping it!"

She tipped her bag over the table, and enough make-up and hair-spray to coat the entire pavilion spilled out.

"Line up!" she barked, "Look up. Get ready! Number four concealer first!"

She grabbed a tube of pale green goo and started down the line, daubing it under each girls' eyes—except for Char Siu who wasn't lined up with the rest of the girls.

"Char Siu!" she snapped.

"Nah, I'm good," Char Siu said.

Lisa narrowed her eyes, black-rimmed wider than a Pharaoh's.

"Char Siu, you know we all agreed I would do the make-up."

"I know. But I told Zader I'd help him with his art project. You guys go to Becky's without me. I'll catch up."

"Char Si-uuuuu! Nooooo," whined Mele. "We need you!"

"Yeah," Becky said, "We can't do the pyramid if you're not on the bottom!"

"Char Siu," hissed Lisa, "Girlz before boyz. Friendz before menz! Now come here; I gotta powder your nose!"

"Nah. It already feels too cake-y. I'd rather just wash my face. I can feel eyeliner on my chin."

"Charlene. Suzette. Apo. No. Make. Mistake."

Lisa ground her teeth and sprayed a cloud of hair spray over Mele and Becky, who tried not to cough.

"Have fun," Char Siu chirped as she slipped into the women's bathroom.

We heard the water splash on.

"Arrgh! Let's go!"

In a haze of perfume, hair spray, and baby powder, the girls sashayed across the parking lot.

"Remember," I heard Lisa tell them, "lead with your hips! Toe, heel, toe, heel, point, point, point! No walking like football players!"

"Are they gone?" whispered Char Siu from the bathroom.

"Coast is clear."

Char Siu stepped out, skin clean and fresh. Her newly bowless hair was swept into a simple ponytail. She kicked off her heels, tossed her jacket on a bench, and sighed.

"You promised to help me with the art project? Since when?"

She picked at some glitter on her fingernails and shrugged.

"Where's Jay?" she asked.

"Nili-boy's surf camp." I jerked my head toward Nalupuki's shore-line. "Nili-boy asked him to help with the littlest kids."

From the pavilion we could see a line of kids holding boards and waiting on the sand while Nili-boy and Jay took three at a time out into the waves.

"So, what's the deal with Art in the Park?" Char Siu asked.

I shrugged. "Mom got a call a couple of nights ago. Lauele Parks and Rec got some money from the county for a community art project and decided to do a mural on the beach pavilion. Since I got honorable mention in the Young Artists Competition last year and lived in the area, the guy in charge wanted to know if I would help him. It's a planning meeting, I think. I doubt we're painting today."

"All the walls or just the main one that faces the parking lot?"

"Dunno."

"You guys gonna do it all yourselves?"

I shook my head. "I don't think so. I think the Summer Fun kids are supposed to help."

Out of the corner of my eye, I saw the guy wearing the Art in the Park shirt put his clipboard down near the showers and pull out a measuring tape.

"So? What are you waiting for? That's the Art Park guy, right?"

I forced the sick feeling back to my stomach and concentrated on breathing. It's harder to barf when you're deep-filling your lungs.

This is different.

It's not like my little carvings at home or even having my art in the Young Artist Competition.

This mural is going to be seen by everybody I know every day.

It's going to be me all over these walls.

What if it's junk?

What if it's ugly?

What if people really hate it?

I touched my pocket and felt the shape of my carving knife through the fabric.

I took another deep breath.

Here goes nothing.

ART PARK GUY

Haole
Someone with a Caucasian complexion; to be Americanized; to assume airs of superiority; foreigner.

As I walked up to Art Park guy, I checked him out.

Everything about him was medium. He wasn't tall or short, dark or pale, and his hair wasn't down past his shoulders or in a military buzz. He was about five foot ten or so, local-looking on the far haole side of hapa, with wispy dark blond hair that poked out from under his baseball cap, curling a little this way and that. Cargo shorts, t-shirt—typical island attire, except for the tennis shoes and low socks.

In a crowd, you'd mark him as a puka shell tour guide or maybe a volunteer soccer coach. He was too old to be a Summer Fun leader, although he had that vibe—early thirties Summer Fun Camp Director or Big Brother sponsor, maybe.

I watched him fiddle with the tape measure as he eyeballed the wall.

Except for the shoes, he blended. He seemed almost unremarkable until he turned and looked at me, and I saw his eyes.

Gold?

Green?

Light brown?

They changed with the light and probably his mood. When he realized I was coming up to him, they softened, turning hazel with flecks of gold.

"Alexander Westin?" he asked.

He sounds like he's from California. Not local.

"Zay-dah," I said.

"Zader," he said.

Definitely not local.

"You don't go by Alex?"

I shook my head. "I go by Zay-dah."

"Zay-dah it is," he said. "Good to meet you."

He held out his hand.

I wiped mine on my shorts and then took his.

His grip's firm, but not crushing.

He tried to say my name better the second time.

Maybe this is going to be okay.

"I see you brought a friend."

"This is Char Siu," I said.

He looked at her, startled.

"Char Siu? Like the Chinese roast pork?"

Char Siu drew herself up to her full height, tilted her head up, and looked down her nose.

"Charlene Suzette Apo." She held out her hand like a queen to courtier.

Art Park guy took her fingers and grinned.

"Milady," he said, sweeping his baseball cap off his head and bowing like a three musketeer. "Your humble servant."

Char Siu giggled.

My mouth hit the floor.

"My friends call me Char Siu," she simpered, then glared. "But NOT like Chinese barbeque!"

He laughed and stood up. "Are we friends?"

"Yep. Just don't call me Manapua."

"Never," he said, releasing her hand.

Char Siu cut her eyes at me. "What?"

I shut my mouth with a snap.

"Nothing," I said. "Not. One. Thing."

Her eyes narrowed to stink-eye, but she let it pass.

"Okay, so it's Char Siu and Zader, right? I'm from the Honolulu Arts Council and the Art in the Park program. You guys ready?" We nodded. "Okay, first things first. Let's get the measurements of all these walls. Looks like we've got a lot of space to work with."

And you are . . .

Typical.

Adults always assumed they were so important that kids automatically knew who they were.

Whatever.

I'm going to call him Art Park guy until he says different.

Char Siu and I took the tape measure and held it along the pavilion's walls, calling out the numbers and re-measuring when he said the tape was crooked or he needed to check a dimension. We could see him sketching and making notes on his clipboard as he walked around looking at everything from different angles and muttering about the light.

We'd finished the last wall when Uncle Kahana and 'Ilima came up from the beach. I smelled the fresh fish in Uncle Kahana's net bag before I spotted him by the showers.

I waved.

"Howzit," he called.

"Eh, Uncle Kahana! Good fishing?" Char Siu called.

He held up the bag. "What do you think?"

"Beautiful," said Art Park guy. "What is it?"

"Dinner."

"I mean, what kind?"

Uncle Kahana's smile deepened when he spotted Art Park guy's clipboard and tennis shoes. He gave me and Char Siu a quick side-eye as he lifted the fish from the bag.

"Uhu," he said. "Parrotfish. Wanna see?" He held out the fish.

Ho, Uncle Kahana! Good one! No mainlander wearing tennis shoes to the beach would touch a fish unless it was served on a platter!

Art Park guy didn't hesitate. He took it by the gills and held it up to the light.

"The blues and greens are spectacular."

Uncle Kahana wiggled his eyebrows at me. I shrugged.

"He's the Art Park guy," I muttered.

"Look at the way the light shimmers on the scales, Zader. We'll need to keep this in mind for the mural." He glanced back at Uncle Kahana. "They eat coral, right?"

Uncle Kahana nodded. "You can tell by the shape of the mouth. So you're the Art Park guy?"

"Justin Halpert," he said and grinned, thrusting out his fish-slimed hand for a shake.

28

ALL IN THE ʻOHANA

Kuʻauhau:

Lineage; to recite genealogy.

H*o!*
Art Park guy got the joke!
Maybe he knows how ridiculous he looks wearing shoes to the
beach.

Uncle Kahana chuckled, caught in his small-kine prank.

"Kahana Kaulupali," he said, changing the haole-style handshake to a local boyz grip. "And this is ʻIlima."

She chuffed, wagged her tail, and went back to the trash.

"You're not from around here."

"No. I grew up in California, but my mother's family is originally from Lauele. I moved into the area a couple of months ago."

Uncle lifted his chin to the pavilion. "To create a beach mural?"

"No," he grinned, "that's just a summer gig. I'm teaching art at Ridgemont Academy in the fall."

"Ridgemont? That's where we're going!" Char Siu said.

Art Park guy startled. "You, too? I knew about Zader—"

"You did?" I whipped my head around.

"Yeah. That's why I called your mom."

"Oh. I thought it was because of the Young Artist Showcase."

"That, too."

"Wait." My head was spinning as I realized who he was. "You're the teacher who saw my art portfolio and got me into Ridgemont!"

"You got yourself in, Zader. You're very talented."

I was overwhelmed.

What I thought was a summer lark was turning out to be an audition for my new art teacher.

I blanched.

Uncle Kahana came to my rescue.

"Halpert, hah? Any relation to Donna Halpert?"

His turn to be surprised again. "Donna Halpert is my mother!"

"No joke? Little Doni is your mother?"

"Yeah! Do you remember her? She said her family came from Lauele."

"Oh, yeah! Her dad and I used to go fishing. You're a Kawena! I thought you looked familiar!"

"Kawena?" Char Siu asked. "My mom's a Kawena."

"My Mom, too," said Art Park guy with a smile. "Cool beans."

He held his knuckles out to Char Siu to bump.

"Donna Kawena Halpert. That would make you—oh, no way," said Uncle Kahana appalled. "Nancy?"

"She's my cousin. I guess you met her."

"Ho! I almost had a heart attack! For a moment I thought you were going to say sister!"

Uncle Kahana wiped his brow.

Justin shrugged. "Nancy's my cousin, but I don't know her very well. I promised my mom I'd look her up. She married a Liu from around here. Do you know the family?"

Liu! That's my mom's last name, I thought.

Uncle Kahana gave me another side-eye.

"Yeah, you could say that. I know all the old Lauele families," he said.

"Do you know Nancy? We heard she moved to Hawai'i with her husband after their wedding in San Diego. He was in the Navy, I think," said Art Park guy.

"You know her husband died?" Uncle Kahana asked.

"Yeah, we heard that. Is Nancy still around?"

"Uh, somewheres, I guess. Last I heard Kaneohe, I think. Here. Let me take that."

Uncle Kahana took the fish and dumped it back into the net bag.

Art Park guy turned on a shower to wash his hands.

"Now that she's older, my mom is all into family history again. She's doing research, trying to trace our Hawaiian line. She's not happy I'm here. I think she wants all her chicks home where she can keep an eye on them."

He leaned towards the water spray and rubbed his hands.

"I haven't seen Nancy in, what, fifteen, sixteen years? She might even be back on the mainland," Uncle Kahana said.

I nudged Uncle Kahana. "Who?" I whispered.

"Nancy Liu. Your Uncle James's wife. Your sister Lili's biological mother."

"Uncle Jamie's *wife*?" I squeaked. "Lili's mother? She's alive?"

"Who told you she was dead?" Uncle Kahana hissed.

"Nobody. I just thought—"

"Liz's brother James is dead. His wife is not, however much your mother wishes her to be," Uncle Kahana whispered.

"So, she what? Ran away?" I asked, appalled.

"Pretty much," said Uncle Kahana. "Said she needed space to find herself."

"I heard it was with a mahu kumu hula from Kalihi," said Char Siu.

"Not," I said.

"Truth," said Char Siu. "My mom said."

"Kulikuli, you two! Not now," snapped Uncle Kahana.

"I heard about her running off with some hula teacher, too," said Art Park guy, shutting off the water.

He must have bat ears like me.

So much for our whispering!

"With Nancy, nothing surprises me," he said. "When we were kids, she used to hold me down and tickle me 'til I puked."

Gross!

TMI!

TMI!

"You knew Nancy and James had a daughter, Lilinoe?" Uncle Kahana asked.

Stunned, Art Park guy stopped shaking the water off his hands.

"No! We heard James died, but nobody said anything about a baby."

"She was adopted by James' sister Liz and her husband Paul." Uncle Kahana gestured to me. "Zader's parents."

"Lili's my sister," I said.

"Char Siu and now you! More family! My mom will be thrilled. I'm thrilled."

Art Park guy gave me knuckles, too.

"Nancy's your cousin," mused Uncle Kahana. "Hard to keep track. Your grandparents have been away a long time."

"They lived in Nevada for a while. Ended up in California. Said they missed the ocean."

Char Siu rubbed her nose. "So that makes you—"

"'Ohana. To you both," Uncle Kahana said. "To all of us."

He started to lean toward Art Park guy like he was going to honi, but cleared his throat instead.

"Welcome home, Justin. I'm sure your new family is going to want to throw you a party. There are a lot of people who will be interested in meeting you."

"Can't wait."

"We need to tell Liz—that's Zader's mom, and Amy—Char Siu's mom—about you! What's your number?" Uncle Kahana patted his pockets.

Like he carries a pen fishing.

No act, Uncle Kahana.

Art Park guy grinned. "I'll give it to Zader."

"Good, good."

Uncle Kahana set his fishing spear on his shoulder.

"Char Siu," he said, "you almost done here?"

She looked at me.

I nodded.

"Yeah, think so."

"I talked with Jay on my way up the beach. You and Jay, my house, half an hour. Zader, I'll see you Thursday around seven. Okay?"

"Shoots," I said.

"'Ilima!" he called. "Time to go!"

'Ilima meandered back from the trash cans, tail in the air. I think she found somebody's plate lunch. I smelled sour macaroni salad, the mayonnaise gone bad, and 'Ilima was sucking her teeth.

Char Siu pulled at her skirt and sighed.

"I better go home and change first," she said, "No way I can spar in this."

"So what? The only time you're going to fight is when you're dressed for it? You gonna tell the mugger, 'Oh, not today, I'm wearing a skirt?'" Uncle Kahana laughed.

"Pshhtt." Char Siu waved her hand and walked to her jacket. "I would fight a mugger, skirt or no skirt. But this is Jay! I don't want him seeing my panties!"

"Ugh. Change. Please," I said.

She bent under the table and picked up her heels. She started to put them on then stopped.

"Stupid things," she said. "I'm not walking home in them."

She rolled the shoes in her Halloween jacket and stuffed the ball into her bag. She wiggled her toes.

"Laters, Zader. See you soon, Uncle Kahana. Bye, Uncle . . . um . . . "

Art Park guy laughed. "We never straightened that out."

Char Siu and I exchanged a look.

Uncle Kahana and 'Ilima stood there, heads cocked.

"If it were up to me, I'd have you guys call me Justin," he said, "but since I'm going to be your teacher, and Ridgemont is kinda formal that way, you'd better call me Mr. Halpert."

Lili's mom's cousin wanted us to call him Mr. Halpert?

'Ilima chuffed.

"California," muttered Uncle Kahana.

She chuffed again, shaking her head. When she saw me staring at her, she turned it into a sneeze and scratched her ear.

Allergies, my foot.

29

BLANK PAPER

'A'a
To accept a challenge; a small root; figuratively, an off-spring.

"Okay, Mr. Halpert," said Char Siu. "I'll tell my mom about you. Uncle Kahana's right. She'll want to throw a party."

"Nice meeting you, Char Siu, Mr. Kaulupali."

"Call me Uncle Kahana," he said. "We're family."

Some more than others, Mr. Halpert, I thought.

"Uncle Kahana, then," said Mr. Halpert.

"Aloha, everybody. Come, 'Ilima; we go. Zader, tomorrow seven pm! Don't be late."

"I'll be there."

And then there was just the two of us.

Mr. Halpert fiddled with his clipboard.

He stared at the wall.

He checked his notes.

I waited, distracted by everything I'd learned.

Finally, he spoke.

"So what are your thoughts, Zader?"

My thoughts?

About the fact that you're my new art teacher, the one that saw my art and fought to get me into Ridgemont?

That you're related to Char Siu and Lili?

That Lili's mom is alive?

That you want me to call you Mr. Halpert instead of Uncle Justin?

That Char Siu and Jay are having their first Lua training session without me?

That Char Siu wears panties she doesn't want Jay to see?

I opened my mouth, then shut it quickly, afraid I would say something about panties.

I couldn't get that thought out of my head.

Finally I just shrugged.

He sighed. "It's all a little overwhelming."

I nodded.

He tapped his papers with his pen. "But remember, just because the walls are big, it doesn't mean they're any harder to fill than a sketch pad. We just have more to work with."

Oh.

The mural.

Not even on my top three concerns list.

I looked at the wall, considering.

He copied some numbers on a new piece of paper and handed it to me.

"Here are the dimensions of the four main walls. Do you have graph paper at home?"

"Yeah. We used it in math last year."

"Good. Figure out a scale, say six inches to one square. Draw the walls. Tape pages together if you have to. We're going to paint all four walls. I want you to think of it as one picture that wraps all the way around. Got it?"

"I think so. I'm taking the walls, combining them into one long wall, and scaling it down."

"Right. Don't forget the restroom doors and windows. We'll have to incorporate them into the design."

"Okay. But Mr. Halpert?"

"Yeah?"

"How is this going to work? I mean, it's not just you, me, and Char Siu painting this mural, right?"

He laughed. "No. You and I will come up with a design. We'll draw it on the walls with pencil and tape. We'll break each section down into areas and number them like paint by number kits. The Summer Fun kids will fill in the biggest areas while we supervise. Later we, and maybe a few others from Ridgemont, will go back and add all the details. Make sense?"

In my mind I could see how this was supposed to work. It made sense—if you never went to Summer Fun.

Those kids were nuts.

"Yeah," I said, "I understand. But what are we drawing?"

"The theme?"

"Yeah."

He flicked my paper. "That's for you to figure out."

I blinked.

He's pupule.

He laughed, "You think I'm crazy."

Close enough.

He laughed harder. "I'm not. You can do this, Zader. I've seen your work. Come up with some ideas."

I'm going to hurl.

I have to come up with the mural on my own!

That's it. I'm just gonna curl under that table and hide.

He saw the fear on my face.

"Zader, relax," he said. "You're talented! With talent you can always fix drawings after you make them, but not even a genius can fix blank paper. Just start! Sketch your ideas without worrying about whether or not they're good. We'll get together again Wednesday morning and see what you've come up with. Deal?"

He's seen my work and thinks I can do this? One turtle carving honorable mention, and I'm supposed to design a beach mural?

I swallowed.

"Deal," I croaked.

Might as well give up my Ridgemont scholarship now.

30

SECRETS

E ʻike e na maka mano
To see through the eyes of a shark—mentally, physically, and spiritually.

J ay and Char Siu had stretched, frog-walked ten laps around the apartment, and side-stepped up and down the stairs as fast as they could another ten times.

Now they were standing on mats in the living room in Uncle Kahana's apartment, trying not to breathe too hard in the stifling humidity as Uncle Kahana walked around shutting all the windows and closing the blinds.

ʻIlima was crashed out on the couch, head back and tongue out.

Now what, Jay thought. *Is heat stroke this week's lua ʻai? Uncle Kahana really needs air conditioning!*

Uncle Kahana grabbed a kitchen chair, turned it backwards, and sat in front of them. Leaning forward on the chair's back, he motioned them to sit on the ground at his feet.

Rubbing his chin and nodding once, he began.

"Huna na mea huna: keep secret that which is sacred. What does that mean to you, Char Siu?"

"It means we don't talk about Lua or what we do here with anyone not in our Lua school."

"Jay?"

"Yeah. The same."

"Who is here today, Jay?"

Jay sat taller. "You, me, Char Siu," he said.

"And 'Ilima," Char Siu added.

"And 'Ilima," Jay said.

'Ilima thumped her tail.

"'Ae, Jay. Who is not here, Char Siu?"

"Zader."

"Zader," echoed Uncle Kahana. "What I am going to teach you is not for Zader."

Not Uncle Kahana, too! Jay thought.

"What! Why?" Jay said. "He's one of us!"

Uncle Kahana folded his arms.

"I know you kids. You probably made a pact that you would share what I'm teaching you separately—"

"Nuh-uh!" Jay said.

"No lie," Uncle Kahana chided.

How does he know? Jay thought. *He doesn't unless we tell him! He's guessing!*

Jay looked down, unable to meet Uncle Kahana's eyes.

"Loyalty is important, Jay. You guys are going to need it. But I need you to trust me and to do what I tell you. You cannot teach Zader what I'm going to show you. You can't even tell him about it. Can you do that?"

Jay thrust out his bottom lip and scowled.

"What if we don't want to?" Jay asked.

"Jay!" Char Siu touched his arm.

"C'mon, Char Siu!" he exploded. "He's acting like 'Alika and Chad! It's another way to exclude Zader. We can't let him do that! You promised me we wouldn't let people treat Zader like that anymore."

Uncle Kahana flicked his eyes at Char Siu.

Well? he seemed to say.

"Uncle Kahana isn't mean like 'Alika or Chad. There must be a reason."

"Okay. So?" Jay asked.

"What?" Uncle Kahana replied.

"Is there a reason?"

"Yes."

"And?"

"And you don't need to know why, you just need to do." Uncle Kahana scratched his arm and sighed. "You can't tell Zader anything about what we do or talk about here."

He can't make me, Jay thought.

"What if we don't agree?" Jay said.

"Then we're pau." Uncle Kahana stood up.

Jay dropped his head. He picked at a piece of lint on the floor, confused and upset.

Char Siu hesitated, then stood up and faced Uncle Kahana.

"Can't you tell us anything more?" she asked.

Uncle Kahana lifted his chin. He glanced at 'Ilima on the couch, then Jay on the floor, his mouth in a stubborn line.

He softened.

"You don't have to lie to Zader, Jay. You can tell him that I said I'll teach him this later, after he learns what Hari's teaching him. He's going to be too busy to care much about what you guys are doing anyway."

"Does he have to keep what you're teaching him a secret from us?" Jay asked.

"No. He can tell you. He just won't be allowed to practice what he learns with you. Too dangerous."

"But we can't say anything?"

"No."

Uncle Kahana reached out to Jay's shoulder and shook it.

"J-boy, I know this is hard for you. But you have to trust me. Zader may never need this knowledge. But you will."

He reached out with his other arm to include Char Siu.

"You both will."

Jay looked up. He frowned, chewing his lip.

Don't blink, he thought. *If you blink the tears will fall.*

"I'll tell you this much more, and then you can decide. I know if you promise to huna na mea huna, keep secret what I teach you, you'll keep your word."

"'Ae, Kumu," Char Siu said.

Jay sighed and nodded.

"I want to teach you ocean lua 'ai, forms that are specific to fighting in water. I want you to learn how to use the sea—the waves and currents—among other things. I think you're gonna need it."

Jay jumped up. "Because we surf? Because Zader can't go in the ocean?"

"Is that why you don't want Zader to learn this?" Char Siu asked.

Uncle Kahana pursed his lips into a hard line. "That's all I'm telling you until you promise to keep it secret. Promise now and mean it or we're done."

Jay and Char Siu exchanged a look.

Char Siu nodded.

Jay closed his eyes.

This is wrong, but I can't make it right.

"'Ae, Kumu," Char Siu said, "I will huna na mea huna."

Jay opened his eyes and squared his shoulders.

"I don't like it, but I trust you, Uncle Kahana. Me, too. 'Ae, Kumu."

The air rushed out of Uncle Kahana's lungs.

He smiled. "Maika'i, haumana, maika'i. Sit, sit."

When everyone was comfortable again, he said, "E 'ike e na maka mano. To see through the eyes of a shark."

'Ilima jumped off the couch and barked.

"Quiet! We talked about this, 'Ilima. I know what I'm doing."

'Ilima huffed and wrinkled her nose. Her ears flattened against her skull.

"Enough, 'Ilima. I'm doing it."

'Ilima shook her whole body from the tip of her snout to the end of her tail like she was flicking water off her coat. She raised her nose to the ceiling, daintily stepped to her dog pillow, and disdainfully flopped down, her back toward Uncle Kahana and his Lua lesson.

Char Siu and Jay exchanged another worried look and waited.

Uncle Kahana sighed. "I'm going to teach you how a shark sees the world and how to defend against it. This is shark lua 'ai."

"Shark style!" Jay said, throwing a one-two punch.

"You going teach us how to punch a shark in the gills or nose?" Char Siu asked.

"No. Yes, that's part of it. It's more about understanding how a shark thinks, his perceptions of how the world works. You'll need to think like a predator after prey."

"Pray? How? Church kine or chant kine?" Jay asked.

Char Siu smacked her palm on her head. "P-r-e-y, Jay. Like what predators hunt, lolo. What a shark eats."

"Oh. Well, what kine shark?" Jay asked. "Some eat squid; some eat fish; some eat—"

"Niuhi," said Uncle Kahana, "the only kine that matters."

"A shark that knows what it hunts," breathed Char Siu.

"Man?" Jay asked. "That's why we need to know, right? Uncle Kahana, you said only Niuhi hunt humans."

"Kids, you're getting ahead of yourselves here. Let's step back. Lesson one: stalking. A Niuhi shark watches and waits. It studies its prey."

"No way. Sharks see food and they bite. That's why people chum," Jay said. "I've seen the Shark Week shows. You should watch some too, Uncle Kahana, if you want to know about sharks."

"If sharks only bite when there's chum—" Char Siu started.

"Then if you don't look like chum, you don't need to worry, hah?" Uncle Kahana threw up his hands. "That's common a shark. I'm talking Niuhi."

Uncle Kahana reached out and poked Jay between his eyebrows.

"Here." He tapped again. "You need to think like a Niuhi. You need to open your shark eyes here."

His fingertip brushed Char Siu's forehead.

"Plenny people all over the world say humans have a third eye, an eye that lets us see things more clearly. I'm telling you have way more than three. We all get choke eyes, haumana, but the one you choose to look through is how you perceive everything—friend, enemy, problem, solution, good, evil—it all changes depending on the eyes you look through."

He paused, regarding them.

'Ilima snorted and rolled over. She put her paws over her nose and narrowed her eyes. Stink-eye to the max.

Uncle Kahana shuddered. "Knock it off, 'Ilima."

She padded over to him and nudged him with her nose.

Uncle Kahana patted her head, working his way down her back.

She leaned into him and rested her head in his lap.

"I worry about them, too," he said. "But they can't hide in the sand any longer. Okay, haumana, everybody up! Time to stalk like a shark!"

31

THE COMPETITION

Hammajang
Broken; used up; old; worn down; junk.

As I crossed the parking lot to the pavilion, I almost dropped my sketchbook.

It was filled with drawings, but I didn't like any of my ideas. The wall space was huge, and nothing I thought of would fill four sheets of paper let alone entire walls.

Mr. Halpert said we could fix anything as long as it was on paper, but I doubted it.

He's going to take one look at these and send me to Lauele High.

He'll give my Ridgemont scholarship to somebody else.

Everyone will know I can't do this.

I wanted to die, but I made myself walk on.

In the shade of the pavilion, Mr. Halpert was waving his hands excitedly as he talked to another kid. When I got closer, I could see pages of what looked like graffiti from a freeway sign spread all over the table.

Oh-oh.

He brought a replacement!

Mr. Halpert smiled. "Zader! This is Owen Porter. Owen, Zader Westin."

Owen gave me a chin lift.

I gave him one back.

For a moment we stood like dogs measuring one another. Owen was taller than me and a little broader through the shoulders. Haole, with blue eyes and blond hair worn in a casually expensive way, Owen wore plaid surfer shorts and a collared shirt. He looked like he'd walked off the pages of an Abercrombie and Fitch ad and smelled that way, too. On his feet were fancy slippahs that didn't come from Longs Drug or Wal-Mart.

I didn't have to follow his eyes as they took in my hammajang t-shirt, boro shorts, and wafer-thin slippahs to know what he was thinking.

That's right, Mr. Haole Man.

But you're in my neighborhood now.

Mr. Halpert rolled on, oblivious. "Owen's going into tenth grade at Ridgemont next year. He heard about our project and wanted to help. Check out his portfolio."

Mr. Halpert shuffled some papers.

Owen and I didn't take our eyes off each other.

"Where do you live?" I asked.

"Kaimuki side," Owen said.

I raised an eyebrow. "You mean Kahala."

"So?"

Rich haole.

Probably an acre or more on the beach.

Bet his maid made him chocolate croissants and fresh-squeezed orange juice for breakfast.

I decided I hated him.

I gave him a Look.

He flinched, but didn't drop his eyes.

Points for that.

Let's see what else you're made of.

"Why not Punahou?" I jabbed.

His eyes narrowed. "Ridgemont's art program is better."

Haole Man had a choice.

I double hated him.

Mr. Halpert cleared his throat.

"There's a lot of street art in your style, Owen. Ever use spray paint?"

He waved one of the drawings under our noses.

Owen looked first. "Not cans. Spray gun."

"This one reminds me of some of the things I've seen around the Newport Beach piers in California."

"Yeah. My mom lives there. I usually spend my summers with her, but this year she went to Italy with her new boyfriend."

Too bad.

Now you're my problem.

"What do you think, Zader?"

Owen lifted his chin and folded his arms.

I didn't want to look, but I did.

The colors were bold and electric—hot pink, neon green, traffic cone orange. Everything was outlined in heavy black and shimmered with chrome highlights. There were tricked out muscle cars, babes in bikinis and high heels, and dudes with dark glasses and gold chains. Everything was slick and stylized and signed OP. Stupid head probably didn't know that around here OP means Ocean Pacific, not Owen Porter.

"It's good."

I wanted to hate it, but the colors and textures grabbed your attention and held it. I felt the California vibe through the paper and almost smelled the fish tacos, limes, and sunscreen on the breeze.

"It's really good," I admitted.

Owen relaxed.

Oh, so you care what I think, Mr. Haole Man?

"For California." I said. "I'm just not sure how it fits in with Lauele."

Bam!

Owen attacked.

He popped the back of my sketchbook so it flopped out of my hand and onto the table.

"Let's see yours," he said.

Jerk.

Lying face up was a reef study I started in pencil and finished in watercolor. Three zebra blennies nibbled on rocks while a snowflake eel curled in a corner under a wana. If you looked closely, you could see the ruffled edges of 'opihi and a hermit crab.

Mr. Halpert flipped pages, and an ulu and a humuhu-munukunukuapua'a swam by. He stopped on my drawing of an octopus nestled between two rocks. Only the eye and one tentacle gave it away.

"Hmmmm," said Owen.

"Yes," said Mr. Halpert. "Zader's style is very different than yours, Owen. His is subtler. See that shading there? He goes for realism while yours is more abstract."

He picked up one of Owen's papers and held it next to mine.

"Even your color palettes are completely different."

"Color palette?" I asked.

"The colors you use," Owen said, his voice adding *duh* on the end.

"Owen, your art is bolder, more in your face," Mr. Halpert said. "It's the difference between Vivaldi and Snoop Dog."

Vivaldi?

Was that good or bad?

If all the students at Ridgemont were smart like Owen and Jay, no way was I going to fit in. Being "last one in" meant I was sitting at the rock bottom of the class. If everybody already knew about things like color palettes and Vivaldi, in less than a month I'd be back at Lauele High with 'Alika and Chad practicing 'You want fries with that?' on career day.

"Word," Owen said. "My art's fresh!"

So mine's not?

"Careful, Owen," said Mr. Halpert. "The art world's fickle. What's fresh and trendy today often lines bird cages tomorrow. You guys could both learn a lot from each other."

He flipped another page.

"Zader, do you work from photographs?"

"No. I spend a lot of time out on the reef. My brother surfs," I said. "I hang out at Piko Point so we can talk in between sets."

"You don't surf?" Mr. Halpert asked.

"I sketch," I said. "I watch. I draw what I see."

"I've never seen a fish like that," Owen said.

It was a small fish with a flame red head, yellow fins, and a black body.

"That's a kind of pao'o. It's out there on the reef."

"Oh yeah?" He gave me side-eye. "Show me."

He threw the gauntlet down.

Mr. Halpert perked up.

"That's a great idea! I've got some art supplies in my backpack. Let me get them from my car, and we'll all head out onto the reef for some inspiration!"

Through his pocket he thumbed his remote, the car chirping in reply.

"I'll be right back."

I looked down at my feet. I didn't have my waders and my slippahs wouldn't protect me at all.

The reef!

I fiddled with my wrist lei, thinking furiously.

I promised Uncle Kahana I wouldn't go near the ocean without all my gear on.

Should I run home?

The image of me in rubber waders, a long sleeved rain coat, and deep-sea diver's helmet popped into my mind. I groaned thinking what Owen would say when he saw it. My stomach fell when I thought about what Mr. Halpert would think.

"Realism? Give me a break. You made that fish up. You may have Mr. Halpert fooled, but not me."

I stood taller and watched Owen's hands.

"It's out there."

"No way. You copied that from Dr. Seuss."

"Whatever. Maybe he copied it from me," I sneered.

Inside I cringed.

Maybe he copied it from me?!

Jay'd never say something that lame!

"You two ready?"

Mr. Halpert didn't pause, but headed down to the beach.

"Coming, Mr. Halpert," said Owen in his best teacher's pet voice.

REEF WALK

Wana

A common spiny sea-urchin known for hiding in cracks. Painful if stepped or sat on.

I was lucky it was low tide.

We could step straight from the sand right onto the first set of rocks that eventually led to Piko Point. I scanned ahead for puddles and splash zones and touched the ti leaf lei I wore inside my shirt, making sure it was there.

I tried to relax and breathe.

Maybe if I keep to the high spots, my feet won't get wet.

Owen caught my hesitation.

"I thought you local boyz ran everywhere barefoot? You got tender tootsies, Zader?"

Forget it.

I get splashed, I get splashed.

I get wet, I get wet.

No water ever killed me.

Yet.

I cocked my head at him. "Just worried about your expensive slip-pahs, Mr. Haole Man."

"Don't call me that," he warned.

A weakness.

Interesting.

Mr. Halpert was standing on the edge of the first shallow pool.

"Wow," he said. "This looks like something out of a fairy tale."

The wind rippled the water, scattering the light. Baby yellow tangs cruised in gangs along the far side, scared away by our shadows looming over the water's edge. A couple of starfish rested near the bottom, and there were colonies of anemones looking like little pink Christmas trees. When a gray blenny hopped from one pool to another, I thought Mr. Halpert was going to fall in.

"Did you see that?" he marveled.

"Yeah," I chuckled. "They do that sometimes."

"What I don't see is any red-headed one fish, two fish," Owen said.

"It's out deeper," I said. "Different pool."

"Uh huh," he said, stalking off.

I was watching every footstep, and half-way to Piko Point, when it happened.

A rogue wave splashed my leg, drenching my shorts and scalding like fire.

Lava-hot acid raced from my knee to my thigh. My calf flashed red, then gray, as the pain arced like lightning between two clouds, sending tingles and shivers down my spine.

I bit my lip and tried not to shriek, but a muffled curse escaped.

"Zader?" said Mr. Halpert from fifty feet away.

"You step on wana, Local Boy?" Owen called from Piko Point. "You need somebody to pee on it?"

"No," I gasped. "I just twisted my ankle."

"You need help?" Mr. Halpert started toward me.

"No, no," I said through gritted teeth. "I'm fine. My slippah ripped. I think I better head back."

"I'll come with you."

Mr. Halpert was forty feet away.

"No need!" I said, holding up my hands and taking a deep breath. "I'm fine. You're almost to Piko Point. You're gonna want to see it."

The fire dimmed to a dull sizzle.

I'll live, just please don't come any closer!

I don't want you to see the freak with the blisters on his leg!

Mr. Halpert stopped coming.

I tried to smile reassuringly and to not think about sizzling.

"He's fine," yelled Owen. "Hey! I think I found an octopus!"

"An octopus?" Mr. Halpert said.

"Yeah! Over here!"

Mr. Halpert caught my eye. "You sure you're okay?"

I nodded.

I reached down and picked up a slippah by its straps, tugging to make sure the worn center post popped out. I held my broken slippah in the air.

"See?" I said. I popped it back in. "It's just loose. I can make it back okay."

Mr. Halpert still hesitated. He knew something was wrong, but the allure of the octopus and my insistence that I was okay pushed him over the edge into believing what he wanted to see.

"Okay," he nodded. "We'll be back soon."

"I'll wait at the pavilion" I said.

With a wave, he turned toward Piko Point.

"Can you still see the octopus?" he asked Owen.

"Hurry!" Owen said.

I jammed my foot back into my slippah and surreptitiously rubbed my leg. Like an idiot I stood there, wondering if I could make it to the beach. That's when another, bigger wave crashed over me, soaking my shirt and face.

This time I didn't yell or curse or even think.

I ran.

I was all the way up the beach near the pavilion showers, trying to tear my shirt off over my head, when it hit me.

I didn't hurt.

In wonder, I skidded to a halt.

I held my arm out in front of me.

Bits of shedding gray blisters clung everywhere like cobwebs hanging from a tree, and when I touched my face, rough flakes fell to the ground like the world's biggest dandruff.

I rubbed my arms and neck and more gray skin fell like confetti.

Gray skin.

I blistered.

So why don't I hurt?

My skin feels a little raw like when you get road rash from a skateboard fall, but with that much water on me I should be unconscious, right?

Did the ti leaf leis protect me?

I patted my head, my stomach, my legs—I was whole.

I leaned against the side of the pavilion, catching my breath, thinking the unthinkable.

The blisters are scary, but did they ever really hurt?

Could it be that all these years, I felt it burning because everyone told me it hurt?

I looked back toward Piko Point. Owen was busy snapping photos with his smart phone, and Mr. Halpert was sketching something.

They didn't see.

I eyed the distance I'd traveled, amazed at how fast I got to the beach. Jay couldn't run like that. I didn't know anybody who could.

Maybe instead of surfing, I can run track.

"Are you stupid, crazy, or do you have a death wish?" hissed a voice behind me.

I whirled around.

Sitting on the rock wall and wearing a too big sundress was Maka, holding a ti leaf in her hands.

She swung her feet, drumming her heels on the wall.

"Maka?" I stammered.

"Oh, good! We're past that silly Dream Girl phase."

She hopped down and walked towards me.

"Just because you can move like that, doesn't mean you should, at least not where people can see you."

"I saw," I swallowed. "I saw you—"

"You saw," she mocked, "but you didn't listen. This reef is danger-ous. You have no idea. You need to stay away from the ocean, Zader."

"I saw—"

"Listen to me, brother. There's more here than you will ever know. You've caught Kalei's eye. That's never a good thing."

"I saw you turn into a shark."

"What an imagination," she teased. "I think you've been eating rare meat again; it's messing with your senses."

"I have your lei," I rushed.

"Keep it," she said, her eyes focused past me.

"Zader!" Jay called. "I saw the wave hit you! Zader! You okay?"

My head snapped toward the ocean.

Jay was running up the beach from Nalupuki; behind him Nili-boy was corralling all the surf camp kids, getting them out of the water and on the beach—one eye on them and the other on me and Maka at the pavilion.

I took a breath to ask a question, but when I turned Maka was gone.

3 3

SECOND DINNER

Amene
What you say at the end of a prayer.

Thursday evening, all the way to Uncle Kahana's apartment, my shoulder blades spasmed as if tiny spiders inched along under my shirt. I felt unnerved and edgy, although nothing looked out of the ordinary.

The Chocks' front yard was littered with bikes. Laundry snapped on a clothesline at 'Alika's grandmother's house, and I could hear somebody picking out *Waimanalo Blues* on an 'ukulele in the backyard.

The parking lot near the beach pavilion was empty; a Foodland grocery bag floated across the asphalt and stuck to the bushes next to a broken bottle. I picked up the rubbish and tossed it into the dumpster near Hari's store.

The street lights were on, but it wasn't quite dark enough for them to make a difference. Twilight shadows lengthened, reaching out like fingers from the edges of the road.

Get a grip.
You're not four anymore.
There's nothing under the bed.

The imaginary spiders skittered down my spine like sand crabs after a wave on a hot afternoon. I felt exposed, caught in the moment when a fish darts from one rock to the next.

I picked up my pace.

When I walked around to the back of Hari's store and started up the stairs, I could smell ginger and fish and, *ugh*, broccoli, coming from Uncle Kahana's apartment. I'd finished dinner about half an hour ago, but my stomach rumbled anyway.

I scratched at the door, waiting for Uncle Kahana to open it.

"Pono," I said.

"Come in, come in," said Uncle Kahana.

'Ilima thumped howzit with her tail on the couch.

"You ate?"

"Oh, yeah. Mom made spaghetti. I'm not hungry, thanks."

"Good. You can eat again."

The furniture was still pushed back against the walls from Char Siu and Jay's earlier training session. When Jay came home, I asked him how it went. He mumbled okay and turned on the TV.

I guess we'll talk about it later.

I kicked my slippahs under a shelf and zoomed in on the two place settings sitting on the breakfast bar, the plates heaping with grilled fish, sticky white rice, and steamed broccoli.

I couldn't wait.

I sat down and picked up a fork, ready for the first bite.

I glanced over at Uncle Kahana's bowed head and paused, bowing my head, too.

"Amene," he said.

"Amene," I repeated, then dug into the mountain of fish.

I shoveled a humongous bite.

Hot, I thought, sucking air.

"Careful, I never cooked 'em cold," Uncle Kahana said. "Plus there might be bones; you never know."

Ginger.

Salt.

Red pepper flakes.

Lemon.

Smoke.

I was in heaven.

"'Ono?"

"Soooooo 'ono," I said around another mouthful. "You speared this today?"

"Of course! Another blue uhu like the one Mr. Halpert admired. Too bad he never tasted it. He would've liked it more!"

He reached over and poured me a glass of ice water from the pitcher. I took a sip, marveling anew at how easy it was now that I didn't worry about getting wet. I could drink a cold glass of water without worrying about spilling it.

I could put my arms on a kitchen table or counter without wiping it down first.

I could walk across the street in slippahs without carrying an umbrella or scanning the sky for a weather report.

Life is good.

I drained the glass and checked the ti leaf lei on my wrist.

Still flexible, no breaks or snags.

Uncle Kahana filled my plate again.

"Eat up. I don't want you hungry."

"Uncle, this is so good, but if I eat too much, I'll get a side-ache when we train."

"Let me worry about that. You'll do better on a full stomach. Trust me."

When I said no thank you to the third plate, Uncle Kahana took my hand and lightly pinched it. I don't know what he was looking for, but satisfied, he nodded and let me put my plate and cup in the dishwasher.

We'd just put the leftovers in the fridge and wiped down the counter when Hari knocked on the door.

A BLADE THAT KNOWS YOUR HEART

Guro
Filipino word often used as a title of respect or a martial arts master or teacher.

"Come in," Uncle Kahana called.

The door pushed open and a slippah flew inside, tapped the side of the bookcase, and fell to the floor. A second slippah followed, landing gracefully next to its mate. A thin black case made of heavy canvas dropped on top of them.

I saw the whiter bottom of a dark foot, then an ankle, and finally a knee creep around the door as a slight figure slid into the room, sweeping it all in one glance and pinning me where I stood in the kitchen.

The man looked like Hari, but he moved like a snake, quick then still, fluid and fast.

Before I knew it, the door was closed, and Hari was standing an arm's length in front of me.

I don't think I saw him move from the door.

"Kahana," he said.

Hari was slim with a willowy build. I thought he was Japanese, Filipino, maybe some Chinese, and about Uncle Kahana's age, which meant he could be anywhere from fifty to eighty. His once dark hair was silvered and thinning and cropped close to his skull. His skin had a weathered look, though not as dark or worn as Uncle Kahana's. This was the first time I'd seen Hari outside of his store. His fingers and teeth were stained with nicotine, and although his eyes had a yellow jaundiced cast, they were bright and missed nothing.

Mongoose, I thought.

No! Hari's a cobra.

"Hari," said Uncle Kahana. He tilted his head at me. "You know Zader."

Hari nodded, his eyes never leaving my face.

"Kahana says you like the blade. Show me."

I cut my eyes at Uncle Kahana.

He raised his eyebrows in a what-are-you-waiting-for look.

Slowly.

This is not the time to move quickly.

Hari looked relaxed, standing with his feet slightly wider than his shoulders, hands at his sides, but there was an energy, an intensity that flowed from him. I could almost see it reaching toward me like an octopus's tentacles testing the currents, gauging the way the wind blew.

Don't look him in the eye; people don't like that.

I set my eyes on his chin and reached into my pocket.

I drew out my knife and put it on the counter, blade folded.

Still looking at me, he asked, "Can?"

I nodded.

I didn't trust my voice.

Hari reached out and picked up my knife.

Snick.

The blade flicked out, and the knife came alive. I swear I could hear it breathe. Hari rolled it in his palm and flashed it left and right, tossing it between his hands. While the knife danced and shimmered in the kitchen light, only Hari's hands moved. He never blinked or shifted his weight; his eyes never left me as they measured and assessed my character.

"Catch," he said, and flung the knife at me.

I didn't think; I didn't have time. My hand reached out and captured the knife by the handle.

Uncle Kahana cleared his throat.

For the first time, Hari smiled.

"I want to see," he said, gesturing at me to hold out my hand.

Like Uncle Kahana, Hari studied the way the blade rested in my palm.

"Relax," he said, repositioning my fingers, pushing the handle forward and back.

He had me swing and slash the air, then fiddled with my grip some more.

"Huh," he said after a while, stepping back.

"What do you think?" asked Uncle Kahana.

"It's a blade that knows his hand, but not his heart."

"Ah," said Uncle Inscrutable.

I was getting a little tired of being kept in the dark.

"What?" I snapped.

Hari chuckled.

"Hari means your knife fits your hand, Z-boy, but it's not the tool you need for fighting."

"This blade is good. Sharp. Strong. But its nature is to create, not destroy. You carve wood, yeah?"

"Yeah. Driftwood mostly. That's why I started carrying it."

One of the reasons.

I looked at my knife and thought of slicing little curls of wood, freeing a sculpture from its prison. The knife warmed in my hand as I remember carving the shark last December, shaping each fin and line.

But when I thought of slicing flesh, of carving into living bone, the knife recoiled; the blade dulled and chilled; and my stomach started to hurt.

I'd never thought of cutting muscle and bone and sinew before, only wood and air dragons.

In my mind I saw a line drawn in blood, splitting, welling, then gushing hot and metallic. I could smell salt and taste its tang in the back of my throat.

I swallowed hard and blinked.

I knew I should be disgusted, but instead I felt excited, energized, and powerful.

Two dragons fought within me—revulsion and glee.

I didn't want to know who'd win.

Uncle Kahana read it all on my face. He walked over and put his hand on my shoulder.

"Things know their nature," he said. "You can't force a fit. Keep that knife for creating art. We'll find you a new one for fighting."

"A tooth or a claw," Hari said.

"Tooth," I said without thinking.

Uncle Kahana and Hari exchanged glances.

I'd said something significant, but what?

"Come," said Hari, motioning toward the open space in the living room. "Leave your blade. You won't need it anymore."

We walked to the mats and stood facing each other. The night was dark outside, but inside the lights lit every corner of the room.

"Alexander Kaonakai Westin, your uncle, Leslie Kahanaonakuna Kaulupali—"

"Leslie?!" I squeaked.

"Watch it," Uncle Kahana said. "John Wayne's real name was Marion."

Hari gave us both stink-eye.

"You guys like fool around? I got better things fo' do."

"He's just nervous, Hari. Kids these days don't understand what you're offering."

"This is serious kine," Hari said.

"I'm sorry, Uncle Hari. Can we start again?" I asked.

Hari sighed, then looked me square in the eyes. "Alexander Kaonakai Westin, your uncle, Leslie Kahanaonakuna Kaulupali, has requested I take you on as my student and teach you the art of knife fighting. Is this true?"

Hari, the convenience store owner, purveyor of 'ukulele and kite strings, macadamia nut candies, and shave ice; Hari, the card playing chain smoker was gone. Although barely taller than me, he towered ten feet tall. Power was here, coiled and patiently waiting.

Stunned, I nodded.

"Speak!" he snapped.

"Yes," I stammered.

"Knife fighting is an ancient art passed down from father to son, from brother to brother. With this knowledge comes responsibility for yourself, for those you love, and for those who look to you for protection. You are studying Lua."

"Yes," I said.

This was the longest I ever heard Hari speak. Until now, I doubted he spoke anything but Pidgin.

"At its core, all fighting, all martial arts, celebrate and protect life. To learn the way of the warrior, you must look unflinching into the darkness that exists. You must learn to recognize it in yourself and in those around you. Do you understand me?"

"No," I said.

Hari cracked a smile. "You're right, Kahana. There's hope for this one yet."

Uncle Kahana scoffed. "Don't undo all my work, Hari! If you build him up too much, I'm just gonna have to break him down again. Poho, that."

I hated when they talked like I wasn't there. It never made any sense.

"Okay, Zader. I'll teach you," said Hari.

"Thank you, Uncle Hari," I said.

"While we're training, call me Guro, not Uncle."

"Guro."

"That's what I called my teachers. That's what my students call me."

"You mean Sargent," Uncle Kahana said.

"The students I pick," Guro Hari said. "Quiet now. Class is starting."

Uncle Kahana rolled his eyes and flopped on the couch next to 'Ilima.

"Okay, Zader, we're going to start with closed fists. Closed fists, always. You have a knife in your hand, remember? Now follow me—"

Tock. Ptwock!

Someone was throwing pebbles at the window.

"What time is it?" Uncle Kahana asked.

I glanced at the stove. "Almost eight," I said.

"Hari, you left the TV on channel 3?"

"Uh, I dunno. The guys were watching *Hawai'i 5-0* reruns when I left."

"Crap."

3 5

SURVIVOR

Menehune

A legendary race of little people who lived side-by-side with the ancient Hawaiians. NOT elves.

"We gotta hurry," said Uncle Kahana, leaping up from the couch and hustling to the fridge. "Zader, I need you to run downstairs and change the channel on the big TV on Hari's Lanai to channel 3. I'll be down in a minute."

He grabbed the leftover fish, a package of cookies, and a couple of cans of guava juice. Rummaging in a drawer, he pulled out a plastic shopping bag and started stuffing it.

"Go!" he said. "People are counting on us! We can't be late!"

I thundered down the stairs, not pausing to put on my slippahs. I whipped around the corner of the building and skidded to a stop on the covered lanai. Eight tables were scattered around, covered with vinyl palaka tablecloths and lighted hurricane candles that glowed with more atmosphere than light.

The massive TV was mounted on the back wall next to the pass-through window to the kitchen and tilted so most tables could easily see it. Football nights were popular, as were sumo matches from Japan. I remember hearing about a haole from Texas who won the grand

158

sumo championship last year, then stunned fans by cutting off his top knot, ending his yokozuna reign before it really began. I would've loved to have seen that. Around here it was the biggest sumo news since Akebono.

The place was almost empty, just a few regulars playing cards, snacking on pupus, and drinking beer as they talked story, and a lovey-dovey couple in the corner by the bathroom.

Nalani, Hari's part-time helper and Nili-boy's secret crush, was wiping down a table and stacking empty bottles on a tray.

"Eh, Nalani, where's the remote?" Guro Hari asked.

I jumped.

He'd slipped down the stairs behind me.

"I think in the kitchen next to the register," she said, tucking her hair behind an ear.

Guro Hari pushed past me and through the swinging door. I could hear him rummaging around, tossing pens and order pads out of the way.

Behind me, Uncle Kahana put all the food he brought from his apartment on a table that was practically in the jungle, smack in the middle of the oleander, hibiscus, and ti bushes that lined the edge of Hari's parking lot. It was a cozy place to sit in the sun away from the busy lanai in the middle of the day, but not where anyone would choose to sit once the sun went down.

Unless they had something to hide.

Wagging her tail, 'Ilima disappeared under a yellow hibiscus bush.

Mongoose?

But she never barked.

"Found it!" Hari called and the TV flipped to channel 3.

"Thursday night," Nalani said to me. "*Survivor* re-runs."

"Make 'em louder. Hard to hear out here," Uncle Kahana said.

The commercial for teeth whitener boomed.

Lovey-dovey Dude frowned.

The card players laughed and started another hand, ignoring it all.

The familiar face of *Survivor's* host wearing his trademark puka shell necklace and boroz-looking safari shirts faded in.

"Last week on *Survivor*. . ."

The hibiscus bushes near the table shook.

I heard a high-pitched voice shout, "Cheeeeehooooo!"

Cheeho? What the heck?

Tribal drumbeats crept in on the soundtrack as the host's solemn narration continued.

"The Mayumba tribe still does not have fire." On screen dirty, cold people huddled around soggy coconut husks and fruitlessly twirled sticks together, rain streaming down their faces.

Behind me someone snickered.

I turned, but all I saw was bushes. Before I could walk over and investigate, 'Ilima whined and poked her head out.

'Ilima? Did 'Ilima laugh? But why is no fire funny?

"Louder," called Uncle Kahana.

Guro Hari turned it up.

Lovey-dovey Dude slammed his drink down. His date fiddled with a swizzle stick and pursed her lips, but his attention was locked on the TV.

As the logo swooped into view, the sound of a conch shell blew, low to high, a rich, full sound that in the old days signaled the presence of a Hawaiian chief.

I swear I heard its echo from the bushes.

That's it. I'm finding out what's going on!

When I started to move, 'Ilima reappeared at the edge of the lanai, blocking my way and grinning her doggy grin.

"Woof," she said.

Oh, so you don't want me to go over there?

We'll see about that!

I moved left.

'Ilima swiveled right.

I moved right.

'Ilima laid down.

I moved to step over her and she jumped up, almost knocking me over.

"Quit it, you two," said Uncle Kahana, coming around the bushes. "This isn't a rumpus room!"

"How's the volume, Kahana?" Guro Hari asked.

"It's good, Hari," Uncle Kahana said. "Nalani, you mind opening a couple of bottles of Primo and leaving them on the table over there? Maybe some sashimi too? Put 'em on my tab, yeah?"

"No problem, Uncle Kahana."

Lovey-dovey Dude snapped his fingers. "Check, please."

"Right away, sir," said Nalani with a final wipe. "Zader, wanna help?"

I looked at Uncle Kahana who flapped a hand at me.

"Go," he said. "Help Nalani. I need to talk with Hari a little. When you're done, come upstairs."

Thick as thieves, Uncle Kahana and Guro Hari disappeared around the corner.

BROKE 'OKOLE OLD MAN

Broke
No more kala.

After stopping by the card players' table, Nalani held the kitchen door open.

She jerked her head at me, and I walked in.

The smell of bleach was everywhere, and the counters were spotless. A commercial grill and deep fryer were along one wall next to an over-sized fridge and an ice maker. Nalani walked to one of the two big sinks, rinsed out her rag, and plopped it into a bucket half-filled with soapy water.

"Wash your hands, Zader. Make sure you use soap."

She tossed me a clean dish towel she snagged from a stack lying on open baker's shelves crammed with mondo-sized containers of spices and seasonings and stainless steel mixing bowls.

"Use this to dry. I need you to make the sashimi while I get all the drinks ready."

I paused for a moment at the sink, checking my ti leaf bracelet and feeling for the lei I wore under my shirt.

It's just water.

Hot water and soap.

You've done this a million times now.

I held my breath as I turned on the water, plunging my hands into the heat. While I knew it wouldn't hurt me, it still made my heart beat faster whenever I got near water like this.

Nalani pointed at the fridge.

"Cabbage," she said. "'Ahi in the blue container. Use a plastic plate, not paper. Sashimi picks up the paper flavor—that's bad. Put the cabbage down first. Lay ten slices of raw fish in a fan along the edge of the plate then put eight more along the inside. Don't forget gloves."

She reached into a tub full of ice and water, fished out four brown bottles, and popped their tops with a church key she carried in her apron pocket. As she set them on her tray, I threw the towel over my shoulder and opened the fridge.

I found the cabbage in a bag and the 'ahi in a double-layered container and carried them to the prep counter. Grabbing a pair of disposable gloves, I noticed a magnetic strip displaying a wicked assortment of kitchen knives. In Guro Hari's kitchen I didn't have to test them to know they were scalpel sharp.

I snapped the gloves on, feeling like a surgeon in an operating room. The light was much brighter in the kitchen than the lanai, and the sterile surfaces gleamed. The cabbage was already shredded, so I laid down a bed of it on a plastic plate and cracked open the container of 'ahi.

The smell of the raw fish was thick in my nose. Fresh and clean, salty like the sea, it lay gleaming like a deep red jewel with just a ghost of blood weeping through the holes to pool in the very bottom of the box. Although I'd never tasted raw fish before, my mouth watered instantly.

It was all I could do to not tip the container against my lips and gulp it down.

Without the second dinner, I would have.

I shook my head, reached into the box, and realized the block of 'ahi wasn't whole; someone had expertly sliced the fish into thin pieces the size of mahjong tiles. I carefully dealt them out like a poker player's hand, slightly overlapping ten slices along the edge of the plate and fanning another eight inside.

Nalani peeked over my shoulder.

"Looks good," she said.

She grabbed two small dipping cups from a stack and set them on the plate.

"Wasabi paste is in the refrigerator door, shoyu-ginger sauce in the squeeze bottle. Check the top's closed and shake the bottle before you squeeze. But toss the gloves before you touch anything else. Don't spread germs."

She breezed back out the door, her loaded drink tray carried shoulder high.

I closed my eyes and crammed the lid on the leftover 'ahi, burping the box to let the air out. Stripping off the gloves, I chucked them in the trash and put the food back where I found it. After adding a little dab of wasabi paste to a cup and squirting sauce in the other, I was done.

Cash in hand, Nalani slammed back through the door and stopped at the register. She punched a few keys and the cash drawer slid out, allowing her to put the twenty in the drawer and slip some coins into her hand.

"Wanna bet this is my tip?" She frowned. "That lovey-dovey guy in the corner is so cheap he only brings girls on half-price Thursdays. Always splits when *Survivor* comes on. Never the same girl twice."

I picked up the sashimi plate and a couple of sets of chopsticks from a bin.

"This is on Uncle Kahana's tab, right?"

"Oh, yeah! No worries, Zader."

I fidgeted. "But if it's on his tab, how is he going to leave you a tip?"

"Uncle Kahana?" She smiled and her eyes lit up, changing her whole face.

Wonder if she ever looks at Nili-boy like that? If she had, he'd be here every night!

"I'll probably find an extra ten or twenty in my paycheck tomorrow. Plus you're the one doing most of the work. I should tip you!"

She held out her hand with the change.

'No, no, no, no, no!"

"You're sweet, Zader, all worried about me and my tips. But it's cool."

"It's just . . . Uncle Kahana never seems to pay for anything around here. It's always on his tab."

Nalani double-checked the change in her hand.

"Oh, that. His little joke."

She shut the cash drawer with her hip.

"What?"

"What you mean, 'what?'"

She tossed her pretty ehu streaked hair.

"You don't pay for what you already own."

My eyes bugged out of my head.

"Uncle Kahana owns the store?"

"Of course! It's all his: the store, the building, the restaurant—everything. His tab is just for inventory. You know, so we can keep track of what's in stock, how many cups, stuffs like that."

"Fo'real? The whole building?"

"Fo'real. Most of the land around the beach, too. I think that's why it's never been developed."

She paused, nibbling on her lip; it was so cute that I almost forgot to listen to what she was saying.

"Zader, Uncle Kahana doesn't like to talk about it. Hari runs the place, but Uncle Kahana keeps track of everything, places all the orders, decides who to hire—everything. I probably shouldn't have told you if you didn't know. I just didn't want you to worry about my tip."

One broke 'okole old man, my left foot!

What else didn't I know?

She picked up a slip of paper and waved her fist.

"Big spender is waiting. Can you take the sashimi to the table for me? You know the one out in the bushes. Just put it there. I'll clean up the mess when *Survivor* is pau."

In a bit of a daze, I carried the plate past the tables on the lanai and out into the darkness. The candle on this table wasn't lit. Outside the circle of light from the lanai, it seemed alone and vulnerable.

This is crazy.

The plastic containers that held Uncle Kahana's leftover fish were empty save for a few grains of rice stuck in a clump. Half of the cookies were gone and all of the guava juice, but only a sip or two of the Primo. I cleared a space for the sashimi and set it down. I didn't know what to do with the chopsticks or even if I'd brought enough pairs.

The bushes rattled.

Cat.

I'm feeding sashimi to a cat.

Another movement caught my eye.

I turned to look across the parking lot toward the dumpster and the street light. For a quick moment as he passed through the light and back into the shadows, I saw him clearly.

Kalei, the Man with Too Many Teeth from my dreams.

My heart beat fiercely; I thought it was going to jump out of my chest. The spider that crawled along my spine raced up and down, and I reached into my pocket.

Empty.

My knife was still in Uncle Kahana's apartment.

Run. Hide.

Like a hound on a scent, he paused.

From the darkness, he swiveled his head in my direction.

I ducked under the table, landing next to a small conch shell drilled for blowing, its cheerful pink smile staring at me. As I scrambled all the way under, I noticed child-sized footprints in the dirt and a single yellow feather that belonged in a chief's cloak.

Menehune?

That's who Uncle Kahana leaves food for?

Menehune watch Survivor *re-runs at Hari's on Thursdays?*

But they're not real!

I blinked, not able to wrap my head around any of it.

"Zader?" called Uncle Kahana.

"Woof!"

'Ilima flew under the table to me, lick, lick, licking my face.

I hugged her tight and buried my face in her neck.

"There you are," he said.

Slap.

My slippahs landed near my feet.

I crawled out from under the table, feeling foolish.

Uncle Kahana handed me my knife.

"Hari had to go. We'll train again tomorrow."

He was talking to me, but his eyes were scanning the parking lot, the beach across the street, and the bushes along the road. I slipped my knife into my pocket and dusted off my pants.

"It's getting late. You shouldn't be walking tonight. I'll drive you home."

In my life I could count the number of times Uncle Kahana had driven me home from his apartment on one hand. Twice because I'd almost got caught in a rainstorm and twice because he'd given me things too heavy to carry.

"Mahalo, Uncle," I said, and got into his car.

BROTHERS

Futless
A condition of boredom, confusion, or frustration; an inability to move forward.

I t was no use.

I flung the papers off my bed, futless.

These were the fourth set of images I'd drawn for the mural and nothing was working. Mr. Halpert had taken one look at the first two sets and said that while he liked taro patches, canoes, and rainbows, he thought it a little passé.

When I asked, Mom told me later that passé meant Mr. Halpert wanted something more original.

I was out of ideas and time. Mr. Halpert expected a final design tomorrow if we were going to get everything ready for the Summer Fun kids next week.

Out the window, I saw Jay carry his surfboard around the house to the backyard and place it in the rack by the door. He threw his beach towel over the railing and bounded into the house.

"Are you tracking in sand?" Mom called from the living room.

"No," Jay said.

"You better not," Mom said. "I just cleaned the floor in there."

There was a pause.

The back door opened, and I saw Jay step outside again and run the hose over his feet and up to his knees. He swiped at them with his towel and wiped the bottoms carefully on the mat.

In the kitchen I heard Mom sigh as she opened the broom closet.

"Sorry, Mom," said Jay, closing the door behind him.

"Go change," she said. "I don't want to find sand all over the house."

When Jay entered our bedroom, I snickered.

"What?" he said, "I didn't know I had sand on my legs."

"You never think."

"What about you and all these papers? Clean up this mess, Dorothy," he said, mimicking Mom. "It looks like a tornado blew through here."

I wadded up a piece of paper and threw it at him.

"Make me," I said.

Jay grinned, grabbed a pair of shorts from our dresser, and headed to the bathroom. A minute later I heard the water turn on and Jay's voice belting *Ka Huliau 'Ana* at the top of his lungs.

Puffing out my cheeks, I bent down and picked up my sketches from the floor. Smoothing them out, I wondered what Mr. Halpert wanted. I'd seen lots of murals full of whales, hula dancers, warriors, Hawaiian gods, surfer graffiti, erupting volcanoes, big waves, and hibiscus flowers. I idly drew a line, then another, but nothing was taking shape.

Jay walked in, wearing the clean shorts and scrubbing a towel over his head. He smirked and snapped it at me, but I caught it and wrapped it around my wrist, tugging back. Jay laughed then let the damp towel collapse in my face.

"It's good you can play," he said.

Not so very long ago, a damp towel in our room was as dangerous as a gasoline torch.

I dumped the towel on the floor.

"Careful. You'll smear my drawings," I said.

"What? Those chicken scratches?"

He sat next to me and shuffled a couple of pages.

"I like this one," he said pointing to a surfer sliding down a wall of water taller than the Aloha Tower.

"You would," I said. "You probably think it's you."

"Nah," he said. "His arms are too small." He flexed his guns and smooched them.

I rolled my eyes.

He flashed his teeth then tapped another drawing, a simple outline of a fish.

"What are these? Practice?"

"Nope. The beach pavilion mural. I have to have a final design tonight."

He nodded then picked at a strawberry on his elbow.

"Sore?" I asked.

"Nah. Just a sand scuff."

"The Great Jay wiped out? I thought you were busy surfing baby waves all summer with Nili-boy's junior surf camp."

He looked at me funny then shrugged.

"I was training with Char Siu and Uncle Kahana this morning. I got a strawberry."

"On sand? In Uncle Kahana's apartment?"

"At Keikikai beach. Uncle Kahana was teaching us lua 'ai in the shore break."

I sat up.

"In the ocean? Training you out in public?"

"Yeah. But we go early, so the beach is pretty empty."

I'd been training with Guro Hari for a few weeks now. I knew Char Siu and Jay had been working with Uncle Kahana, but this was the first time I heard anything about the beach.

"You guys doing conditioning? Running up and down the sand like soccer players? Or are you kicking waves like that karate school from Mililani?"

He hedged. "Kinda. It's pretty lame."

"But you're in the ocean, right? Is that why Uncle Kahana won't let me come?"

"Maybe."

"Don't you think it's weird that he's training us apart? Why train you with Char Siu?"

Jay brushed it off. "What's the big deal? It's not all fun and games, Zader, making 'A' with Char Siu on the beach, even if nobody's around to see it. That tita is tough! Thanks to her I have sand in places I don't want to talk about!"

"Make 'A'? Why're you embarrassed? You guys rolling in the whitewash?"

I watched Jay look everywhere but at me. He fidgeted with the papers, then hooked his towel off the floor with his foot and swung it around his ankle.

Maybe Char Siu was kicking his 'okole.

"Did Guro Hari find you a knife yet?" he asked.

I looked at my pocket knife sitting on my nightstand. While I no longer carried it with me everywhere I went, I still sharpened the blade every day.

Guro Hari was teaching me the importance of respecting the old ways. According to him, what sometimes seemed crude at first, like a stone age tool or a sliver of bamboo, was really very elegant—and deadly. Obsidian blades dated back to caveman days, but were so sharp that some modern surgeons preferred thin slices of obsidian to steel. When I first learned about them, my fingers itched to get a chunk of obsidian so I could practice striking the core just *so*, flaking off a blade with the keenest edge in the world.

Then there were legendary samurai swords, the steel so fine that the blade could sever a man's neck while leaving everything in place. The stories said a man would live until he took his next step, tumbling his head from his shoulders.

I'd studied medieval swords, Egyptian scythes, and Australian aborigine-style boning knives, but so far nothing felt right.

Guro Hari told me to be patient, that when I was ready the right blade would come.

I just wished it would hurry.

"No, I don't have a knife yet," I said, picking up a pencil and flicking at few lines across the paper, sketching a blade in flight.

Jay took my pencil and added a blob.

I squinted.

"Kung-fu star?" I asked.

"Yeah. I figured a wannabe ninja like you would have more than just a knife."

The star was lopsided and the edges too thick. There was no way that anyone could throw that.

"You really suck at this," I teased.

"That's why you're doing the pavilion, not me."

He got up from my bed and opened the closet door. On the top shelf a row of surfing trophies gathered dust. Dad wanted to build a case for them in the living room, but Jay said no and stuffed them in our closet.

While Jay liked all the free stickers, leashes, and wax from Da Kine, Local Motion, and Lauele Surf Designs, the only time he wore a shirt that said champion was right after a surf contest for the winner's photo in the paper. After that, he stuck it in the Goodwill bag for Mom to drop off the next time she went to Honolulu.

Once when I asked him about it, he said, "No reason to tell the world what I already know."

Humility or pride, I was never sure, but it was all Jay.

He wiggled his 'okole at me as he scrounged around the bottom of our closet and liberated a t-shirt. He sniffed it, and satisfied, pulled it over his head.

"If it were up to me, I'd paint the pavilion with invisible paint," he said.

I jumped.

"What?"

His head poked through. "What you mean, 'what?'"

"Invisible paint?"

He slipped his arms through the sleeves. I could see a small dot of blood from his elbow's broken scab on the hem. It started to glow.

"Zader? You okay?"

I shook my head. "Yeah."

How long since I ate?

"I just mean I wish the pavilion wasn't there. It blocks the view of the mountains and Piko Point. If it were up to me, I'd use invisible paint—like Wonder Woman's airplane."

Wonder Woman's airplane. That's it!

"Jay, you're a genius!"

"I know," he said.

FIGHT LIKE A SHARK

Run-fu
The first rule of fighting: don't.

Jay was winded, and his ribs hurt as Char Siu's foot crashed into the same spot for the twelfth time.

I'm never going to get that block right—was it slide, shift, turn, send back the energy, or was it turn, shift, slide back? Jay wondered, doubled over and holding his side. *If I can't get it right in Uncle Kahana's apartment today, no way I'm getting it right tomorrow in the water at the beach.*

"No love taps, Char Siu!" Uncle Kahana barked. "Full speed! Again!"

I can't breathe, but Uncle Kahana wants more.

If Char Siu hits me any harder, I'm gonna cry; I don't care who sees.

This hurts!

While Uncle Kahana had never been cheery when they trained, now there was a grimness to everything he did. He was much more intense, especially when they trained at the beach, making them push against the waves and crawl along the shore on hands and knees, not caring if they got sand or salt up their noses. He smiled less and snapped more.

But it was 'Ilima that had Jay worried.

On beach training days, she stayed near the edge of the grass, never venturing down the sand to sniff around crab holes or trash. While Jay and Char Siu sparred in the apartment, she stayed on the couch feigning indifference, gazing out the lanai door, her ears never relaxing.

It used to be when a hard punch landed, you could count on a consoling lick from 'Ilima.

No more.

Now the bruises just stung.

Pain—that was another difference; rarely did Uncle Kahana allow them to pull punches now when they sparred. Three times Char Siu walked home with a swollen lip or bloody nose, and Jay once limped for the better part of a week. Scuffs and bruises were the new normal; bags for ice packs, bandage wraps, and ibuprofen stayed out on the counters now since Uncle Kahana said it didn't make sense to waste time putting them away.

Jay watched Char Siu's leg as she spun, the kick coming full speed and power right at him.

A split-second decision, Jay ignored his instincts and retreated, slipping to the side and allowing her foot to harmlessly slide by.

"Better," Uncle Kahana said. "You're watching her foot. But the counter-move to what you did allows her to get too close."

Jay replayed it in his mind. "How? Her body's going the other way."

"Body, yes. Head, no."

Jay laughed. "What's she gonna do? Strangle me with her ponytail?"

"Teeth," Uncle Kahana said.

He's messing with me! Jay thought.

"Teeth?" Jay asked.

"Teeth," Uncle Kahana said.

"Uncle Kahana, people don't bite! It's not fair," sputtered Char Siu.

"You know what they say about a fair fight?" Uncle Kahana asked.

"No," Char Siu said.

"If you're in a fair fight, your tactics suck."

He let that sink in.

"We're not doing WWF Wrestlemania, kids. If you can't run-fu, then your only option is to fight. Nobody's going home with belts or trophies, just blood, bruises, and bandages, you or him. Finish it and finish it fast. You better use whatever weapons you have, 'cause guaranz the other guy's going to use 'em even if you don't."

"But teeth," Jay said. "Fo' real?"

"No laugh. You ever get bit?" Uncle Kahana asked.

"Yeah, mosquito," Char Siu said.

"I'm not talking mosquito," harrumphed Uncle Kahana. "Teeth can be a weapon. You guys ever heard of Mike Tyson?"

"Who?" Jay asked.

"Never mind. If you control the head, you control the bite. Watch."

Uncle Kahana wrapped his hand in Char's Siu's ponytail and gently tugged.

"See? Where my hand goes, her head goes. So does her mouth."

He released her and rounded on Jay.

"Pulling hair? You want us to pull hair?" Jay yelped. "You want me to fight like a *girl*?"

Bam!

Char Siu grabbed Jay's hair in her fist and threw him to the mat.

"Yeah, Jay, you better pray you can learn how to fight like a girl 'cause this girl is kicking your 'okole!"

Too much, Jay thought. *I don't care if she is a girl, I'm killing her!*

In one motion, he jumped to his feet and threw a sharp jab at her face.

Uncle Kahana caught it.

"That's enough sparing for today," he said.

Char Siu headed to the kitchen and grabbed a paper towel.

"Gross, Jay! Your slimy boy sweat is all over my hand!"

"Then I better wash it off!" Jay stalked to the kitchen sink, turned the faucet on full-blast, and jammed his whole head under the spray, splashing water all over Char Siu.

"I'm gonna be sick," she gagged.

"Just not where I have to clean it up," Uncle Kahana sighed. He checked the clock. "Kids, we only have a few minutes left. Get a drink and catch your breath. Then it's review time."

Sitting on the training mats in front of the couch, Jay prodded his ribs, hoping they weren't broken.

Not, he decided. *Otherwise I couldn't stand to poke them.*

Char Siu flopped down next to him and popped the lid off her juice. She took a sip, then held her cold juice bottle against her elbow, wincing.

Yeah, that's what I thought, Tita. You're hurting, too!

Jay downed his juice in one long gulp and wiped his mouth on his sleeve. Leaning toward Char Siu, he barred his teeth.

"Think he'll make us bite next week?" he whispered.

Char Siu shuddered. "Don't give him any ideas!"

Jay fiddled with his juice wrapper, picking at an edge until he could pull it off in one piece.

I'm not sure I like this. Uncle Kahana is changing the way I think. Things were easier when I could just say hello and not worry about someone's teeth.

Wadding the wrapper into a ball, he cataloged his injuries starting with his forearm.

Yep. Gonna bruise. Better than taking a punch in the face, though.

He sniffed.

Char Siu's right, I need a shower.

I don't care if Lili gets mad; I'm staying in until the hot water runs cold!

Drink in hand, Uncle Kahana nudged 'Ilima to make room for him on the couch.

Jay sighed. *He's sitting down. It's gonna be a long one.*

"A shark circles its prey," Uncle Kahana said. "It watches and waits. Why?"

"'Cause it's chicken," Jay said.

"'Cause it's smart," Char Siu said. "It wants to make sure it can win before it fights."

"Maika'i, Char Siu. Sharks, especially Niuhi sharks, take run-fu one step further. Not only are they going to run when they aren't certain they can win, they aren't going to attack unless they know what they're hitting and that they can get away." His eyes twinkled for the first time that day. "Jay, you're the expert. What do your shark shows say?"

"Sharks are ambush predators."

"That's right. That's why you don't swim in murky water or near the mouths of rivers or splash around on the surface when there's a lot of white-top chop."

"All sharks or just Niuhi?" Char Siu asked. "Only Niuhi bite humans, right?"

"Under the right conditions any kind of shark can bite you," Uncle Kahana said. "Common sharks bite when they're cornered or if they mistake you for something else. Niuhi don't make mistakes. They take the time to figure out what they're stalking. If they're unsure or want to make a point, they'll bump before biting."

He paused and patted 'Ilima on the head.

She tucked her nose under her tail and ignored him.

He sighed and dropped his hand.

"Bump before bite?" Jay repeated. "Is that why you and Nili-boy asked if the Niuhi shark I saw bumped my board?"

"'Ae, Jay. Last fall when you first saw the little Niuhi shark off Piko Point, I wanted to know if it circled or bumped because—"

"Because circling means it's interested," Char Siu said.

Uncle Kahana nodded. "Circling is curious, not bad, but not good either. You never want to pique a Niuhi's interest. Better to stay under the radar."

Uncle Kahana's right. Having a Niuhi look at me was bad enough. I can't imagine getting bumped. I'd never come near the ocean again.

Uncle Kahana spotted Jay's shudder and grinned.

"Glances are bad. Circling is scary. Bumps can make you mental!"

"You been bumped?" Char Siu asked.

Uncle Kahana pursed his lips. "No. Not by a Niuhi. But I know someone who was."

"What happened?"

Uncle Kahana opened his mouth, but before he could speak, 'Ilima sat up on the couch and barked, glaring at Uncle Kahana. With the hair up on the back of her neck and her ears thrust forward, she looked as though she didn't like where this was going, not one little bit.

Uncle Kahana flinched, but didn't move over or off the couch. He wiggled deeper into the cushions and focused on a spot over Jay's head.

After a moment he said, "I'm not sure what happened."

'Ilima chuffed and flopped back down.

"The Niuhi bump? Was it a warning or a test?" Jay asked.

"Dunno. Doesn't matter. The point is to keep under the radar. Nothing good ever comes from piquing a shark's interest."

"Uncle Kahana, what are you trying to tell us?" Char Siu asked. "Why all this stuff about sharks?"

'Ilima growled low in her throat, a sound that Uncle Kahana felt more than heard.

He carefully placed his hand on her head again as a peace offering.

She gave him stink-eye, but stilled.

"Long time ago, Hawaiians understood sharks. There's a reason so many of the chants and meles call blood-thirsty chiefs sharks."

'Ilima didn't growl again, but all the hair stood up on her neck.

Feeling her coil to spring, Uncle Kahana gave 'Ilima side-eye.

'Ilima looked him in the eye, then down at his lap, and back to his face. She raised an eyebrow; precious things were in easy snapping reach.

Uncle Kahana cleared his throat and casually placed his arm across his thigh, creating a barrier that would only slow, but not stop a determined attack.

He shifted his weight.

Her point made, 'Ilima snorted and tucked her nose under her tail, but Uncle Kahana didn't let his guard down.

He knew how fast she could move.

"Self-centered and self-serving, chiefs that walked and hunted and thought like sharks were feared. A chief's word was law. His whim was law. Shark-like chiefs were the ultimate bullies. Threats, real or imagined, were eliminated. Territories were expanded and held at all costs, despite what was best for the people. If the shark chief felt threatened, he'd retreat, but would return to stalk, wait, and watch. And when the moment was right, he'd attack swiftly, brutally, completely committing until the threat was gone."

"Uncle Kahana, if shark chiefs were so bad, why are we learning to think like sharks?" Jay asked.

"Know your enemy, Jay. If you know how he thinks, you'll know what he'll do. Anticipation is key to defense."

'Ilima raised her head.

Uncle Kahana tensed his arm, keeping it ready.

When she suddenly leaped up, Uncle Kahana snapped into a defensive block.

"Aiyah!" he shouted.

'Ilima yawned, then gracefully jumped over Uncle Kahana's outstretched arm and onto the floor. Tail in the air, she daintily pranced to her dog pillow, not even giving him a backward glance.

"Harrumph," muttered Uncle Kahana.

'Ilima chuffed and flopped down, her back to Uncle Kahana.

"So sassy," he said. "Like butter wouldn't melt in your mouth."

She sneezed and started to snore.

"Uncle Kahana, who are our enemies?" said Char Siu in a small voice.

"Times have changed," Uncle Kahana said, "but sharks still walk like men."

39

HOPING IT'S HAUPIA

Palala:
To honor a child with a gift.

M r. Halpert stood back from the wall, scanning it from right to left, and holding two paint brushes like chopsticks.
"I think this is going to work."
We were on the last section of the last wall at the pavilion. The outlines were penciled and taped, and we were daubing small brush strokes of color in each of the main sections to guide the Summer Fun kids tomorrow. Owen couldn't make it today—he had a golf lesson. I was *so* disappointed, but I managed to get over it.

After the day on the reef, Owen hadn't been around much and stayed just an hour or so when he came. He suggested a few things, like how the light would look on the water and how to draw a surfer in the distance with just a few brush strokes, but mostly he let me take the lead. I liked to think it was because my art skills dominated, but the truth probably had more to do with his ride not wanting to hang around waiting. Lauele was light years away from Kahala suburbs.

Mr. Halpert and I were moving fast. We had about fifteen minutes to finish and clean up before people started arriving for the neighborhood party. Mom and Aunty Amy were already setting up tables on the other side of the pavilion. From what I heard, the whole town was coming to meet Mr. Halpert and to check out the design for the mural.

My stomach felt like a mass of moray eels in a typhoon.

I daubed a little bit of red on the wall and stepped back.

Amazing.

Last week, when I brought Mr. Halpert a blank piece of paper and said this was Jay's idea, at first, he didn't get it. Disappointed, he tried not to show it.

"Zader, it's a blank piece of paper. I get it. You're out of ideas," he said. "It's okay. I'll come up with something. I just wanted to give you a chance."

"No!" I said. "The design is invisible! Imagine if the pavilion wasn't there!"

He looked at me like I was crazy.

Then it clicked.

"Genius," he said. "We'll draw what a person would see if the pavilion wasn't there!"

It was perfect. On the east side of the pavilion the mural showed a sandy stretch of Keikikai beach, the waves gentle and kind, with little kids playing in the whitewash and building sand forts and castles.

Going clockwise, from the southern parking lot the mural showed the rocks north to Piko Point with surfers in the distance riding massive waves all the way to Nalupuki beach.

On the west side the view was mauka from Keikikai beach, so the mural showed the hillside where we tried to go grass sledding and the tall pali cliffs that framed Lauele valley. Stunt kites danced against the sky and a few wispy clouds rimmed the mountain tops.

The last wall, the one on the north side, was the trickiest. In reality, the mural should have shown the ugly parking with Hari's in the distance. Mr. Halpert said no way we're painting an asphalt parking lot, so the mural started at the edge of the road. We cheated and added more plants and flowers, making it look like Hari's was peeking out from the jungle. We drew people sitting at the tables on the lanai and two kids carrying large rainbow shave ices as they walked toward the front of the store.

Mr. Halpert called it artistic license.

Much better than the parking lot, streetlight, and dumpster.

We all need a little art to hide what's ugly.

I stepped to the wall and added a last dot of purple to a shave ice.

That looks so 'ono.

My stomach growled. I was always hungry these days.

I put my brush down and stepped back from the mural.

I hope this works.

While I kinda understood how the Summer Fun kids were going to paint large swaths of color, and we'd go back later and add all the details, I was skeptical. I'd seen a lot of Summer Fun arts and crafts projects over the summers.

Mr. Halpert reached down and tapped his paint can closed.

"It's going to be great, Zader. I think your idea of painting the doors, window trim, and roof line bright yellow instead of my original black will make them stand out. It'll look like they're floating in space, just like a minimalistic theater set."

I had no idea what Mr. Halpert was talking about. I think that meant he liked it.

I nodded knowingly. It was easier than asking.

Each side of the pavilion had an easel with sketches of what the wall was going to look like. They were supposed to help people see how the colors and shapes would come together to create the mural, but we'd already made a lot of changes when we outlined the walls. Mr. Halpert said our proofs were suggestions, not blue prints; that we were artists, not architects.

Whatever.

It looked good.

"We're as ready as we're going to be," he said. "I'll go rinse the brushes at the showers if you'll put away the paint."

"No problem," I said.

I was on the north side of the building, tapping the lids closed, when I felt someone come up behind me.

"This is the last can, Mr. Halpert," I said. "Go join the party! I can carry these to your trunk."

"Kaonakai," said a woman's voice.

I glanced up.

She was stunning.

Standing there in a simple old style sarong, ti leaf lei on both wrists, long dark brown hair swept back in a simple long braid, she looked like a photograph for a tourist brochure or an old time ad for pineapple. It wasn't what she was wearing so much as how she carried herself.

Hula dancer. Tall and graceful even just standing.

She smiled and held out a flat package wrapped in banana leaves.

"Mahalo, Aunty," I said.

I looked down at my hands splattered with paint.

"But I can't take that now. My mom's setting up the food on the other side. I'm sure she'll find a spot for it there."

"Aunty?" she said, quirking an eyebrow at me.

Oh, no.

She called me by my Hawaiian name and acts like I should know her!

She's family!

But why is she so annoyed I called her Aunty?

I looked closer, searching for a clue.

She looked about thirty, too young to expect me to call her tutu. Besides, few grandmothers minded being called aunty, but aunties sometimes clicked their tongues at being called tutu. Aunty was always the safest bet.

She pursed her lips for a moment, then sighed as she presented the package to me again, saying, "Palala."

Palala?

I don't remember an aunty or cousin named Palala.

Must be one of mom's friends from work.

Better go with it!

"Oh, of course! Aunty Palala! How good to see you!"

She frowned, the lines on her forehead suddenly appearing as her mouth tightened. She hefted the package.

"The others were for your mother. This one is for you. It's a little early, but I thought you could use it now."

Wait?

For me?

Haupia!

Aunty Palala made my favorite dessert and wrapped it in banana leaves old-style.

Score!

"Oh, thank you so much! I'm sure it will be 'ono," I said.

My stomach growled again.

"May you never need it," she said.

"Okaaay," I said.

Did she say, 'may I never eat it?'

What the heck?

Who brings coconut pudding to a party and then says don't eat it?

"It's special; just for you. Since you're busy, I'll leave it in the usual place."

"Sounds good, Aunty Palala. Thank you for thinking of me! You're right; haupia's my favorite. Like I said, the dessert table's just on the other side. My mom should be over there, too. She'll be happy you're here."

I turned to pick up the paint cans.

"Aloha e Kaonakai," she said, and when I stood up, she was gone.

Weird.

Like anybody calls me by my Hawaiian name.

40

DESSERT

Kaona

The hidden meaning; the concealed reference to a person, thing, or place; innuendo.

The party was in full swing, and Lili was glowing.

Mr. Halpert was so excited to meet her. When he found out she danced hula, nothing she said made him stop pestering her until she finally consented to dance.

Uncle Jerry and his boys had brought 'ukuleles and guitars for a backyard kanikapila, and pretty soon Mele and Char Siu were pulled into the act.

"Harriet!" called Uncle Jerry from the musician's circle. "Aunty Harriet! Come up! We'll play *Maui Girl* for you!"

Aunty Harriet shook her gray head no, no, no, as people begged and whistled for her to hula.

"C'mon! No shame!" teased Uncle Jerry.

Hiding her mouth behind her hand and giggling like a teenager, Aunty Harriet made her way to the area in front of the makeshift stage.

"Okay, but I'm not doing this alone. Mitsy! You come too! Let's show these young folks how it's done!"

As the band strummed the intro, Aunty Harriet and Aunty Mitsy— really *Tutu* Harriet and *Tutu* Mitsy—lifted the hems of their long dresses in one hand, and, as graceful as waves rolling to shore, sashayed out into the audience, mesmerizing with their eyes, hands, and hips.

"I love a pretty Maui girl . . ." sang Uncle Jerry.

Aunty Harriet caught his eye with a come hither glance.

In that moment the years melted away.

Beautiful.

When they dance you forget that they're grandmothers.

"She lives at Waikapu . . ."

Aunty Harriet turned and winked at Dad as she dipped and rose, teasing with her fingertips.

Aunty Mitsy floated over to Junior-boy and pretended to sit on his lap.

"Hooooooo!" roared the crowd.

Wolf whistles and cat calls turned his teenage face bright red.

Oh, man! She got him good! He has to dance with his grandma now!

Blushing darker than lomi-lomi salmon, Junior-boy stood up and danced with Aunty Mitsy.

"Cheehooooo!" somebody yelled.

"That's the way, Junior-boy!"

"Her waist is oh, so slender . . . Her 'opu too much nui nui."

A few in the crowd chuckled as Aunty Harriet mimed a big stomach.

Stomach.

That reminded me.

I walked over to the dessert tables looking for the haupia in the banana leaf package.

Mom was talking to Uncle Kahana.

"Eh, Liz, you know most Hawaiian songs are not about what most people think they're about, right?" Uncle Kahana asked.

I looked under some foil wrap.

No banana leaf.

Mom turned toward him.

He nodded his head at the dancers. "They know. You watch the old folks. When they're busting a gut over songs about fish or rain or hunting, that's your big clue that something else is going on."

"Why, Uncle Kahana!" Mom said, play swatting his arm.

She's happy tonight.

"What? You think old means dead? Sheesh." He lifted his eyebrows. "Someday you'll see." He glanced back at the dancers. "Ho, that Harriet! Some wahine, no? I remember her when she was sixteen. She's even better now."

Mom clicked her tongue. "Oh, my ears!" she giggled.

Aunty Mitsy pulled Lili from the audience and with a side-dip spin, left her dancing with Junior-boy.

Sly!

Poor Lili; it was hard to tell whose cheeks were redder.

Uncle Kahana sipped his drink.

"Our Lilinoe is growing up," he said.

Mom frowned and straighten the napkins.

"Mr. Halpert—sorry, *Justin*—the kids call him mister—anyway, Justin said Lili's grandmother wants to meet her."

"Nancy's mom?"

"Yeah. She claims she never knew Lili existed."

Mom adjusted a serving dish.

"You don't believe her."

"I can't imagine not knowing about a grandchild."

She lifted a bowl and scraped mac salad a little too thoroughly into a smaller dish.

So much for Mom's good mood.

Drat!

Where's that haupia hiding?

It better not be gone already!

"But what if?" Uncle Kahana pressed. "What if you had a granddaughter you didn't know about? You'd be excited, right? You'd want to meet her."

"I'm not sure it's the right thing for Lili. Why now?"

"Because now they know." Uncle Kahana nibbled a bit of purple sweet potato. "I love these. I'm gonna talk to Hari about putting these on the menu. 'Ono on a plate lunch."

"I don't want Lili involved with them. That family's twisted."

"Nancy's twisted. Maybe the family's okay. Justin seems all right," Uncle Kahana said.

He picked at some tako poke on a platter. The octopus smelled good, but I couldn't have any. Besides, I was on a haupia hunt.

I lifted another lid.

"What if Nancy comes back?" Mom said.

"Liz, stop worrying about what ifs. Nothing you can do. Tomorrow comes tomorrow. You worry too much."

"And you too little," she snapped.

I could hear *broke 'okole old man* in her tone, but she didn't say it.

If she only knew.

Looking under a cake pan, I bumped Mom with my elbow.

"Zader! Why're you under my feet?"

"Haupia," I said.

"No more," she said. "There's liliko'i cake or chocolate dobash over there."

"It's all gone?" My face fell.

"Never had," she said.

"Then what did Aunty Palala bring?"

Uncle Kahana whipped his head around, pinning me with his eyes. "Who?"

"Aunty Palala: tall Hawaiian-looking woman with two wrist leis. She had something wrapped in a banana leaf package. She wanted to give it to me, but I told her to take it to the dessert table."

The blood drained from Uncle Kahana's face.

The kanikapila had moved onto to another song, but as far as Uncle Kahana was concerned, we were the only two people at the pavilion.

"What happened to the package, Zader?" he asked.

I blinked.

"She brought it over here," I said.

Heedless, he flicked covers and wrappings to the floor, scrambling through the leftovers and dishes.

"Hey," protested Mom.

"It's not here, Zader. What—exactly—did she say?"

"She said," I paused, thinking back. "She said she would leave it in the usual place."

"'Ilima," Uncle Kahana whispered.

In a flash she shot out into the night, heading down the beach to Piko Point.

TOOLS, NOT TOYS

Niho ʻoki
A blade like a shark's tooth.

When ʻIlima brought Uncle Kahana the banana leaf package, Mom paled.

"Who was that woman?" she asked, eyes mempachi-wide and cheeks the color of oatmeal.

Is she going to faint?

Do I catch her?

What if I miss!

I looked at the pavilion's hard cement floor and braced myself.

"Not here; not now, Liz," murmured Uncle Kahana.

"But—"

"Later."

He held out the package to me, green and smelling faintly of reef, like a priest with an offering.

"She said it's for you, Zader. It's from your Hohonukai ʻohana," he said.

What!

I stood there with my eyes bugging and my mouth open like a bufo catching flies.

Uncle Kahana nudged me and my jaws closed with a snap.

"Take it," he said. "Don't make a scene."

I took it from him, holding it on my palms like a tray. I didn't know why I didn't recognize it before; it was just like the package I opened last year, the one with a Tahitian pearl the size of an eyeball.

Mom and Dad told me I'd received a package each year around the day Uncle Kahana found me on the reef at Piko Point. Except for a shark tooth strung on a cheap leather thong, each gift had been a treasure too valuable to keep at home. They were waiting in a safe deposit box in Honolulu, but for what, I didn't know.

Early. She said it was early because my birthday's a couple of weeks away.

With trembling fingers, I popped the knots and the rest of the leaves fell away like petals from a flower. Resting in the center was a slender piece of ivory the size and color of expensive hotel soap. It was curved slightly on one side with a depression in the middle and a slit along the top.

"Ivory," said Uncle Kahana. "Very old."

Its pale yellow gleam sparkled against the pavilion lights as lighter streaks of white moved through it like waves or the rings of a tree.

"What is it?" I asked.

"Take it in your right hand, Zader," Uncle Kahana said. "Careful. Give Liz the wrappings."

As I reached to pick it up, I swear it leaped into my hand, the curve melting against my palm, my forefinger slipping just underneath the leading edge, and my thumb rolling into the depression. It looked and felt like a high-tech car remote or the key to a futuristic flying car.

Mom bent down to pick up the discarded leaves.

It was easier, I think, than watching.

"Hold it away from your body," Uncle Kahana said. "Make sure it's not pointing at anybody. Good. Now slowly, gently, press with your thumb"

Snick.

From the slit a blade slid out, a blade unlike any I'd ever seen.

It was short—no longer than half my thumb. On one side a serrated edge curved wide, the tip ending in a point that hooked back at an angle, then rounded out to smaller serrations. It looked like—

"Shark tooth," Uncle Kahana said. "The shape, I mean. It's like a tiger shark's."

It looked like my necklace hidden in the box with Maka's lei under my bed. I shifted the knife in my palm, but it didn't move much; it fit like it had grown in my hand all my life.

I held it up to the light, in love.

I pressed the center again.

Snick.

The blade disappeared.

Snick.

Out again.

I'd never seen anything so beautiful.

"Give it here," Mom said.

No! It's mine!

Cut her if she tries, said a new voice in my head, low and sweet.

Unlike my pocket knife, this knife didn't mind blood.

Shocked, I tried to drop the knife, but my hand wouldn't release. I pressed the action again and the blade disappeared into the handle.

Shaking, I handed it to Uncle Kahana.

"Give it," said Mom, holding her hand out to Uncle Kahana. "That's no toy for a boy."

He wrapped his fingers around my knife, hiding the whole thing in his hand.

"No, it's not," he said mildly. "But it's meant for Zader."

"A knife? What kind of toy is that?"

"You said it yourself, Liz. It's not a toy. It's a tool."

I held my breath.

If Mom said no, it was over.

I tried to look indifferent, but failed.

Just keep your mouth shut. Let Uncle Kahana do the talking, I thought.

"It's from his other 'ohana," he said.

"I know," Mom said.

Tears?

Were those tears in her eyes over a knife?

"Two?" A tear rolled down her cheek. "I really have to lose two?"

Uncle Kahana wrapped his arms around her, pulling her head into his shoulder.

"Nobody's losing anybody," he said. "Not on my watch."

He gave me a head shake, telling me to leave.

'Ilima nudged me with her nose and licked my hand.

"My knife," I mouthed.

"Later," he mouthed back.

I wanted to stay and fight for it, but I knew if I did, I would lose.

Time to run-fu.

A TASTE OF RAW FISH

Ho'oha'i
To flirt.

I scanned the crowd for Jay and found him sitting at a table with Dad, Lili, Nili-boy, and Mr. Halpert.

I wandered over.

"Zader!" Lili said, "Did you know Mr. Halpert met Nili-boy years ago?"

"He called me a stupid head coconut," Mr. Halpert said, "because I was brown on the outside and white on the inside."

"Truth," Nili-boy said.

"And that makes you . . . " teased Dad.

Nili-boy grinned. "Me? I'm a dobash malasada. Golden brown on the outside and full of rich chocolaty goodness on the inside. Irresistible!" He wiggled his eyebrows and laughed.

In the parking lot, we heard a car alarm chirp, and a svelte figure with long brown legs in white short shorts walked out of the darkness and into the pavilion's light.

"Speak of the devil," muttered Nili-boy. "Nalani!" he called.

"Am I too late?" she asked.

"No, no! Let me show you the mural."

Smooth as Haleiwa strained poi, Nili-boy swept Nalani off to the other side of the building.

"Hello, Zader," said another new, but familiar voice.

Carrying a platter and coming around the other side of the car was Ms. Robinson, our eighth grade teacher.

Jay and I exchanged glances, stunned. While we knew teachers lived outside their classrooms, it always freaked us out a little to see them at the store or beach.

"I hope you don't mind me coming to see your project. I'm so excited for you! Nalani told me all about it."

Mr. Halpert stood up and ran a hand through his hair.

"I don't think we've met," he said.

Dad did the honors. "Anne Robinson, Justin Halpert. Justin, Anne. Justin is the new art teacher at Ridgemont. Anne was Jay and Zader's teacher last year at Lauele Intermediate."

"A pleasure," said Mr. Halpert holding her hand a little too long.

"Nice to meet you," her smiled dazzled.

"Ms. Robinson, how do you know Nalani?" Jay asked.

"Nalani's my cousin. She told me about the project and said you were going to be here. I had to see it."

I scanned Ms. Robinson's petite frame, blues eyes, and light brown hair looking for traces of Nalani. Other than the fact that both were cute and deceptively sweet, I didn't see it.

Calabash cousin, I thought, although it really didn't matter.

"We're glad you came," Dad said.

"I wouldn't miss it." She turned to Mr. Halpert. "New art teacher?"

"Starting in the fall."

"Your first time in Hawai'i?"

"Is it that obvious?" He smiled ruefully. "I thought I was blending better."

"It's your accent," Ms. Robinson said. "It gives you away."

"Me gotta for speak more da kine."

Jay winced. "Don't," he said.

"Me no can like speak good?" Mr. Halpert asked.

"No," Ms. Robinson said, "you can't!"

"Can we like stay—"

"Just stop! You're making my ears bleed," Jay said.

Dad handed Mr. Halpert a Spam musubi.

"Eat that. It will help wake up your local genes."

Mr. Halpert took a bite.

"Good," he pronounced. "You think there's really something in the genes? With my mom's family coming from here—"

"He's my cousin!" Lili said.

"—you think I'd have some racial memory of how to surf or pound poi."

"Have you tried pounding poi?" Ms. Robinson asked.

"Once at a touristy lu'au. I made a monster mess."

He swallowed the last bite of musubi and licked his fingers.

"I've actually been in Lauele once before, about fourteen years ago. I was engaged."

"A destination wedding?" Dad guessed. "On the beach at sunset, I bet."

"It was supposed to be our honeymoon," he said.

"Supposed to be?" Ms. Robinson asked.

"My finance decided to run away with the wedding planner."

"Ouch."

"I got over it," Mr. Halpert said. "I had help."

"What made you decide to move here?" Dad asked. He gestured at the walls. "Art? Ridgemont?"

"A woman."

Ms. Robinson's eyes lit up. "Really," she said.

"I her met during one of my beach walks. She was beautiful, lying on the sand. At first, I thought she was hurt—I'd never seen anyone just lie on the sand without a blanket or towel, just curled on her side like a mermaid. When I realized she was okay, I blurted out, 'Can I paint you?' I'm still amazed she didn't call the cops." He turned to Ms. Robinson. "I mean, wouldn't you if you opened your eyes and saw a strange dude looming over you?"

"It would depend on the dude," she giggled.

Teachers giggle?

"I would," Lili said. "I'd throw sand in his face."

"I'm glad she didn't," Mr. Halpert said.

"Was it love at first sight?" Ms. Robinson said.

"For me it was."

"Let me guess. After fourteen long, lonely years, you've reconnected on Facebook," Ms. Robinson said.

"And came all the way here," Dad said, "to discover she's a hundred pounds heavier with three kids and a mortgage!"

"No. Much worse. I went back home, painted her portrait, framed it, and put it on my desk. I look at her every day, but I've never been in contact with her since I left her on the beach, drove to the airport, and flew back to California."

All the adults and Lili cracked up.

I caught Jay's eye, and he shrugged.

He didn't get it either.

Mr. Halpert wiped an eye.

"I'm glad I'm here. I love what I'm doing with Zader, and I can't wait to teach a full class, but I'm an idiot," he said. "I don't know what I was thinking. I had some romantic, foolish notion that I'd walk the beach one morning, and she'd be there, and it would be like time had stood still. Too many Hollywood movies."

Ms. Robinson touched his arm. "You're a dreamer," she said. "The world needs dreamers."

He shook his head. "It's time for me to wake up. I need to leave these kinds of dreams in the past."

"I'd like to help you try," Ms. Robinson said.

Mr. Halpert stood.

"Want to see the invisible pavilion?" he asked.

"Love to," she said.

They left.

"What just happened?" Jay asked.

"I'll explain it when you're older," Dad said.

"You always say that," Jay said.

"Yeah," I said, "when are we going to be old enough?"

"You'll know you're old enough when I no longer have to explain it," Dad said. "I'm getting some cake."

"Me, too," Lili said, following Dad to the dessert table.

"Grown-ups," Jay said.

"Tell me about it," I said.

"I want cake. You want some?" Jay asked.

"No. You go, though."

Someone was yelling hana hou, hana hou, but Uncle Jerry and his boys were setting down their instruments, and people were gathering sleepy kids and diaper bags.

In the darkness, by the showers, I could hear Tunazilla crooning to herself, practicing some 'ukulele chords Uncle Jerry had shown her.

Listening I had to admit she can really sing.

Godzilla with the voice of an angel.

Maybe the only person as out of place at Ridgemont as me.

Nili-boy and Nalani hadn't made it all the way around the pavilion yet, and I could hear Mr. Halpert explaining something to Ms. Robinson about light and shadows and forced perspective.

I bit my lip and sighed.

I couldn't ignore the scent of ginger, shoyu, and garlic on the plates in front of me any longer. On Lili's abandoned plate I spied a single slice of sashimi, forgotten when she was called to dance.

I picked it up.

The 'ahi glowed translucent pink like a ruby lit from within.

I held it up to my nose and smelled the brine and blood.

The raw fish smell was clean and sweeter than cake.

Kapu.

I swallowed.

Delicious.

I didn't care.

Tonight I was going to get answers.

I was going to make my Dream Girl, Maka, come.

43

RAW FISH DREAMS

Moe'ino
A bad dream.

Maka didn't come.

But my dreams that night were strange and unsettling.

I was standing on sand with twisting towers rising around me; for a moment I thought they were giant petrified trees, but they arched, twisted, and bridged in ways no jungle canopy does.

The light was mottled and dim, like wearing goggles in the rain.

I felt pressure crushing my chest—a sumo wrestler sat on me, his oiled topknot crawling up my nose, his pomade stinging my eyes, smothering me so I couldn't take a lungful of air.

I'm dying!

Air raid sirens went off, blaring and pounding a metal spike through my brain.

Tsunami! I thought. *Get to higher ground!*

I reached down and grabbed the sumo's loin cloth and heaved him away.

Panicked, I started to run, but the sand held me back.

I tried to climb the towers, but whatever I grabbed popped off in my hand; nothing would bear my weight.

Looking for higher ground, I ran in circles, gasping for breath that never came, while all around me the sirens shrieked danger, danger, danger!

Run!

Hide!

Overhead, the sky darkened like a hawk's shadow over a weak sun.

I scrambled faster, feeling like a hamster in a wheel going nowhere fast.

In desperation, my hand slapped my pocket. Through the rough fabric I felt it, the oblong shape of my new knife.

Salvation.

But when my eager hand reached inside, my pocket was empty.

Uncle Kahana had my knife.

The darkness gathered thick and black, roiling around me like smoke.

A giant hamburger cruised by, bleeding ketchup and sesame seeds. I opened my jaws, wide, wider, widest, starving to take a bite.

Snap!

Hot juice flooded my mouth and washed down my gullet as I chomp, chomp, chomped through flesh and bone, not stopping to chew.

"You'll get a stomach ache if you eat like that," Uncle Kahana said.

I rushed heavenward flying through the sky, the murk clearing as I rose.

Jay's surfboard hovered above me, its ti leaf lei design reminding me wait, stop, don't, his brown, slender leg dangling over the side.

Delicious.

44

LIPSTICK WARRIOR

Paio
To fight; combat; battle.

"**W**hat's the matter, Zader?" Guro Hari called through the door. "No shame," he chuckled.

I didn't want to come out of Uncle Kahana's bathroom.

Both Guro Hari and Uncle Kahana had made it clear that if I wanted my knife, I had to do this.

For anything else I wouldn't.

I opened the door and side-stepped out into the living room. Maybe if I were built like an Olympic swimmer, it'd be okay.

I wasn't.

I kept my eyes on the floor.

"Eh, Z-boy, not bad," Uncle Kahana said. "Fits okay."

He slurped on his straw, probably his second or third sprunch of the day.

From her dog pillow, 'Ilima chuffed and grinned her doggy grin. When I looked at her, she flicked an ear at me and settled deeper into her bed.

I tugged at the back. The shorts were giving me a major wedgie.

"It's just a speedo, Zader. All the guys in Brazil wear much less." Uncle Kahana cracked his knuckles.

"If it's better for you, we can do 'em bare," Guro Hari offered. "But it's really hard to fight naked. Most guys feel too exposed."

I blanched.

They laughed.

I narrowed my eyes. "How come I gotta wear this and you don't?"

"Oh, you like me strip?" Guro Hari threw off his shirt and reached for his pants.

"No, no, no, no, no!"

"Just joking," said Guro Hari, snapping his waistband. "Skin is easier to wash than clothes. Today you learn what a blade can do. I already know. Come."

I walked over to the counter where Guro Hari had an assortment of training knives laid out. They were balanced and shaped like real knives, but dull. You could still get hurt practicing with them, but you probably wouldn't bleed out or cut someone's finger off.

He selected a trainer knife that looked like it had been shaped out of Styrofoam. A few quarters were stuck to the handle for weight and the whole thing was wrapped in layers of duct tape.

Ug-ly.

"Just like your shark tooth knife, yeah?"

Guro Hari handed it to me.

No. Not at all! I thought.

I palmed it and took a few token swipes. It seemed the right size, but I'd only held my knife for such a short time, I couldn't be sure.

"I think so," I said. "It looks like my Shark Tooth."

"It's not a shark tooth," Uncle Kahana said. "Don't call it that."

"All fighting blades have a name, Kahana. What's wrong with Shark Tooth?" Guro Hari flashed his tobacco stained teeth. "Sounds tough."

Shark Tooth.

I liked it.

"He doesn't have to name it now," Uncle Kahana grumped. "He never even used it yet. Besides, it's not a shark tooth."

"What's the big deal? You Lua guys use shark tooth-bladed clubs. I've seen 'em in Bishop Museum. You probably got one hanging over your bed."

Uncle Kahana grunted. "What I have hanging over my bed is nobody's business."

"I call 'em like I see 'em, Kahana. Zader's right. His knife looks like a shark tooth. Shark Tooth knife."

"You've seen it?" I asked Guro Hari.

He nodded. "I've used it."

"Where is it?"

"Safe," Uncle Kahana said.

'Ilima thumped her tail and yawned.

"Can I have it?"

"Bumbai. When Hari thinks you're ready."

Guro Hari cocked his head at me.

"Zader, it's an odd blade. I've never seen anything like it. It should be unbalanced, but it's not."

He ran a finger along the edge of my training knife.

"See here? Your blade has a convex shape like an ulu knife."

He picked up the knife that looked like half a donut with a wood plug where the hole should be.

"Inuit—"

"North Pole braddahs," Uncle Kahana interjected, "the guys who used to live in igloos."

Guro Hari ignored him.

"For centuries, people living in the Arctic shaped these kinds of blades to slice skin from blubber. It's a skinning knife."

"Good for cutting pizza, too," Uncle Kahana said.

Guro Hari gave Uncle Kahana small-kine stink-eye as he waved the ulu knife in the air, miming gutting a fish or skinning a seal.

"As each slicing stroke finishes, the curved shape takes the energy and forces the cut deeper. But an ulu blade is one long surface. Yours is serrated."

He put down the ulu and picked up what looked like a steak knife. He pointed to the tiny barbs along the edge.

"Serrations grab and tear as they cut; each one is like another tiny knife. They are a little tricky to use, but a sharp serrated blade can go through cloth, leather, skin, and muscle like a blow torch through butter."

My Shark Tooth is cool.

"But you need to understand, Zader, that Shark Tooth is more than a curved serrated blade."

"It's not a shark's tooth," Uncle Kahana rumbled.

"Your *blade*," emphasized Guro Hari, "is just as deadly as a stabbing tool."

Guro Hari picked up a stiletto, a knife with a long thin blade and needle-like point. He thrust the stiletto in the air in short, quick jabs.

"Like a stiletto, a shark tooth's narrow tip pierces easily, but see how the point hooks back like an arrow or a barb?"

I looked at the mess of cardboard and duct tape in my hand and saw what Guro Hari meant, although on my trainer it looked more like a blob than the elegant curve I remembered.

"Kinda," I said. "You mean right here?"

"That's it. When you pull Shark Tooth out, it will tear a much bigger hole. Bigger holes mean more damage."

"There's more, Zader." Uncle Kahana pinched the bridge of his nose like his head hurt. "Hari and I think the handle is fossilized ivory, but the blade is something else, not metal. We have no idea how to sharpen it, but so far nothing seems to dull it, not even rolled cardboard."

"You cut cardboard with my knife?"

I felt insulted.

Guro Hari counted on his fingers. "And cloth, bamboo, sugar cane—"

"—soda can, turtle shell—" Uncle Kahana added.

"Turtle shell?" Guro Hari asked.

"I had one lying around the house. What, you think I'd walk up and just stab a random honu on the beach?"

"Just checking."

"My blade can do all that?"

I looked at the wimpy training knife in my hand, wishing it was real.

"Yeah," Guro Hari said. "Plus it's small and light. When you're bigger you can hide it in the palm of your hand. Nobody will see it until it's too late. It's lethal."

Lethal?

Like kill somebody?

Could I really do that?

Maybe I don't want to learn about knives and fighting.

Maybe I should just stick to drawing.

But another part of me was thrilled.

I can protect myself against anything.

"That's why we need you to understand, Zader. Like your mom said, it's not a toy." Uncle Kahana slurped more sprunch.

"I know," I said.

Uncle Kahana said, "I know you think you know, but we're gonna make sure. Let's do this, Hari."

"Usually this comes much later in training, Zader. I was a grown man before my Kali master sparred like this with me." Guro Hari reached into his gear bag.

Holy crap, what's happening?

Is he going to cut me?!

I don't need to be cut to know that knives are sharp!

"Guro Hari? I'm not feeling—"

"Do both," Uncle Kahana said.

"Both? I thought just his," Guro Hari said, feeling around a side pocket.

"You never know. I see those gray hairs, Hari. You getting makule, yeah? Slow. He might get you instead," he chuckled.

Guro Hari's going to get me?

That's it; I'm outta here!

I started to inch toward the door.

'Ilima sat up, her eyes following me.

"Bubbles, Kahana," Guro Hari said, still poking around in his bag.

"I knew you'd say that. That's why I want proof. Both blades!"

"Ah! Got it," Guro Hari exclaimed, pulling his hand out of his bag and brandishing—

A tube of lipstick?

He popped off the top.

"Fire Engine Red number forty-three," he announced.

It looked like something an old tutu would wear to a lu'au, the kind of red that stayed in a lip print on your cheek fo'days.

"Red? I told you I didn't like red," Uncle Kahana grumbled. "You were supposed to get coral or pink!"

"It's authentic," Guro Hari said.

"Too authentic."

"No way," I announced. "I'm not doing it."

Guro Hari turned to me, puzzled. "What?"

"This is some kine joke, right?"

"What?"

I gestured along my body.

"First you get me in a speedo. Then you make me wear lipstick. Is Jay going jump out of the broom closet with a camera?"

They both blinked at me.

Guro Hari waved the lipstick at Uncle Kahana, and they both collapsed laughing.

Uncle Kahana had to lean on the counter to keep from falling down.

Guro Hari wheezed and coughed so much, I thought he was going to bring up a lung.

'Ilima padded away from her pillow and leaned against my leg.

"You never told him?" howled Guro Hari.

"J—J—Jay!" gasped Uncle Kahana. "Camera!"

I reached down and patted 'Ilima's head annoyed, but relieved.

Guro Hari wiped his eyes with a dish towel. "You're gonna wear red, Zader. But not on your lips. Watch."

He lifted a training knife from the counter and rolled the lipstick along its edge.

Quicker than I could follow, he struck at Uncle Kahana's eyes.

Uncle Kahana blocked it from touching his face, but when he showed me his arm, I could see an eight inch slash of red lipstick scrawled from wrist to elbow.

"Eh!" complained Uncle Kahana.

"Blood," Guro Hari said.

"A scratch," sniffed Uncle Kahana.

"Incapacitated."

"Not," Uncle Kahana said, flexing his wrist and rotating his shoulder. "All muscle, no tendon."

Guro Hari smirked. "Makule," he said.

"The boy's blade, too," Uncle Kahana said, smearing the lipstick on his arm with the dish towel. "We don't have all day."

Guro Hari took my training knife and inked its edges in red.

"Waste of lipstick, Kahana," he said, and handed it back to me. "Now Zader, remember: distance, position, precision. You don't need a lot of strength. You need speed and agility. Always move, move, move."

I nodded.

"We fight!"

Slash!

Like a vampire, Guro Hari's knife grazed the side of my neck.

Uncle Kahana tsked. "You make-die-dead already, Z-boy."

45

JACKIE CHAN WANNABE

Puhi niho wakawaka
Literally a sharp-toothed eel; figuratively fierce warriors.

Stunned, I stood like a statue, not moving, not defending.

Guro Hari bobbed and weaved, his knife a magician's wand.

Swoosh!

"Fight or die, Zader," Uncle Kahana said cold and remote. "Choose."

I looked at the slick red line severing my shoulder from my body.

Incapacitated.

Useless.

My arm went numb, and for a moment, in my imagination, the red line welled and bled.

All over the tile—my blood's going everywhere.

What a mess.

Guro Hari and Uncle Kahana exchanged a worried look.

Slowly, too slowly, Guro Hari went for my face.

I blocked.

I took the energy from the blow, turned it, stepped inside, and swung my trainer, but Guro Hari was no longer there.

Another blow: this one mocking and light to the back of my head.

I pivoted, but felt his trainer brush just above my heel.

He rolled to his feet, picked up the lipstick, and re-applied it to his knife's blunt edge like a cheerleader getting ready to give the quarterback a kiss.

I lunged.

He casually leaned back as my trainer swung in front of his face and calmly twisted the lipstick back into the tube.

I lunged again.

He side-stepped and pilfered a sip of Uncle Kahana's sprunch.

"Hey! No give me your germs!" Uncle Kahana took the dish towel and wiped the end of his straw.

I side-stepped, and Guro Hari tapped me with his open hand on my cheek.

I took a step back.

He stepped forward.

I inched back.

He crept forward again, but his eyes weren't on me; they were on Uncle Kahana pouring another drink.

I saw an opening and went for it.

As easy as sitting in a beach chair on a lazy afternoon, he trapped my hand, took my knife, and grinned.

I could count the flecks of tobacco in his teeth.

I twisted away and fled to the bathroom, slamming and locking the door.

"That's his best move yet," Guro Hari said.

I heard ice rattle in a glass.

"This one's mine?" Guro Hari's voice.

"No. You get the old one over there with your gulas on the straw. This fresh one's for me," Uncle Kahana said.

"Gulas add flavor."

"Keep your flavor to yourself."

I heard Guro Hari's wheezing chuckle and more ice rattle.

"Cigarettes are going to kill you," Uncle Kahana observed.

Guro Hari said, "Probably. I would've quit in my twenties if I knew I was going live this long."

"Psshtt. I would've started if I knew I was going to live this long!"

I heard a straw sucking air in the bottom of a glass.

"Zader still in the bathroom?" Uncle Kahana asked.

"Would you come out?" Guro Hari asked.

"Zader! Again!" called Uncle Kahana.

For the second time this morning, I didn't want to come out of the bathroom.

"Zader! It's okay! Just come out."

I looked in the mirror.

The lipstick lines traced the damage; I was staggered when I counted; most of them I never felt. If this was fo'real I'd be make-die-dead for sure. I was too slow, too clumsy, and if I wanted to get better, I'd have to train hard.

"You can do this," I whispered to the mirror.

I opened the door.

Guro Hari pounced.

Slash!

Swipe!

Slice!

I felt something flutter to my feet.

I ignored his trainer's blade and struggled to shut the door.

He let me.

I leaned against the door breathing hard, my eyes wide and staring in the mirror.

My lei!

I looked down at my feet.

"You cut my lei!" I roared.

"I took your knife," Guro Hari called through the door.

I kicked it.

He wheezed again.

I felt him move away.

"Eh, Kahana," he said in the kitchen, "get more sprunch?"

No way was I opening that door again.

My eyes settled on the window. It was a typical bathroom window with frosted glass jalousies and a screen. I wiggled the glass strips out of their metal clips and set them next to the sink.

"Zader, come out. Fo'real this time," called Uncle Kahana. "We just want to talk."

Talk my 'okole.

When I snapped the final clips, the screen popped out, fell two stories, and bounced in the parking lot.

I hoped it bent.

Knuckles rapped on the door.

"Peace, Zader. Promise," Guro Hari said.

I climbed on the toilet tank and stuck my head out the window. The drop was near the front door to Hari's—I mean Uncle Kahana's—store. A little below me and to the left was the edge of the hand railing for the upstairs lanai that ran along Uncle Kahana's living room.

I was pretty sure I could make it.

Pretty sure.

I was outside the window frame and hugging the wall, reaching for the railing with my foot when I heard a *plop*.

I looked down.

A young haole girl with a sunburned nose was looking up at me. A large yellow and orange shave ice was melting at her feet.

"Mom!" she yelled. "There's a naked boy covered in lipstick climbing out a window!"

I froze. I

couldn't go back and I couldn't go forward.

"Jeanie!" a woman's voice scolded from the store.

"Mom! He's got weeds wrapped around his ankle and wrist!"

Please, let me die and end this, I prayed.

But whatever happens, please don't let anyone show up with a smart phone or camera.

If this gets out, I'll never live it down.

"Go away!" I mouthed at her.

"He wants me to go away!"

"What did I say about telling stories?" the woman said.

"But Mom, this time it's true!"

I sensed more commotion under me, shadows and light flickering like schools of fish on the reef.

I peered down.

"Jeanie! Look what you did! Your snow cone's all over—" the voice trailed off.

Bleach blond hair and mega-sized sunglasses stared up at me.

I closed my eyes.

Next to me the sliding door swept open and a strong brown arm wrapped around my body, lifting me over the railing and onto the lanai.

Uncle Kahana leaned down.

"Aloha! So sorry about the shave ice! Tell the girl at the counter Kahana said to give you a new one! On the house, of course! Have a nice day!"

As he pushed me through the open door and into living room, I heard the woman say, "Hush, Jeanie, hush! I told you it's another culture! The whole island is like going to Chinatown in San Francisco. Now do you want a free snow cone or not?"

Behind me Uncle Kahana slammed the sliding door closed and locked it.

Guro Hari was leaning against the kitchen counter, drink in hand.

Uncle Kahana's eyes traveled from my toes to the top of my head. My hair was wild, my knee scraped, and the lipstick had streaked and smeared like ocean waves all over my body.

"So what now, Jackie Chan?" he asked.

I hung my head. "Guro Hari cut my lei," I mumbled.

"'Ae. He also took your knife, jumped you when you thought you were safe, and sliced you like a loaf of bread. What's the problem?"

"I need my lei."

Guro Hari walked over.

He tipped my chin up.

He said, "Anything you have—anything you love—can be taken away from you. Anything."

Uncle Kahana draped a blanket over my shoulders and guided me to the couch. He wrapped his arm around me and pulled my head to his chest.

Some of the chill I felt eased, and the adrenaline that pushed me out the window ebbed.

'Ilima nosed my leg, then jumped in my lap, her head tucked under my chin. I sat there breathing her warm doggy breath, wanting to disappear.

"It's okay, Z-boy," Uncle Kahana whispered. "Let the tears come."

LAUELE GIRLZ

False Crack
An expected hard blow, usually to the face.

From the pavilion down to Keikikai beach was a zoo.

Wet sandy towels, sandwich bags, Hawaiian Sun cans wrapped in layers of tinfoil and paper towels, potato chips, kakimochi, and iso peanuts littered every surface. The showers ran non-stop as kids filled plastic cups and water balloons and played chasemaster around and around the picnic tables.

The Summer Fun leaders were counting down the days until they could return to college. They kept one eye on the kids, making sure nobody got out into the parking lot or past the lava rocks to Nalupuki Beach. There was a mondo-sized shaker of meat tenderizer in the first aid kit if jellyfish showed up, but mostly they talked story with each other and refereed sand fights and squabbles over whose turn it was to work on the mural.

That morning Mr. Halpert had counted noses and said that every kid had ten minutes to add their touches to one of the walls, eight kids at a time. An hour later most decided they'd rather play in the surf than wait their turn to color in the lines.

Fine by me. Less chance of a paint fight that way.

I don't think it occurred to Mr. Halpert that paint brushes could be used on more than walls and canvases. Unlike public school and Summer Fun, in his teaching experience all of his students actually wanted to be in his class.

Lucky 'Alika and Chad are too old for Summer Fun this year. We'd be cleaning paint off the pavilion floor until school started.

Looking down the beach, I saw Nili-boy's junior surf campers taking a break and eating a snack in the shade under a quick-set canopy. Jay was sitting on his board with a soda can in his hands talking to bikini clad Lisa Ling and Becky Walters.

I did a double-take.

I'd seen them up at the pavilion a million times, but never on Nalupuki beach or on the reef. Neither of them surfed. I doubted they could swim. Lisa tossed her hair over her shoulders, laughing at something Jay said.

Interesting.

As I came around the corner, Char Siu was standing on a step stool working alone on the wall facing Hari's. She wasn't part of the Summer Fun crew; Mr. Halpert had her doing the more delicate work of filling in round shapes with a blend of dull charcoal and muddy yellow that would eventually become part of the reef at Piko Point.

"Eh, Char Siu, wassup!"

She sniffled and wiped her nose on her arm, turning away from me.

"Zader, could you just go away?" she croaked.

"Char Siu?"

She turned red-rimmed eyes on me, her face splotchy and swollen, her mascara puddled under her eyes, looking like she lost a boxing match with the world flyweight champion.

Dipping her paint brush, she methodically stroked color on the wall, studiously avoiding me.

"What happened?" I asked.

"Nothing."

"Something."

"I don't want to talk about it. I just want to be alone. Go paint somewhere else. Please." She added it like an afterthought.

I stood there for a minute, not knowing what to do. Char Siu just kept dipping and stroking, pausing only to wipe her eyes or nose on her sleeve.

I opened my mouth to try again when Mr. Halpert walked around the corner.

"Oh, Zader! You're back! Done with your karate lesson?"

It wasn't karate.

I'm not sure what it was, but it was easier to say karate than try to explain Lua or Kali. Everybody'd seen the movie, but nobody would ever confuse Uncle Kahana or Guro Hari with Mr. Miyagi.

Guro Hari was right; skin did wash easier than clothes, although even after showering at Uncle Kahana's, I could still see faint red lines here and there.

Some marks never wash off no matter how hard you scrub.

"Yeah," I said.

"Did you get lunch? I have an extra sandwich in the cooler."

I patted my tummy. Uncle Kahana had filled me full of chicken katsu and rice until I could barely get up from the table.

"Don't leave hungry," Uncle Kahana had said. "I don't ever want you hungry. You ever feel the need to eat, see Hari. He'll fix you a plate no matter the time and put it on my tab."

"Thanks, Uncle Kahana. But I'm stuffed. I couldn't take another bite."

"Good, good," he'd said.

"I'm good," I said to Mr. Halpert. "I ate. How can I help?"

"Grab the other step stool and work on the sky. I don't dare let the Summer Fun kids climb a ladder, so they've done all they can on this wall. Why don't you work here and keep Char Siu company?"

I shot Char Siu side-eye, but she wouldn't take her eyes off what she was doing.

"Okay," I said.

After checking the chart, I poured a little of the sky blue into a paint tray and went to work.

"Check it, 'Alika. It's Char Siu and her *boy*friend."

I clenched my jaw and didn't turn around. I didn't have to; I knew it was Chad Watanabe and his partner in crime, 'Alika Kanahele.

Jerks.

All last school year, the Blalahs made my life miserable. Jay ran interference for me, even breaking 'Alika 's nose and smashing him with his surfboard, but like my mom said, these guys were special kine stupid.

After what happened last spring at Piko Point, 'Alika didn't hassle me, but not even a muzzle and a choke chain could keep Chad from grinding on me every time we met.

Ignore them.

They'll get bored and leave.

"Let's go," nudged 'Alika. "Stale, already. I wanna check out the waves Nalupuki-side."

"Nah," drawled Chad, "Not boyfriend and girlfriend. More like one dog and his—"

Crack!

Chad's head rocked back as Char Siu's roundhouse kick caught him right in the temple. She threw her paintbrush at 'Alika and sat on Chad's chest. Her arm was cranking back for a kill shot when I tackled her.

She was wild like a cat, clawing and scratching at me and trying to kick me in the alas. I folded her into a Lua hold to keep her from biting.

Chad was on the ground and woozy.

'Alika stood there with paint running down his shirt. I gave him a Look.

"We going do this?" I asked.

"No," he said. "I'm cool."

He picked Chad up and headed toward the parking lot.

Beneath me, Char Siu raged.

"What's the matter, Char Siu? Are you crazy?"

She went limp for a second, then burst into tears.

Surprised, I let my grip go slack.

She sat up and punched me in the gut.

"Auwi!" I sucked air through my teeth. "Why'd you do that?"

"You skinned my knee!" she spat.

"Better a skinned knee than jail!"

I hiccupped.

"It would've been worth it!"

"Next time, I'll remember you feel that way!"

Her nose was running again. She lifted the bottom of her t-shirt and used the inside hem, giving me stink-eye the whole time.

"I am not in love with Jay," she announced.

I blinked at her.

"Of course not."

She sniffed. "Just because we do Lua together, it doesn't mean I'm going to marry him or anything!"

"Marry him? Jay? No way. You can do soooo much better. I pity the girl who marries Jay. Have you seen his side of our room?"

I rubbed my stomach and groaned.

It worked.

She cracked a smile.

"Who said you love Jay?"

"Lisa Ling. She told Becky and Mele that I spend so much time with him, I must be in love."

I looked back down the beach. Jay was heading back out into the waves with a couple of kids in tow, but Lisa and Becky were still hanging around, standing with their hands on their hips and their heads thrown back, swinging their hair in the breeze.

Posing.

"I don't think you're the one in love with Jay."

Char Siu wiped her eyes, smearing the last trace of black eyeliner into a bruise.

"I'm sick of wearing tape on my eyelids. I hate high heels. I like to dance, but I don't wanna be Krystal QT."

"So don't," I said.

She looked at me with pity in her eyes.

"Oh, Zader. Guys never get it."

BUMP

Maka ʻike
To see supernatural things.

Owen and I were finishing the last touches on the mural's stunt kites when a horn beeped in the parking lot.

I'd painted mine to look like "Iolani, the custom quarter-Hawaiian stunt kite Uncle Kahana gave me for my birthday last year. It made me feel good to think that years from now, I could come back to the pavilion and see my kite flying over the same green hills no matter what developers decided to do.

That's the beauty of our invisible pavilion; it only reflected what we wanted to see.

Owen's kite was rad. It looked like an anime hero's pet fish and twisted like a Chinese lion dance. I doubted it would actually fly, but it looked really cool.

Guess that's part of whatever artistic license Mr. Halpert keeps yammering about as he tells us to paint more flowers and bushes in front of Hari's store.

When the horn beeped a second time, Owen dropped his brush in the rinse bucket and yelled, "I'm coming!"

Much softer to me he said, "That's my ride. I gotta go."

He threw his hands up at the open paint cans and drop cloths scattered around us.

"Don't worry," I said. "I got it."

"Thanks, Zader. See you tomorrow?"

"I'll be here."

"Me, too, if I can get a ride."

He grabbed his backpack and headed to the parking lot, but not before the horn beeped again.

"I'm coming!" he shouted, breaking into a trot.

"Thanks, Owen," Mr. Halpert said. "We made good progress today."

"Laters." Owen waved without looking.

"Ready to clean up?" Mr. Halpert called from the other side of the pavilion. "It's getting dark."

"Yeah," I said, tossing my brush in the rinse water.

I'd folded the drop cloths, stuck them in a crate, and was reaching for the rinse bucket when I felt it.

The itchy, twitchy feeling between my shoulder blades was back.

I didn't look, but listened.

I heard a sound like slippahs sliding across sand on cement. A shower turned on. I swiveled around to see a lone surfer washing the salt off his board.

It's all in your head.

The sun's going down.

You always feel squirrelly and light-headed this close to dinner.

I picked up the screwdriver and double-tapped all the lids on the paint cans to make sure they were sealed. The chicken-skin feeling kept creeping like fog down my arms and legs and settled like a cold wind on the back of my neck.

I tried to casually roll my head on my shoulders like I was stiff from painting, while my eyes and ears swept the area, scanning for what didn't belong.

I heard a car alarm chirp and a trunk pop open.

I almost jumped out of my skin when Mr. Halpert touched my shoulder.

So much for my mad ninja skills.

"Zader?"

"Aaahhhh!"

He put his hands up. "Whoa! Didn't mean to startle you like that. Everything okay?"

I swallowed. "Yeah. I'm just a little . . . chilly."

"The wind's picked up. As long as it doesn't blow so hard it lifts sand, the breeze will be good for the mural."

He held up one of the lanterns we used when it got too dark and swung it toward the wall.

"Let me guess. This one's yours and the neon fish with the googly eyes is Owen's."

I didn't bother answering. Owen and I had worked out an armed truce; we could paint together, but we wouldn't hang out after school. The differences between Kahala and Lauele were more than our zip codes. We were both okay with it. While Mr. Halpert wasn't exactly thrilled with us, as long as we were civil, he didn't push it.

He stepped closer, examining the fine lines I'd drawn to suggest 'Iolani's rigging.

"Owen's is pure fantasy. But this one," he pointed at my kite, "I've seen this kite flying over this hill before."

The hair on the back of my neck started to crawl.

I ran my hand over it, but it wouldn't lie down.

I tried to concentrate on what Mr. Halpert was saying, but I missed it.

"Am I right?" he asked.

Oh, crap.

"Zader, it's okay. I did the same thing myself on the other wall."

Yes or no. Choose!

"Y-y-yes?" I said.

"Thought, so," he said. "I can tell this came from the heart."

I guess yes was right!

I must have looked puzzled because he moved straight into lecture mode.

"Art can also be a record, Zader. Historians glean a lot of valuable information from art—everything from what people wore to the tools they used to what they ate—all of those things can be discovered in paintings and sculptures. Art helps fix in time what human memory cannot."

Oh, great. More stuff to look up when I get home.

He stepped back from the mural.

"I think it's fantastic that you drew your kite in the mural. Let's clean up. Then I want to show you my piece of history."

ORIGINS

Ka leo
The voice.

We'd stored the paint cans in the back of his trunk, and I'd policed the area picking up all the assorted beach litter—gum wrappers, empty soda cans, and paper shave ice cones—I could find. It was getting late, and I hurried, not wanting Mom or dinner to wait any longer.

As we cleaned, I'd ignored the spider running up and down my spine and the insistent buzzing that settled somewhere low in the back of my brain, but when I heard the voice, I couldn't ignore it any longer.

"Boy," it said.

The voice of the Man with Too Many Teeth.

I dropped the brush I was reshaping and stood up.

The sun was long gone; it was full night now and the moon was rising over the mountains. The breeze off the ocean was humid, and the sound of the surf crashing in the background mingled with the Jawaiian reggae beat from a passing car.

I frantically turned in circles, wondering where he would strike.

Everything Uncle Kahana and Guro Hari taught me flashed through my mind.

I slapped my hand on an empty pocket and cursed.

I started to move.

I spotted the silhouette of a tall man near the trash cans. He side-stepped toward the beach, limping slightly.

Bum, my mind shouted. *It's just a crazy homeless person. You're fine.*

But the chicken skin on my arms told me different.

Get an adult.

I raced around the side of the pavilion to where Mr. Halpert was stacking the last of the crates.

"Come see," he said, not looking at me, and held the lantern up to the mural of Keikikai Beach. "I'm really excited about this."

I closed my eyes and tried to slow my galloping heart and runaway breath.

"A long time ago I met a woman named Pua-O-Ke-Kai on the beach here at Keikikai. I'm sure that for her it was nothing more than a vacation fling with a temporary tourist." He shook his head, remembering. "I should've realized it when she never told me her last name, phone number, or where she lived. For all I know, she was married or on vacation, too."

I heard his voice and registered his words, but my senses were straining to hear footsteps on the other side.

"But I was supposed to be on my honeymoon. Romance was in the air. I fell hard. Back in L.A., she was never far from my thoughts. I painted her portrait—you'll see it when school starts. I keep it on my desk."

One breath in, hold it, release.

In.

Hold.

Release.

I shifted my weight back and forth, standing ready on the balls of my toes.

Don't lose it now, I thought. *Not in front of Mr. Halpert.*

I squeezed my eyes tight.

"Anne—Ms. Robinson—has helped me see that I've built Pua into someone so perfect that all I could think about was being with her. I wasn't seeing what was right in front of me. So I decided to paint her in the mural lying on the beach the way I first saw her. That way she'll always be here waiting for me if I need her. What do you think?"

I had time for an impression only.

Maka? No, too old.

I blinked and Aunty Palala swam into focus as the world came crashing down.

I ran.

REVELATION

Ho'oia
To confirm; verify; profess.

From the bottom of the stairs, I could see the light on in Uncle Kahana's apartment and smell the Spam sprinkled with a little ground cloves frying on the stove top. The rice cooker dinged, and a kitchen drawer opened and closed. The radio was on, and through the window I heard Dan the Man giving the last traffic report of the night.

"Good news, everybody! Our traffic cam shows the accident with the Honda Civic on H1 just before the Kap'Iolani off-ramp has finally cleared. Mahalo to the boys in blue for their quick kokua! Looks like clear sailing all the way to Hawai'i Kai on Kalanianeole. Cheehoooooo!"

'Ukuleles strummed, and Braddah Iz's silken pipes filled the air.

"Take me home, country roads . . ." Uncle Kahana sang along, his old man's voice true, but not as full and rich as Iz's ghost voice singing from the grave.

The records we keep haunt our lives, I thought. *The past never stays there.*

I shivered and started up the stairs.

'Ilima met me at the door.

"Zader!" Uncle Kahana said with his back to the door. "I wasn't expecting you tonight! Jay and Char Siu are coming later, but this is a good surprise. You hungry? I made plenny. Get Spam and rice and corn."

He was flipping the slices in the pan, getting ready to slide them on a plate.

"You eat this. I'll slice some more for me."

'Ilima didn't sniff or wag her tail or lick my hand. Instead she barked. For the first time I can remember, she didn't look at me with love.

Uncle Kahana jerked around, his warrior eyes assessing.

I was breathing too hard, my eyes were bugging out of my head, and my limbs were shaking.

Without taking his eyes off me, he tipped the crisp slices onto a plate already loaded with rice and waiting on the counter.

"Here," he said. "Eat."

He changed his grip on the frying pan, but didn't set it down.

The smell washed over me in waves.

Pork.

Salt.

Cloves.

Fat.

I could see each flavor rolling through the air in bands of color.

'Ilima's cold nose touched my leg, and I moved.

I ignored the fork and used my fingers to bring a slice to my mouth, the sizzle of the fat scalding my tongue and blistering my lips, but I didn't care. The pain was part of the experience, and I wanted it all.

I gulped and swallowed, not bothering to chew. Bits of sticky white rice clung to my fingers. A rice paddle appeared, dumping a new payload of rice onto my plate.

I hissed, wanting more crisp and tender pork.

The food kept coming, the Spam now sliced cold from the can, the jelly salty and slimy like fresh opihi or oysters.

It was the best thing I'd ever tasted.

One second, I was ravenous. The next, I was done.

I pushed back mid-bite and reached for a napkin.

Uncle Kahana stood near the fridge, watching me.

I burped and sipped juice, and he poured me some more.

The rage was gone. All I wanted was a nap, but the questions wouldn't stop circling my mind.

"Uncle Kahana, who was Aunty Palala?"

He sat the frying pan on the stove and turned off the burner.

"Aunty Palala? I don't know who you're talking about."

He picked up a dish rag and started wiping the counter.

"Please don't lie to me anymore," I whispered. "I'm not a child."

He hung the rag on the oven handle and got out the broom.

"Nobody said anything about you being a child."

"I know she's part of my Hohonukai family. I know someone has been leaving gifts for me on my birthday for you to find and bring them to Mom and Dad. You know more than you're telling me."

"The gifts are left with Pohaku, the 'aumakua stone, at Piko Point."

"You mean by."

"No, I mean with."

He passed a hand over his face.

"Come sit at the table," he said. "Bring your juice. I can't think surrounded by all this mess."

Uncle Kahana took the chair that faced the door and not dinner's remains in the kitchen.

I slipped into the chair next to him, wary.

'Ilima curled under the table, resting her head on my foot. She was solid, warm, and comforting, and I ran my toes along her back.

Feeling my way through a game of chess, I led with a pawn.

"Aunty Palala."

"Tall, you said? Graceful like a hula dancer? Hmmmm." Uncle Kahana was stalling.

"At Piko Point, Maka gave me—"

"Maka *gave* you?" The blood drained from his face, and his right eye began to quiver. "You've talked with Maka *in person*? I thought you said she was a dream?"

I pounced. "For years I called her Dream Girl, until she turned out to be real."

I didn't give him a chance to think about it, I attacked again. "Maka says Aunty Palala—"

"Pua," he blurted. "Her name is Pua, Pua-O-Ke-Kai. Palala is a Hawaiian word meaning a gift intended for a child. It was what she was carrying, not her name."

"Who is Maka?" I asked.

"Her daughter," Uncle Kahana said. "The one she kept by her side."

"At the pavilion, Pua had a gift wrapped in banana leaves. It was for me."

"The knife," Uncle Kahana confirmed. "The one Hari is training you to use."

"I want it."

'Ilima crept out from under the table and stood near her dog pillow.

She chuffed.

"I don't think so," Uncle Kahana said.

"Why not?" I pressed. "It's mine."

'Ilima whined in the back her throat.

"He's not ready," Uncle Kahana said.

"Who's not ready?"

"You. Me. None of us."

"I need my knife."

"Why? What do you think you can do with this Shark Tooth of yours, hah?"

"I can protect myself against Kalei."

At the name, Uncle Kahana trembled. His lips turned blue as he slowly toppled out of his chair. He held a hand to his chest, gasping for air.

"No," he moaned.

I should have rushed to his side.

I should have lifted him back onto his chair, called for help, got him some water—anything, but what I did.

A switched had flipped inside me.

He was weak and that made me strong.

"Maka calls me brother."

"No."

"Pua is her mother."

"Don't say it," he begged.

'Ilima barked, sharp and insistent, digging with her paws on her pillow.

"'Ilima! Don't do this!" Uncle Kahana started to crawl toward her.

Weak.

The dog pillow flipped.

Shark Tooth gleamed on the tile.

I'm yours, it said.

I picked it up.

Snick, went the blade.

"Anything you have can be taken away from you," I said.

"Zader, please listen. Let me help."

"You can't run very far on an island, Uncle Kahana. At some point you gotta face the bully."

'Ilima stood between me and the door. Her coat shimmered and sparkled like she'd rolled in glitter. It dropped from her coat and pooled at her feet.

Uncle Kahana's not going to like that mess, I thought. *It's a lot worse than beach sand.*

"'Ilima, don't let Zader leave," Uncle Kahana said.

She tilted her head at Uncle Kahana then turned to me. She was trying to tell me something, but I didn't get it.

In a flash she was gone, out the door and down the stairs.

"'Ilima!" shouted Uncle Kahana.

Weak.

And I am strong.

"Pua is my mother," I said. "And Maka is my sister. And that makes me Niuhi."

I stalked out the door.

THE WRITING ON THE WALL

Ho'omaka'ana
The beginning; to begin.

Uncle Kahana

"Uncle Kahana, what's wrong?"

Char Siu kicked her slippahs off at the door and rushed to his side. He was sitting on the floor near the kitchen table, pale and sweating. She checked his pulse, certain it was a heart attack.

"Uncle?" Jay asked, hovering in the doorway.

"Go get Hari," Char Siu said. "NOW!"

"Wait," Uncle Kahana said. "It's okay. I'm okay. Come in and shut the door."

"Uncle Kahana, you are not okay," Char Siu said. "Does your arm tingle? Do you have a stabbing pain in your chest?"

He sighed and started getting up.

"I have a terrible pain in my heart," he said, "but it's not a heart attack."

He stood a little unsteadily and pulled a chair from the table.

"Sit. Both of you. It's time we talked."

ZADER

I kept Shark Tooth in my hand, but I didn't think it would help.

Kalei was much stronger and bigger than me, and anything I had, anything I loved, was his for the taking.

Guro Hari had taught me that.

The streetlights were on, but the light of the full moon was brighter. The adrenaline pumped in my blood, electricity snapped, and suddenly the shadows were as bright as day.

The pavilion stank. The sweat of human bodies, old food, and fish slime overwhelmed me.

When I looked at the mural, I could see waves of paint fumes wafting from the walls like a cartoon image of Pepe Le Pew. They burned my lungs, making me cough. I covered my nose and mouth with my hand and searched the drawings on the wall.

Just a few brush strokes—shades of sienna, cinnamon, and charcoal, a couple of dots of orange and yellow for a dress—up close it looked like nothing at all.

But I knew it was the woman who gave me Shark Tooth, the one I'd called Aunty Palala, the one Mr. Halpert called Pua, the one Maka called mother.

My mother.

UNCLE KAHANA

Char Siu put the glass of water she insisted he drink in front of Uncle Kahana.

"Mahalo, Char Siu," he said, not touching it.

"I think we should call somebody," Char Siu said.

"My mom?" Jay asked. "Or you think a doctor?"

"No. I told you, I don't need a doctor," Uncle Kahana said.

"His color's better," Jay said.

"Sit," Uncle Kahana patted the table. "Just stop, both of you, and sit."

Char Siu glanced around. "Where's 'Ilima?"

Uncle Kahana closed his eyes. "Gone," he said. "Out."

"Where?" Jay asked. He stuck his head out the door. "'Ilima!" he whistled, "Come home!"

"She's not in the yard," Uncle Kahana said.

"But she's coming back?" Char Siu stood up and went to the door. "She's not lost, is she?"

"That's not important," Uncle Kahana said.

"What? How can you say that? Jay, I told you something is really wrong! We need to get a grownup involved."

"No grownup can help," Uncle Kahana sighed. "I prayed I'd never have to tell you, but you need to know. You need to know about Nana'ue."

ZADER

"The likeness is good," the Man with Too Many Teeth said. "It shows great skill."

Kalei stepped out from the shadows of the pavilion. He shook a can of spray paint, the ball bearings inside roaring like thunder in my too sensitive ears.

"But we can't have it."

He sprayed a spot of black paint, obscuring Pua on the beach. The paint bubbled, then ran as black streaks raced down the wall to puddle on the ground. He rattled the can again and swept his arm in a wide circle over the wall, then filled the space with triangle teeth. A few more swipes and a giant shark's head rose from the middle of Keikikai beach.

"Now, that's more like it," he said. "Although I'm sure you could do better. Art was never my thing."

"Who are you?" I whispered. "What do you want?"

"Who am I?" he mocked, his mouth too full of teeth. "The question is, who are you?"

UNCLE KAHANA

"Nana'ue?" Char Siu echoed. "I've heard that name before."

"Me, too. What grade is he?" Jay asked. "Does he surf?"

"You're thinking he's one of Nili-boy's friends, Jay?" Char Siu asked.

"Yeah. Hapa-Hawaiian guy, usually surfs Sunset, wears a puka shell necklace, has a tattoo around his ankle—"

"Will you two just cool your jets for a minute? You don't know Nana'ue!" Uncle Kahana pinched the bridge of his nose. "Nana'ue lived a long long time ago. It's a legend. Nana'ue's father was Kamohoali'i—"

"Pele's older brother! My kumu hula talked about him! Kamohoali'i was an ocean god who could take the form of a shark!"

"'Ae, Char Siu. Kamohoali'i has many names and many forms. That's not what's important now. I need you to focus. What the legends say are true, although over the years some of the basic facts have gotten scrambled. All storytellers are liars in the end."

ZADER

The blood pounded in my head.

The low angry buzz hovered in the base of my skull like a swarm of killer bees.

Run, they said, *hide.*

I shifted my weight, ready to take flight.

Another voice in my head shouted, *Wait! Don't act like prey!*

Kalei's eyes lighted; his brow quirked; his eagerness spilled over me like waves.

"Are you going to run?" he asked.

I choked back the fear and pushed back the buzzing. In my hand I gripped Shark Tooth tight, hiding it behind my thigh.

"No," I squeaked.

"Good," Kalei said. "I'd rather not chase you. I might lose control. That wouldn't be good. Well, at least not for you."

UNCLE KAHANA

"Nana'ue was born to a human mother and a shark father who was a god. The legend says he looked like a normal human except on his back he had a hole that resembled the mouth of a fish."

"Are you telling us the story behind another lua 'ai?" Jay asked. "I'm confused; is this a defensive or offensive move? Are we making a hole in someone's back or are we using it to hide something?"

"Jay, you will be the death of me yet."

Uncle Kahana sipped his water and cleared his throat.

"If you give me a moment, you'll understand. I'm telling you the reason behind all the training you've been doing."

"Sorry, Kumu," Jay said.

"Listen: Nana'ue's shark god father lived with them for a time, but eventually he had to return to the sea. He made Nana'ue's human family promise to never feed him meat and to keep a kihei, a short cloak, over his shoulders to hide the hole."

"The hole that looked like the mouth of a fish," said Char Siu.

Uncle Kahana nodded. "Everything was fine until Nana'ue went to live and eat with the men. It was in the men's hale mua that he first saw pork and asked for some. His grandfather loved him so much, he couldn't deny him anything. He fed Nana'ue pork, wanting him to grow big and strong."

"But feeding him meat was bad, even though Nana'ue wanted it," Char Siu said.

"People don't always do what they should when it comes to love," Uncle Kahana said.

"What happened when Nana'ue ate meat?" Jay asked.

"The more he ate, the more he wanted. His little fish mouth grew until it covered his whole back. Razor sharp teeth appeared."

"Holy crap!" Jay said.

"His father was a god, remember? It happens," Char Siu said.

"One day, while he was bathing in a pond with his mother, he changed. Nana'ue the boy was gone. Nana'ue the Niuhi shark was born."

"Niuhi shark!" Jay yelped. "Nana'ue was Niuhi?"

"'Ae, Jay. A shark that knows its prey."

ZADER

Kalei dropped the spray can and moved to his right, forcing me away from the pavilion and toward the beach.

"You are hanai," he said.

"I'm adopted, yeah."

Where is this going?

"Are you the ho'oilina?" he asked.

"I don't know what that means."

"Each generation knows less and less! Ho'oilina! Are you his apprentice?"

Apprentice?

Like the Sorcerer's Apprentice? *Are we talking Mickey Mouse?*

"I still don't know what you're asking," I said.

"Is Kahana filling your head with genealogy stories, telling you when to plant taro, and how to navigate by the stars?"

"N—n—no," I stammered. "He's teaching me Lua."

Kalei threw his head back and barked.

"Ha! Even less useful," he chortled. "I really shouldn't be amazed."

A quick movement in the bushes by the trash cans—with my heighten senses, I smelled her before I saw her—'Ilima, crouching in the shadows.

UNCLE KAHANA

"As Nana'ue grew, so did his appetite for meat. Eventually, the little fish he caught as a shark in the pond and the pork he ate as a boy weren't enough. In ancient Hawai'i nei there weren't many options."

"He started eating humans," Jay said.

Uncle Kahana put his head in his hands. "And he didn't want to stop."

"But did he?" Char Siu asked.

Uncle Kahana didn't look up.

"Yes," he said to the table. "And that's where you guys come in."

ZADER

Kalei pressed forward, limping a little, and I retreated backward, keeping a good grip on Shark Tooth. I didn't think he'd seen it hidden in my palm.

If he gets close, I'll cut him.

"Hanai, but not apprentice," he mused. "Who are your parents?"

"Liz and Paul Westin," I said.

Pua-O-Ke-Kai.

Mr. Halpert, I thought.

"No. Liz and Paul's son is James Kapono. A rising surf star. I've seen him on his board out there, the board marked with a ti leaf lei around the bottom drawn by you. Why would you draw such a thing on a surfboard?"

"To keep Jay safe."

"Safe from what?"

"N-N-Niuhi," I whispered.

He stilled.

I could see his pulse hammer in his temple.

His tattoos rippled.

"And what are Niuhi?" he asked.

"Aware," I said, and tripped.

I fell backward over the edge where the grass ends and the sand begins, tumbling with Shark Tooth trapped beneath my thigh.

I smelled my blood before I felt Shark Tooth's bite.

Kalei's nostrils flared. "Niuhi!" he roared.

From the bushes, 'Ilima attacked like a bullet in the dark, trailing sparkles of silver and gold. Her fangs sank deep into Kalei's arm, knocking him to his knees.

Run!

His arm cocked back and fired like a torpedo.

"That's the last time you interfere with me, you 'e'epa dog! I'm sending you back to the underworld where you belong!"

'Ilima yelped, the pain ringing loud and long in my ears, but I didn't look back; I ran heedless over lava rocks, splashed through puddles, and didn't stop until I was standing at the edge of the big saltwater pool at Piko Point.

UNCLE KAHANA

"You talking bubbles, Uncle Kahana," Jay said. "We don't have anything to do with an ancient Hawaiian legend about a shark-boy. Char Siu, get the phone. We're calling my mom. Uncle Kahana's delirious."

"But you do have something to do with a shark-boy, Jay. You're Zader's brother."

ZADER

I was standing in saltwater, in a shallow depression in the reef not deep enough for anything but hermit crabs to live.

My feet sizzled, sending waves of energy pulsing up and down my spine.

I gasped, trying to catch my breath in the humid night air, the stars so bright above me they hurt my eyes.

I held my arm out to block the moon; it dazzled like the noon day sun.

There was no pain, but I felt things loosening, moving inside, my organs shifting to new places, bones creaking and sinews stretching.

I was excited and scared and my heart beat so hard I could see it pounding in my chest.

This is it.

I was surrounded by ocean, the only way back blocked by Kalei.

Do or die.

I jumped.

Zader's adventures continue in
One Truth, No Lie
Book 3 in the Niuhi Shark Saga trilogy.

GLOSSARY

THE NIUHI SHARK SAGA

-dem | Refers to a group of people or things identified by one part of the group.

'a'ole pilikia | No trouble; it's no problem.

'ae | Yes.

'ahi | Tuna.

'aina | Land.

'alas | Masculine family jewels.

'au'au | To bathe or swim.

'aumakua | Guardian spirit of an ancestor that can take many forms, such as animal, bird, fish, rock, or wind.

'e'epa | Hawaiian word for supernatural and legendary beings.

'ehu | Reddish tinge in hair that is usually brown or black.

'Ilima | The name of a delicate orange flower and also the name of Uncle Kahana's poi dog.

'Iolani | The name of Zader's kite. Literally, *heavenly* (or royal) *hawk*.

'ohana | Family, those you call family.

'ohana nui | Extended family; clan.

'okole | Rear end; buttocks.

'olapa | A type of tree.

'olohe lua | A Lua master; head of a Lua school.

'ono | Delicious, delightful; to relish or crave.

'opihi | A type of limpet.

'opu | Stomach; tummy.

'uku | A flea or body louse. When combined with a number such as 'uku-billion it means many or more than you could count.

'ukulele | A stringed instrument similar to a small guitar.

5-4-4 | A play on words meaning "go to the bathroom." When spoken, the numbers 5, 4, 4 in Japanese are go-shi-shi.

act | To show off, to act like a big shot.

ai ka pressah | Refers to overwhelming sense of stress or performance anxiety; literally, *oh, the pressure!*

aiyah | Expression of dismay or alarm.

akamai | Smart.

Akua | God; na akua means gods.

Ala Moana | A giant outdoor shopping mall near Waikiki.

alas | Slang for the family jewels.

amene | Amen; to say amen.

an'den | Literally, *and then*, meaning 'So what?' or 'What's next?'

anykine | Any which way or style; also confused or uncaring.

Aunty | Title of respect used for female adults.

auwe | Expression of disappointment or grief.

auwi | Ouch!

babooze | A fool; someone who is stupid or goofy.

bamboocha | Big, huge, ginormous.

bento | A box lunch.

boro / boroz / boro-boros | The oldest, most worn-out clothes.

brah / braddah | Slang for brother.

bufo | Bullfrog.

buggah | Bugger; source of frustration.

bulai | A blatant untruth; a bull lie.

bumbai | Sometime soon; in the near future.

calabash | A bowl or container often made of wood or a hollowed gourd. When used to refer to people, it implies a close friend or relative, i.e. someone who would eat out of the same serving bowl.

char siu | Chinese-flavored barbequed pork often used as filling for manapua or as a garnish for saimin. Also a nickname for Charlene Suzette Apo.

chasemaster | A variation of the playground game tag.

chee | You think so? You notice?

cheehooooo | Wooohooo! Wheeeeee!

chicken skin | Goosebumps; an eerie feeling.

chillax | Combination of chill-out and relax.

choke | Lots; plenty; more than enough.

cockaroach | To steal or take something, to act like a cockroach. Literally, *cockroach.*

codeesh | Good grief; sheesh.

confunit | Exclamation of frustration; literally, *confound it.*

cuz | Cousin.

dobash | A chocolate chiffon cake with a rich chocolate pudding-like frosting; any rich chocolate filling or frosting.

false crack | An expected hard blow to the face.

fo'days | A very long time. Literally, *for days.*

fo'real | Said to question or establish truth, reality, or teasing. Literally, *for real.*

fut / futs | A fart; figuratively people who are elderly or unexciting.

futz / futzed | To toy with.

grind | Slang for eating; to eat very quickly.

guaranz | Guaranteed; no doubt; for sure.

gulas | Flem.

Guro | Filipino word for teacher or master.

ha la | Interjection.

hae | Wild; fierce; savage; ferocious; to provoke to rage.

hala | Pandanus tree; the leaves can be woven into mats, bags, etc. The fruit looks like pineapple. A common joke is to tell tourists that hala trees are pineapple trees.

halau | A dance troupe and/or school, usually of hula.

Halema'uma'u | Volcanic crater home of Pele, Hawaiian goddess of volcanoes and fire.

hammajang | Broken; old; run down; confused; every which way.

hana hou | Do it again! One more time!

hanabata days | Youth; small kid time. Literally, *the time when your nose ran.*

hanai | Adopt; adopted; to adopt into a family.

haole | Modern usage refers to someone with fair Caucasian skin.

haole-style | Americanized; Westernized; to do something like non-locals.

hapa | Half.

haps | Slang for what's going on; what's up.

hau | A type of lowland tree.

haumana | Student; pupil; apprentice.

haupia | Thick coconut pudding served in slices like fudge.

Hawai'i nei | All of Hawai'i, encompassing all the land, people, and traditions.

hele, hele'd | Hawaiian word meaning to go, come, walk, move, or travel.

ho | Wow.

ho'i hou | To return; in Lua, it refers to the concept of looking to the past to understand the present.

ho'ohuli | To cause or induce change.

ho'oilina | Apprentice or heir.

ho'omaika'i | Hawaiian phrase meaning to give thanks.

ho'omau | Always; steady; perseverance.

Hohonukai | The place where Zader's birth family lives. Literally, hohonu: *deep, profound*; and kai: *ocean, sea water.*

honi | To kiss. In ancient times to touch noses and exchange breath in greeting.

honu | Turtle.

howzit | Hello; hi. Literally, *how's it going?*

huhu | Angry; offended; mad.

hui | A group or club. Also to call out to get attention or to gather people together.

hukilau | To fish cooperatively as a group with a large net. Literally, *pull ropes.*

hula | A style of dance native to Hawai'i.

hula halau | A school or group formed to study and perform hula.

hulihuli chicken | A type of marinated BBQ chicken.

imu | An underground oven, a pit where heated rocks and food are layered and covered until the food is cooked, similar to a clambake.

iso peanut | A snack food; peanuts encased in a rice flour cracker shell and flavored with soy sauce and seaweed.

J'like | Just like.

Jawaiian | Refers to a type of Hawaiian music with a reggae beat.

junkalunka | Old; rusted; junk; said especially of cars.

K-Pop | An abbreviation referring to South Korean popular music.

Kahala | Wealthy neighborhood on 'Oahu.

kahuna | One who is an expert in a skill, labor, or body of knowledge. Also a priest, sorcerer, wizard, or minister.

Kailua-Kona | An area on the Big Island.

kakimochi | A snack food, rice crackers seasoned with soy sauce and seaweed.

kala | Cash; currency; money.

Kali | Filipino martial art that focuses on bladed weapons or stick fighting.

kalua pig/pork | Kalua refers to food cooked in an underground oven or in that style.

kama'aina | Native born; local. Literally, *land child.*

kanaka | A person; a human being. Usually refers to someone Hawaiian or part Hawaiian.

kane | Male; man.

kanikapila | Backyard jam session; to gather informally to make music.

kaona | The hidden meaning of a song, poem, chant, dance, etc.

kapa | A type of cloth made from mulberry bark. Also refers to modern fabric with ancient Hawaiian designs.

kapakahi | Confused, mixed up, without order, a mess.

kapu | Hawaiian word meaning taboo or sacred, forbidden or prohibited. Also to sanctify or consecrate.

kaukau | Slang for food or to eat.

keiki / keikis | Child / children.

Keikikai | Family / kids' beach.

kiawe | Hawaiian name for a species of mesquite tree often used as charcoal.

kikepa | A long, wide strip of cloth similar to a sarong.

kine | Kind; type; style.

koa | A type of hard wood indigenous to Hawai'i used to make surfboards, weapons, furniture, bowls, etc. Also a warrior.

kokua | Help; assistance.

kolohe | Mischievous; naughty; a rascal.

konane | An ancient Hawaiian board game played with black and white pebbles similar to checkers.

Kuka'ilimoku | Ancient Hawaiian god associated with war and human sacrifice.

kukae | Excrement.

kuku | A thorn, barb, or something thorny or prickly.

kukui | Hawaiian for a large spreading tree with nuts similar in size to walnuts or macadamias. Figuratively, kukui refers to enlightenment.

kuleana | Refers to right, responsibility, privilege, authority, or stewardship.

kulikuli | Noisy; deafening; meaning be quiet, keep still, or shut up.

kulolo | A thick taro and coconut pudding often served in slices like fudge.

kumu | Hawaiian word for teacher, tutor, the beginning or origin.

kung fu | A Chinese form of martial arts.

kupuna | Grandparent; elder; ancestor.

lanai | A porch or patio; an outdoor living area.

lau | Food wrapped in leaves and baked in an imu or in that style.

Lauele Town | Name of the town where Zader lives. Literally, *to wander mentally; to imagine.*

lauhala | Pandanus leaf. Used to weave hats, mats, bags, etc.

lehua | A type of flower sacred to Pele. It often looks like a red puffy ball. Picking it is said to make it rain.

lei | A garland.

li'dat | Similar to; literally, *like that.*

limu | A general name for all kind of plants that grow in water, usually referring to edible seaweed.

local-style | To do something in a manner typical of the local island culture.

loco moco | An island dish with sticky white rice, a hamburger patty, and a fried egg covered in brown gravy.

lolo | Feeble-minded; stupid; crazy.

lolo-palooza | Pidgin word used to describe what happens when a bunch of feeble-minded, crazy people get together.

lomi salmon | A dish made with salmon, onions, and tomatoes.

lu'au | A Hawaiian feast.

Lua | A hand-to-hand fighting in ancient Hawai'i. Modern usage of the word also refers to a bathroom.

lua 'ai | A hold, move, or form in Lua.

mahalo | Thanks.

mahalo nui loa | Thank you very much.

maika'i | Good. Well done.

maile lau li'i | A type of vine that grows in the rainforest.

makai | Toward the ocean. The opposite of mauka.

make 'A' | To screw up; to embarrass oneself.

make-die-dead | Poetic way of saying very dead.

makule | Old; elderly.

malasada | Similar to a sugared doughnut, but without a hole.

malihini | A newcomer to Hawai'i, sometimes referring to tourists.

mamo | Hawaiian sergeant fish.

manapua | Hawaiian name for Chinese char siu bao.

manini | Small, tiny.

mano | Shark.

mauka | Toward the mountains, inland. The opposite of makai.

Mele Kalikimaka | Merry Christmas in Hawaiian.

mempachi | A type of fish with over-sized eyes; also a glassy-eyed stare; someone pretending to be stupid or dazed.

menehune | A legendary race of little people said to have built fish ponds, roads, and temples overnight. Do not confused menehune with elves, pixies, or fairies.

moe 'ino | A bad dream; a nightmare; to have a bad dream; to toss and turn.

momona | Big; fat; large. Usually not complimentary.

mondo | Big; a lot; over-sized.

musubi | A type of sushi.

nalu | Ocean wave; in Lua, it refers to acceptance of things you cannot change or control, like an ocean wave.

Nalupuki | A big wave beach in Lauele.

Nana'ue | The name of a Hawaiian boy of legend said to be the son of the king of the sharks and a beautiful woman.

naupaka kahakai | A shrub that grows along the beach.

niele | Nosey; to keep asking questions; busybody; curious in a rude way.

Niuhi | Man-eating shark. A shark that is aware of himself as a predator.

Nu'uanu | A place on 'Oahu.

nyah | The sound made when sticking out your tongue.

oli | Hawaiian chant that is not danced to.

pa lua | School for Lua training.

pahu | A type of drum.

palaka | A checkered fabric, often blue or red on white.

palala | A gift intended for a child.

pao'o | Hawaiian name for blennies, a small fish commonly found in tide pools.

papa konane | A wood or stone game board for playing konane, a game similar to checkers or chess.

pau | Finished; done; completed.

pau hana | Retired; end of work day or week; the work is completed.

Pele | Fire Goddess.

piko | Navel or umbilical cord. Figuratively a blood relative or a beginning.

Piko Point | The farthest tip of land on the lava flow between Keikikai and Nalupuki beaches.

pilau | Rotten; rank; stinky; rancid.

pilikia | Trouble.

pipihi | A type of sea snail.

plenny | Plenty.

pog | A drink made from passion fruit, orange, and guava juice.

Pohaku | The name of a guardian stone; the Hawaiian word for stone.

poho | Waste; in vain; without profit.

poi | A paste made from cooked taro roots mashed with water.

pono | Hawaiian word meaning good; upright; moral; correct; in perfect order or peace; virtuous; successful; balanced in equity.

potato-mac salad | A combination of potato and macaroni salad; a staple in island-style plate lunches and picnics.

pshhtt | A sound of derision or disbelief.

Pu'uwai | A town on the island of Ni'ihau.

puka | A hole; dent; ding. Also a door or opening.

pupule | Hawaiian for crazy; reckless; insane.

sashimi | Japanese word for sliced raw fish.

shaka | A hand gesture meaning *hello* made by extending your thumb and little finger and with your other fingers folded into the palm.

shambattle | A type of dodgeball game.

shibai | A lie; a fib; a story; a statement meant to deceive or hide the truth; something shady or insincere.

shoyu | Japanese word for soy sauce, a very common seasoning and condiment in island cooking.

side-eye | To give someone a knowing look; to non-verbally express criticism or skepticism.

sifu | Cantonese word for teacher, often used to address a martial arts master.

sistah | Term of endearment; sister.

slippah | Flip-flops; zori sandals; thongs; rubber beach sandals.

spak | To spy, see, or identify, particularly when someone is hiding something.

sprunch | Drink made of Sprite and Hawaiian Fruit Punch.

stink-eye | A scornful glare or dirty look.

ti / ti leaf | A type of plant used for wrapping things such as food or offerings, to bind wounds, or to mark sacred places.

tita | A tough, strong, independent woman or girl.

titah | Term of endearment used for girls, especially if they are sassy and precocious.

tutu | A term of respect for an elder.

tutu kane | A term of respect used to address an older man; grandfather.

tutu wahine | A term of respect used to address an older woman; grandmother.

ugi | Something that is disgusting; the feeling you get when your skin crawls.

uhu | A type of parrotfish.

Uncle | Title of respect used for male adults who are older than you.

uwehe | A hula move.

wahine | Female; woman; girl.

Waikiki | A tourist area on ʻOahu.

Waimanalo | An area on ʻOahu.

wana | A spiky sea urchin that lives in crevices in the shallow reef.

wasabi | Japanese condiment usually crushed or grated into a light green paste. It's very spicy like horseradish.

wassa mattah | What's the matter? Often followed by like beef?

wassup | What's up; a casual greeting.

wen | Used to express future tense.

DISCUSSION GUIDE

ONE SHARK, NO SWIM

Spoiler Warning: These questions may reveal important details about the story. Be sure to finish the book before reading on.

1. Describe Uncle Kahana's relationship with 'Ilima. How does 'Ilima let Uncle Kahana know what she's thinking and feeling? How long do you think they've been together?

2. Char Siu faces pressure from her friends to dress and act a certain way. Do you think she wants to do all the things her friends do? Why or why not? Have your friends ever wanted you to be more like someone else? What did you do?

3. If Uncle Kahana owns the store and is not really *a broke 'okole old man,* why do you think he hides behind Hari?

4. Uncle Kahana teaches Jay, Char Siu, and Zader about *run-fu,* which is running away and avoiding confrontation when possible. Do you agree or disagree with this idea? Have you ever faced a situation in which you thought you had no choice but to fight?

5. Uncle Kahana begins to train Zader alone and Jay and Char Siu together. What different kinds of things does he teach them? Why do you think Uncle Kahana forbids Jay and Char Siu from teaching Zader what they learn, but Zader can tell them what he learns?

6. Throughout the story, Kalei watches Zader from afar. Why do you think he's interested? What catches his attention?

7. Zader thinks Mr. Halpert is his biological father and Pua is his biological mother. Do you think he's right? Why or why not?

8. What do you think happens when Zader jumps into the water at Piko Point?

9. If you could change one thing about the story, what would it be? Why?

For more classroom materials and information about Hawaiian culture, history, and island living, please visit www.NiuhiShark-Saga.com.

ACKNOWLEDGMENTS

I could not have made the journey from book one; *One Boy, No Water;* to book two; *One Shark, No Swim;* in the Niuhi Shark Saga without the love, support, and encouragement of many people, including:

Kevin, my husband and companion of more than 30 years and counting.

Our kids, Dylan and Shelby. I'd promise to cook more meals, clean house more often, and actually fold all the laundry, but you guys know book three is coming. Don't worry; pizza's on speed dial now.

My parents, Kathy and Steve Covalt who always ask, "how the writing's going?" and show up at book signings when they already have copies.

My amazing beta-readers and critique crew: Christine Haggerty, Teri Harman, Jennifer Griffith, Eric Bishop, Tyler Miranda, and Camille Price. They are all fantastic authors and editors—be sure to check out their work; you'll be glad you did.

Special *mahalo nui loa* to Tina Cabiles Carden for her translation of *E 'ike e na maka mano*; the Hui Hawai'i O Utah Civic Club and Na Keiki Ka Ua Kilihune Hula Halau under the direction of Kumu Hula Barcarse for their performances and support at book signings; and Dr.

Leslyn Hanakahi who first suggested what a Niuhi shark fighting style might look like.

Lastly, thank you to all my friends, family, and kupuna who continually remind me what it means to be a 21st century Hawaiian. Any inaccurate portrayals of Hawaiian history or culture are a result of my own imagination and imperfect memory—*e kala mai ia'u*.

Lehua Parker

ABOUT LEHUA PARKER

LEHUA PARKER writes Pacific literature stories for kids and adults that explore the intersections of Hawai'i's past, present, and future. Her published works include the Niuhi Shark Saga trilogy, Lauele Universe Stories, and Fairy Tale Ink Serials, as well as plays, poetry, short stories, and essays. *One Boy, No Water*, Niuhi Shark Saga #1, was a 2017 Hawai'i Children's Choice Nene Award Nominee.

As an author, editor, and educator trained in literary criticism and advocate of indigenous cultural narratives, Lehua is a frequent presenter at conferences, symposiums, and schools. Her hands-on workshops and presentations for kids and adults are offered through the Lehua Writing Academy.

Originally from Hawai'i and a Kamehameha Schools graduate, Lehua now lives in exile in the Rocky Mountains. During the snowy winters, she dreams of the beach.

Connect with her at:

www.LehuaParker.com.

Subscribe to Talking Story Newsletter at
www.LehuaParker.com/newsletter

facebook.com/LehuaParker

instagram.com/LehuaParker

twitter.com/LehuaParker

ALSO BY LEHUA PARKER

Zader Stories

Niuhi Shark Saga Trilogy

Book 1: One Boy, No Water

Book 2: One Shark, No Swim

Book 3: One Truth, No Lie

Niuhi Shark Saga Prequels

Birth/Hanau (Zader's Birth)

Pua's Kiss

Niuhi Shark Saga Sequels

Rell's Kiss (Rell Goes Hawaiian)

Lauele Universe Stories

Tourists

Nani's Kiss

Under the Bed

Other Titles

Maverick

Red

Voices

CPSIA information can be obtained
at www.ICGtesting.com
Printed in the USA
LVHW091452260719
625483LV00007B/85/P